Annie Begins

Annie Begins

a novel

MICHELLE TOTH

Paige,

I'm so very happy
you're here to share
this moment. I
hope you enjoy
Annie!

xo
Michelle

(sixoneseven)BOOKS

Boston, Massachusetts

In loving memory of KMZ

SEPTEMBER 1995

CHAPTER 1

It's a long-standing part of my identity to drop everything if I'm needed by someone else—to be one of those people who is "always there" for you. Like a yearbook platitude come alive. I'm embarrassed to admit that I can be *especially* available if the requester of my time is charming or funny or both. Or male. (And if he's handsome, too? Done.) That is how I found myself racing across Harvard Yard in my impractical shoes, heading for dinner with Paul Dennison at a restaurant in that part of Harvard Square where street parking is a bitch and garages are in short supply—and I was far too broke to valet-park my bottom-of-the-line Toyota. I'd settled for a questionable parking space and prayed my resident sticker would get me some slack, and eventually made my way across the cobblestone alley and into the dim entryway of Harvest. Hopefully Paul would forgive me for being late; his invitation had come only a few hours before and it was a minor miracle that I'd escaped from the office at all.

Easing out of my jacket, I let my eyes adjust. I saw Paul, over by the bar, wedged between competing groups of thirty-something women. He was oblivious to the buzz he created with his good looks—floppy dark hair, gray-green eyes, uncommonly white teeth—looking as if he'd just stepped out of a J. Crew catalogue. This last fact would be intolerably cliché if it weren't actually true—two summers before, between our first and second years at Harvard Business School, Paul worked on a financing deal with the company that owned J. Crew and somehow ended up on page sixty-two in the Winter 1994 issue, in a Harrington-stripe Jersey Polo and Dress Chino Trousers in British Khaki. That was the kind of thing that happened to Paul.

I made my way over, prepared to tease him for inviting me out at the last minute. He saw me and nodded hello, then stood to his full six feet two inches. When I came within arm's length he pulled me to his chest, and seemed to cling a few seconds too long. He finished with an awkward pat-pat-pat on the back and I got the distinct feeling that something was wrong.

"Hi, Paul. It's so good to see you. It's been too long."

"Hey, Annie." He forced a grin, when it would normally be so natural. His eyes were tired and his smile dull, in spite of its white glow. "It's good to see you, too. Sorry I've been out of touch."

He sounded so serious. And sweet. Nothing like his regular easygoing, sarcastic self. *What* was going on?

We settled into a small corner table covered in creamy linen. Grateful for the flattering candlelight, I relaxed into my chair, sipping water and studying Paul. I hadn't seen him in months, since our graduation in June, and something was different.

"Do you want wine?" Paul asked, as the waiter placed menus in front of us.

"Sure. Whatever you think."

"I think a bottle. Red?"

I much preferred white; I hated how red stained my teeth purple. "Red sounds perfect," I said.

Paul ordered pinot noir and asked for bread and olive oil, too. He was so easy with the waiters. I remembered that his office was nearby and imagined him lunching here often, cozying up to the staff and getting extra bread and attention.

"So, are you wondering what my big news is?" Paul asked, playing with his utensils. He had perfect hands, strong fingers, nicely shaped. I realized I needed a manicure and tucked my hands in my lap.

"Ahhhh, you're pregnant?" I instantly regretted my stupid joke when I saw his face freeze. I wasn't particularly good with witty repartee.

"Ah, no. That's not it. Although we were trying," Paul said, half under his breath.

The waiter interrupted to introduce the wine, from the Otaga region of New Zealand. I was distracted by the elaborate display of unscrewing instead of uncorking the bottle, but the waiter explained—probably in response to my puzzled look—that many New Zealand wines were screwtop nowadays. This break in our conversation gave me a few minutes to organize my thoughts. Paul and Susie, his wife, *were* trying to get pregnant? Not trying anymore? Talk about a foot-in-mouth comment. Was everything okay? Susie, the pretty schoolteacher with the heart of gold and the body of a *Playboy* model, was regarded as the ideal wife by virtually all of the men in our business school class. Totally sweet and totally hot. I wanted to hate her, but I couldn't because she was so genuinely nice. It would be sad if she was having trouble having babies.

"Sorry, that was not a good joke," I said, once the waiter left.

"No, it's fine. How's work?"

"Work? Come on, Paul. We can't talk about work now. You seem upset. Tell me what's going on." For the first time in the years I'd known him Paul looked unsure of himself, even vulnerable. It made me nervous.

"Well, I don't know how else to put it, but Susie is leaving me. She wants a divorce."

I choked a little on my screwtop New Zealand pinot noir. "Omigod. *Oh. My. God.* You're kidding! But you're perfect together! I thought—I mean—I can't believe it." Holy crap. I had only ever known Paul and Susie Dennison as the annoyingly perfect poster-couple of commitment. Paul Dennison, *single*? It had simply never occurred to me this could happen. Not to him. WAIT! Paul, the guy I had always regarded as the perfect man, suddenly *available*? Then, just as quickly as it arrived, I shoved that line of thinking from my mind. I was there as comfortess, not to take advantage of the situation. Plus, Paul was starting to talk again.

"Well ... I knew we had some issues, I worked too much ... you know ... but I never expected this. And I don't know if I should be relieved or pissed off that she left me for the damn Tree Guy." He gulped down some wine.

"Tree Guy?"

"Uh huh. Frankie. Someone she went to high school with. She hired him to do some work on our yard, and they started talking ... "

"Paul, this is just bizarre. And you're saying Susie actually seems happier with the Tree Guy than with you? So much so that she's asking you for a divorce?"

"That's my ego you're trouncing on over there. And yes. The answer to your question is yes."

"Oh, sorry. Really, I'm so sad to hear this. It's just that it's hard to believe. Impossible, really."

"I don't know if it will last, but they've been together for months already. She says she really loves him."

"Loves him! But what about you? She must love you, too." Didn't everyone?

"Yeah, but she says she likes *herself* better with him. How *Oprah*, huh?" He paused and sank a little in his chair.

Our waiter was back. Distracted by the unfolding drama, I had barely glanced at the menu. "You go," I said.

Paul occupied our waiter with questions about the panko-crusted Berkshire pork loin and the Long Island duck breast. I just wanted to get back to our conversation. I scanned the menu, mentally sorting entrees by price and weighing the odds I'd have to pay for myself. Paul had invited me, so he'd probably pick up the check. But it would be totally reasonable to go Dutch, since we were just friends, and I couldn't risk *that*. This was not the time in my life for forty-dollar steaks, and the waiter was hovering. "I'll have the Eggplant Napoleon, please." The cheapest thing on the menu and still twenty-five dollars for a stack of vegetables. It was exceedingly embarrassing to be the owner of an advanced degree and still penniless at nearly twenty-nine years old.

"Is that it?" Paul asked. "Come on, it's my treat."

I should've gotten the steak. "I love eggplant," I fibbed and turned to the waiter. "And I will start with the lobster tail appetizer, thanks."

After gathering our menus, the waiter took an interminably long time to drift out of earshot.

"Paul, this is just unbelievable. I just can't picture Susie having—" Paul's face immediately dropped and I cringed. "Oh, gosh, sorry," I stuttered. "What I meant to say—where is she living? Where are you living?"

"She's at the house. I couldn't stand it there. I'm staying with a friend here in Cambridge."

While the waiter refilled our wine glasses I peered across the table at my friend. He looked depleted, and sad. I couldn't blame him. The situation was absolutely scandalous. I wondered for a fleeting moment how our mutual friends would react when they found out. They'd be as shocked as I was.

"So . . . honestly . . . how are you holding up?" I asked.

Paul paused, gnawing on a hunk of sourdough. "Um, not so great. But I thought to myself, who would be the easiest person to talk to and the best listener I know? And I thought of you."

Hours later, waking up from a short sleep on the office futon and feeling already behind schedule, I tossed aside the fleece jacket I'd been using as a blanket and tried to stretch out a few kinks in my neck. I squinted in the dark, the space around me lit only by the bluish glow of computer monitors. Late last night, after dinner with Paul, I'd come back to the office to finish a few critical tasks. But two bottles of wine and hours of intense conversation in my official capacity of best-listener-that-Paul-knows had left me sleepy, and I'd decided to nap before attempting any work. But now it was six a.m. and I'd gotten nothing done. My caffeine-withdrawal headache was setting in; I was so *not* a morning person.

A few feet away a half-dozen computer programmers, up all night and fueled by free cans of Coca-Cola and bags of Munchos, plugged away at lines of code and murmured good mornings as I crept back to my desk.

"You were snoring again," teased Jeet, the brilliant junior from MIT, our youngest and possibly most talented programmer. He was certainly the most awake. My comeback was restricted to a tired eye roll. I didn't have quite the same get-up-and-go that I had a decade ago, when I was Jeet's age and could pull all-nighters with ease. These days I could still handle a sleepless night, but it caused substantially more pain. *Did I really snore?*

The windowless loft space that housed our start-up company was pungent and stifling at times, filled with hot computers and sticky programmers, most too engrossed in pursuing their technical ambitions at "Internet speed" to take time out for basic personal hygiene. They tended to lose track of time, something easy to do without any natural light and with the constant whirring of fans that moved the stale air around, lulling the team into a state of suspended reality. And with precious little capital, at least in those early days, the whole start-up situation left us working twice as much and three times as hard as at any regular job. I loved it.

"Okay, guys. I've got a few hours. Who needs me the most?" I asked no one in particular.

Jeet spoke up first. "I do. Come take a look."

At nine a.m., after reviewing the latest version of our website with Jeet and sending a few dozen emails, I headed for the door to go home, shower and change so I could come back and do it all again. On my way out I peeked into the boss's office where I could normally find Stephen, but it was empty. Damn! I was dying to tell him about my dinner with Paul. Then again, even if Paul didn't seem particularly concerned about who knew, I didn't want to be a total gossip. Along with the obvious sadness of the situation, and my genuine sympathy for Paul's pain, I was utterly taken aback by the never-before-dreamed-of possibility that Paul Dennison could, one day soon, be available. To anyone other than his wife. And maybe even to me. On some level I knew it was ill advised to be thinking like this, but I just couldn't help it. And now *I* needed someone to talk to.

Jeet wandered by, apparently in search of more caffeine, and jolted me out of my thoughts. "Haven't you left yet?" he asked.

"I'm going, I'm going. Call me if anything comes up. I'll have my cell with me. And I'll be back in an hour."

I negotiated the curb near the front of our apartment while talking into my new cell phone, feeling hip and cutting-edge and only slightly aware that consciously *feeling* hip and cutting-edge probably meant that I wasn't. I'd made it halfway home before my phone rang with one last request from Jeet.

I let myself into the apartment and broke the silence of an otherwise-empty home. At the landing at the top of the stairs I passed Stephen's room and his unmade bed and then Mallory's room, virtually empty. This was a real problem. She'd moved out weeks ago and we still hadn't found a replacement, which was yet another thing weighing on me. My big, sunny bedroom was sparsely decorated with a few used pieces of furniture and a handful of family photos, mostly of me with my siblings at various weddings, baptisms, cookouts. My brother, Andy, younger by two years, was a classic middle child—on the surface charming and fun, but perpetually feeling underappreciated. He'd left home for college in Connecticut and had never come back, but he could be counted on to call our mother every Sunday and to show up for all family events of any significance. Jodie, the baby of the family, was five years younger than I was and still lived at home with Mom and Dad, and despite her proximity, was the least reliable for making appearances at family gatherings. Jodie was used to doing whatever she pleased.

In the bathroom I stepped into the shower—a favorite luxury, especially when I was home alone and didn't have to worry about people knocking on the door to brush their teeth or retrieve something from the medicine cabinet, when I didn't have to concern myself with how the outline of my butt or my boobs looked from the other side of our cheap shower curtain. So I had a special appreciation for being alone in my apartment, but generally preferred the company of roommates. We usually had three, but with Mallory now gone, it was just Stephen and me. We needed to get our act together about filling the third bedroom, and fast.

I threw on jeans and pulled my wet hair back into a ponytail, grabbed my backpack, and descended the apartment stairs as the heavy wood door at the bottom opened with an unexpected and vigorous whoosh of air, creating a minor wind tunnel in the foyer that kicked up stray mail on the floor—Trader Joe's flyers and unpaid Nynex bills. The elusive Stephen Kanner, my friend, former classmate and now boss, was standing there flipping through a stack of mail that had surely been accumulating for days, possibly weeks.

"Hey, roommate," I smiled, glancing at my watch. We were both supposed to be at the office in fifteen minutes for a meeting with a *Boston Herald* reporter. Stephen hardly looked worried. I wanted to tell him about Paul, but there wasn't time.

"Hi, Annie. How's it going?" Stephen was casual and relaxed in a way that I envied deeply. His stress tended not to show, unlike mine, which was popping up in wrinkles around my eyes. Though speaking of wrinkles, I noticed that Stephen's shirt was crumpled and mis-buttoned and bore the signs of haste or dressing in the dark, or both.

"Nice shirt," I said. "Don't tell me, you crashed at Courtney's again?"

Stephen looked smug and semi-guilty, or perhaps better said, *pseudo*-guilty. Stephen didn't really do guilt.

"You're so bad!" I was only half kidding. I felt overprotective toward all the women whose hearts would inevitably be broken (after their beds were inevitably graced) by my charmer of a roommate. Stephen was tall and sexy in a hard-to-define way, and he had a killer smile and a magnetism that pulled all kinds of people to him—women and men alike. Kids and animals, too, come to think of it, and hopefully, investors in his start-up Internet company that I was now betting my own career on. I took some comfort in the belief that the kind of attractiveness that Stephen had in excess was inborn, and therefore impossible to cultivate in myself.

"Stress relief. You should try it," he smiled.

"Courtney's not my type."

Stephen tapped me on the head with his mail as he moved past.

"Hey, we've got that *Herald* reporter meeting in fifteen minutes," I said.

"I know." He plodded up the stairs and talked over his shoulder. "Two-minute shower and then I'll head over."

"Do you want me to wait and give you a ride?" I called after him, looking again at my watch. He was the founder and CEO; our first real publicity interview couldn't start without him.

"Nope, thanks. I'll ride my bike. See you in a few."

I found it hard to imagine he'd arrive in time, but stranger things had happened. Eight minutes later, while I sat at the fourth or fifth traffic light between our apartment and the office, I saw Stephen fly by me on his bike with a friendly, superior wave.

CHAPTER 2

Early-stage start-ups in 1995 tended to be long on titles (chief excitement officer, anyone?) and short on cash, compensation, and other particulars, like desk chairs and paper. Stephen and I would pause occasionally and laugh about the absurdity, how every self-described entrepreneur was, by necessity, a jack-of-all-trades. You could be negotiating a partnership theoretically worth millions of dollars in the morning, rotating your zero-percent-interest credit cards by midday, picking out staplers or filing cabinets in the afternoon and deciphering corporation papers from the state of Delaware by night. I thought they should give an elective in business school on how to choose a rental photocopier—*not* a small or uncomplicated decision.

We were early-stage enough to not have a name. We called the company Sally.com, the name of Stephen's first dog, while searching for a "real" name. The pressure to figure this out was upped significantly by this first newspaper interview, arranged by our public relations firm.

The reporter, Blake Hadley, had asked to come to our space, and arrived promptly at eleven in a slim black suit and heels that contrasted sharply with the jeans-and-T-shirt culture of our office. She was attractive but not pretty, and her packaging was flawless—perfect hair, makeup, nails, bag, shoes.

I met her at the door. "You must be Blake," I said, extending my hand. She shook it, and I noticed she had the cool, delicate hands of a girly girl. The kind of hands that someone like me could crush without much effort. "I'm Annie Thompson. We spoke on the phone."

"Oh, yes. Nice to meet you." Her demeanor was chilly, just like her hands.

"Come on in. Stephen's in the, um, conference room." We walked past the lineup of programmers and interns who barely looked up from their workstations, and rounded the corner into the makeshift space we called the conference room, partially blocked off from the rest of the office by rows of filing cabinets and a rolling whiteboard. Stephen was sitting at one end of the fake-wood table with Charlotte from Whisper, our PR agency, doing some last-minute preparation for the interview.

I made the introductions while Stephen stood and extended his hand and his most charming smile, and I could almost feel Blake's coolness let up a little. She was no more immune to Stephen's charms than any normal woman, including Charlotte, who seemed to notice Blake's tilted head and silky voice as she reciprocated Stephen's introduction.

Blake pulled out a notebook and a small tape recorder and went over the agreement about the focus of the article, then jumped in.

"Stephen, can you tell me what Sally.com is all about?" Blake asked.

"Sally.com is the temporary name for our online matchmaking start-up. Sally is actually the name of my first puppy, *my* first love," Stephen laughed. "We're trying to revolutionize the dating process by putting it entirely online."

"I've heard this before. Suddenly every Internet entrepreneur wants to revolutionize one thing or another," smiled Blake.

"Right, I know. But we do believe that's what we're doing. We can see the potential so clearly—I mean, who doesn't think there's room for improvement on the dating scene?" He asked this with a chuckle and a raised eyebrow and I thought I saw Blake shift in her seat. "But we also understand that we have some major cultural taboos to shift if we are going to succeed in our mission."

"What are those taboos, exactly?" Blake asked.

Stephen responded with his prepared answer. "Formal matchmaking tends to be a bit awkward and tacky and there's often a sense of desperation about it. We want to change all that, to make it completely credible and desirable and logical to meet people online."

"And how did you get started?"

"We started more by chance than anything. A year and a half ago I was working for the summer with a technology company and I met Jeet, who was this whiz kid, a computer science intern from MIT. So Jeet turned me on to some of the database technology that was just getting going, and when you combined it with the fact that Internet connectivity was taking off, you could see that it would enable all kinds of online services that wouldn't have been possible even a couple of years before."

"And how did you decide to focus on matchmaking?" Blake asked.

"It hit me one night in a bar watching my friends strike out again and again trying to meet women who were just wrong for them. We could apply this new technology to what was, in my opinion, the highly inefficient process of dating."

"Do you have strong views about dating?" Blake asked and Stephen's face opened into an easy grin.

"I do, actually. My personal philosophy has always been that instead of being linear, or sequential, dating should be a simultaneous, parallel processing experience. At least in the early days. Once you meet the right person, then of course you want to focus just on her. Or him."

Stephen himself had long since mastered the ability to keep multiple fledgling relationships going until he found someone to date exclusively. He preferred to think of his approach as merely efficient, and it had always worked—for him. But the Web's potential to speed everything up meant even regular people could meet lots of prospects and date them at the same time.

Stephen continued, "My other personal mantra is to work through your friends. The idea behind Sally.com is to make it easy for people to find potential dates through ever-expanding and overlapping circles of friends. Or, they could focus on shared interests or other important characteristics, like religion, or education."

"Is that the basis of Sally.com, your personal dating experiences?" Blake asked. She was gentle, but challenging.

"No, though that is where we started. But then I studied the market and did surveys and confidential interviews. That confirmed for us that it is going to take some time and effort to get people to overcome the stigma of using any kind of dating service. But the truth is, Blake, the research also told us that, secretly, people were excited by the idea of an easier way to find a date or their life partner. So that was pretty encouraging, and here we are."

Well, to be clear, there were a few steps in between. Feeling optimistic, Stephen had abandoned the formal recruiting process during our second year of business school and instead made a bet on starting Sally.com with his credit cards and a loan from his cousin Denny, who'd won the New Jersey State Lottery a few years before.

Blake was jotting notes, and Stephen kept going. "What

about you, Blake? Are you single? What do you think about dating?" Stephen asked his questions with genuine interest, and you could see Blake almost answer them.

"Not so fast, Mister. I'm the interviewer."

Stephen just smiled and returned to answering her questions. He was comfortable enough in situations like this, but he was anxious about getting too much publicity too soon. He believed that Sally.com had to be the first in this space, and had to get really big, really fast in order to ensure that people would dramatically change their dating behavior and that he would make a boatload of money. It was complicated from a timing perspective: he didn't want to tip his hand to potential competitors too soon, via publicity or any other means. But we needed to attract investors and to populate the site with early adopters to make the whole thing work. It was all a gamble that required brilliant timing and execution.

The interview ended with Blake giving her card to Stephen "in case anything else came up" and promising to follow up on Monday to get the new name of the company so she could include it in the article. That, of course, meant we had to actually agree on a name, which had so far proven impossible. We wanted to find the perfect brand.

Complicating the matter of naming our company was the emerging "land grab" for Internet domains. Every good dot-com name seemed to be already taken. And it was my job to use the name to develop a logo and marketing materials, to begin building the look and feel for our website, and to design our official launch party, which was scheduled for just before Valentine's Day. It was almost October. We had eighteen weeks to go, and it was looking to be a stretch.

Stephen, Jeet and I gathered in the conference room and erased the rolling whiteboard so we could start fresh.

"We need to get our name right." Stephen uncapped a black dry-erase marker and sniffed it. "But we're running out of time."

"Stephen, I know you love Connect.com, but the lawyers say it's already the name of a telecom company in Moscow. Of course they're willing to sell the URL for fifty thousand dollars."

"Glad to hear the Russians have caught on to capitalism. Next!"

Once we got into it the possibilities flowed, and the three of us generated dozens of options by shouting and building on each other's ideas. But we hadn't hit on The One. Within three-quarters of an hour we'd covered an entire whiteboard with potential names. Stephen pointed at a section of his scribbles.

"The straightforward names sound the best to me," Stephen said. "We're going to have a hard enough time getting people to try online matchmaking, so we can't make it sound too goofy. We need to call it like it is, no shame. Tell the truth."

"Call it like it is?" I said. "Tell the truth? Okay, well in that case, if we're talking about almost-thirty-somethings, how about . . . oh, oh, I've got it," I nearly shouted. I was a little punchy—perhaps it was the dry-erase markers. "For the *really* ready—Compromise.com."

Stephen laughed and added: "Or, Lastresort.com, maybe Settlenow.com?"

"Warmbody.com."

"Aliveandbreathing.com."

"www.getmymotheroffmyback.com."

"Justnakedfriends.com." Jeet was howling at his own contribution, and Stephen and I cracked up because Jeet was known for having a constantly renewing lineup of "naked friends."

"Okay, seriously," I said. "I agree, simple and direct is good." I made some squiggly green lines around a group of names.

"Catch. Match. Good Catch. Good Match. GoodMatch.com, I like that," Stephen said, and I nodded. Jeet was still enamored of Justnakedfriends.

"I think GoodMatch.com could work," said Stephen. "It says it's less about the hunt and more about just finding the right kind of person for you. I like that." The three of us were nodding in agreement, though my personal—and mostly bad—dating experience suggested it *was* more about the hunt. But that small matter need not influence our choice of name; I was well aware of aspirational marketing.

"Okay, Jeet," I said. "Let's see how the URL search goes and we'll pick this up first thing in the morning."

Stephen and I walked back down a hallway toward his office. "Stephen, do you think it's a problem that we're trying to launch the first major innovation in matchmaking and we're all single workaholics with essentially no social lives?"

"Nah. It's Internet-inspired irony, that's all. It's rampant," Stephen said with his usual confidence.

"I guess," I said. "But with my PR hat on I am a little concerned that we're not practicing what we preach, not at all. You'll definitely get those questions in future interviews, I think."

"Yeah, you're right. But what can you do?" His voice trailed off, sounding unconcerned.

"Maybe we can sponsor some sort of live and in-person social events. High visibility. To build off the launch party." We reached Stephen's desk.

"Yeah, but that sounds like more work," he noted.

This gave me pause. Didn't everything take work?

"We have so few resources," Stephen continued. "We have to focus." He then plopped into his chair, and leaned forward to stare at his computer monitor.

I didn't disagree with him. We did need to focus. We had a fraction of the people and time and money we really needed to do this right. As it was, I was looking to do the job of five people myself in the coming few months. I'd give it some more thought before pursuing my ideas.

When I got back to my desk I checked my email and felt my stomach flip when I saw Paul's name in my inbox. I clicked the message open:

> *Thanks for having dinner with me last night. It was great to talk to you. Are you free any night next week? How about drinks on Tuesday at the Thirsty?*
> *-PJD*

PJD? His initials? What did the J stand for? When did he start signing his messages like that? So many unknowns. I wrote back to Paul:

> *Anytime, seriously. Especially if you're treating. Kidding. Tuesday is great. How about 9?*

I contemplated signing my initials—ACT—but decided against it. First, it spelled an actual word and that was just awkward and could conjure up weird associations in Paul's mind, like I was ordering him to do something, and fast! Second, Paul might interpret me as making fun, which on one level I would be because, really, who signs their name like that other than a pretentious ass? Had he always done that? Surely I would have noticed and made some effort to get him to stop. For his own good, of course. Maybe it was just an email thing. So on the one hand I thought the whole signing PJD was a silly thing for him to do and on the other hand I thought it conveyed just the kind of cool, privileged confidence that I found really attractive. Only people with a markedly strong sense of themselves thought their name important enough to actively draw attention to it. Regular people didn't do that. Only parents who had especially high expectations for their offspring gave them weighty names like Garrison and Xander and Braxton. Paul's given name was Paulson, in point of fact. I had to confess, though, that I liked those names. The kind of name that was better suited as a last name than a first. Where gender was sometimes unclear. The kind that hinted at advantage and wealth, and suggested a lack of worry about money. Maybe I was just envious, feeling bad about my own tedious name and the averageness it conveyed. Annie. Annie Thompson. Maybe I should switch to my formal name, Anna. That had a certain sophisticated ring to it that might suit me better. Or at least the me I aspired to be. Yes, it would be the aspirational marketing of myself.

I hit send and Paul replied an hour or so later to confirm with multiple exclamation points that made me think he was really looking forward to it (yes!!!), and another *–PJD*. Like a trademark, or at least an annoying habit.

For the rest of that day, and the next and the next, everything was easier. Or everything was the same but I didn't notice the hassles and headaches and I didn't care about hardly sleeping and I was lighter and happier because I would soon see Paul again. On Tuesday.

CHAPTER 3

I headed over to the Thirsty Scholar at eight forty-five p.m.—the earliest I'd left the office in weeks except for the other time I'd seen Paul recently. I found a parking spot on the street—something fairly easy to do in Somerville—and fixed my lipstick in the visor mirror, hoping Paul wasn't anywhere nearby.

Inside the low-lit Irish pub there was sports on the televisions above the bar and a jukebox playing U2. I settled at a barstool around a barrel converted into a table, appreciating the solidness of the wood and the smooth, curved seat with slight indentations that provided an individual spot for each butt cheek. While I waited I debated whether I should take off or keep on my sweater. That morning I'd scoured my closet for something half-decent to wear and poured myself into a daring—for me, anyway—black sleeveless sweater with tiny cut-outs that showed skin in several places. For work, I'd worn an almost-matching cardigan over it which covered the cut-out parts entirely. In a moment of boldness I slipped out of the cardigan and hung it over the back of my barstool.

Paul walked in a minute later, and from my seat I couldn't see him well or read his mood. "Annie." He came closer and struggled to smile. I tried to place his expression but it was perplexing. He kissed my cheek and sat next to me, shrugging out of his jacket.

"How are you?" I spoke with empathy and sympathy and

all the "mpathy" I could muster. He looked like shit. Well, actually he *looked* hot, but he *seemed* crappy, depressed, a little lost.

"I'm the same. Still getting divorced. Still can't believe it," he said, then looked me up and halfway down. "Hey, I like your top."

The look I gave him was *What, this old thing?* but in reality, with him both noticing and *commenting* on it, I felt exposed and stupid in my attention-getting top. Even if they were only tiny slivers of skin showing through the cut-outs. Within a few minutes I pretended to be cold and put my cardigan back on. My fingers caught in the sleeve and it turned into a production until I finally wriggled myself back under appropriate cover.

"Are you hungry?" Paul asked.

"Starving," I fibbed. I had lost my appetite at the sight of him.

We waved at the waiter and ordered burgers and fries and beer—neither of us had eaten since lunch. The beer arrived and we clinked our glasses.

"To getting through life crises intact," Paul said.

"It really is a bona fide crisis, isn't it?" I said.

"Hell yeah. I'm trying not to dwell but this is so fucked up." He said it in a harsh but sort of sing-song way, as in "this is SO fucked UP" with a bit of a groan at the end. Like he was still trying to wrap his brain around it, but couldn't quite get the ends to meet.

"Paul, are you sure this is over? Are you really sure there is no way you can work this out with Susie?" I was surprised at myself for putting this thought in his head. I might just be a certifiable idiot, or at least a wholly incompetent schemer. I saw his face turn from dazed and sullen to certain while the waiter approached and deposited our platters of food.

"Yeah, I'm really sure. 100 percent."

Maybe that's what I'd sensed on his face when he first walked in: resignation, and I was *psyched*. Paul squeezed ketchup on his plate and proceeded to dab his burger in it two or three times before each bite. Why I thought this was worth noticing I had no idea, but it seemed since my crush had taken over in the brief period of time that I'd known about his divorce that anything Paul did was worth noticing and being intrigued by or, worse, turned on by. Look how he dabs . . . *Stop it!* I really needed to get a grip. The poor guy needed a *friend*. I was finding it challenging to be worthy of my best-listener status while feeling such private hope about his pending singledom.

I took the onion off my burger and ate a French fry. Perfectly crisp on the outside and steaming mush on the inside.

"The Frankie thing is a fiasco," Paul went on. "It shocked the crap out of me that Susie would cheat. I never saw that coming." He emphasized the main words of the sentence by jabbing a French fry into the air between us. "But the really big part is that she's practically non-apologetic. It's like she sees it as justified based on my years of supposedly neglecting her." He fell back on his stool in defeat. "And she really prefers this guy. She's much happier with him."

"Do *you* think you neglected her?" I asked rather innocently, and non-judgmentally, I thought.

"Well, I didn't see it that way at the time, but yeah. I probably did. We'd been together for a long time. We didn't talk as much. We didn't laugh as much. We didn't have sex as much. And I was working day and night while she was off screwing around with Tree Guy."

I was trying to pay good attention to the current conversation but in my private, parallel one it occurred to me that all the things I got from Paul when we'd hung out in school—easy companionship, laughter, *time*, attention—weren't things his own wife was necessarily getting from him.

"Well, it seems like there was some definite growing apart," I said. "But what about Frankie? Do you think Susie just fell in love with someone else?" Susie was hot, and I hadn't dared ask but was guessing Frankie was one of those tan, handsome, dense types with strong arms and an easy smile. I could see them falling for each other over flirtatious exchanges while he manicured their lawn, but for them to continue in a relationship seemed highly implausible.

"I know it sounds bizarre," Paul said. "But she seems really into him. And the part of me that's loved her since I was twenty likes seeing her happy for a change." He paused, and bit, and chewed while his statement hung in the air, and all I could think was that *I* wanted someone to love me since they were twenty.

"That's only when I'm not completely pissed off that this all happened while she was goddamn married to me," he said.

Paul ate the last of his fries and finished his burger, swallowing the rest of his Guinness in a single gulp and wiping the foam from his lip with his napkin. When the waiter walked by he ordered us another round of beers.

"I don't know," he said. "I have to say I feel relieved that I don't have to stay in our relationship. We could've worked on it, but it was pretty stale. Even taking the affair aside, at thirty-one, I'm not sure she'd be the woman I'd choose for myself now."

Oh, now we were getting somewhere. Now I simply needed Paul to reach the obvious conclusion: What about someone you have a real foundation of friendship with? Someone who gets your ambition? Someone who would make sure you didn't stop having sex? How about *me*?!

What I said was: "Really. What would you choose differently?" Could I *be* more boring?

"I don't know exactly," said Paul. "But in my more optimistic moments—and I know I might be deluding myself—I feel like I could be lucky that this happened now. I have ten years of relationship history with someone I thought was perfect for me that I can learn from, and now I'm a lot more mature and I can find someone who really fits, not just looks the part."

I tilted my head and said "Hmmmm" so he would keep going.

"I don't think I ever realized how draining someone else's insecurities could be. Especially when that person is really attached to those insecurities, you know?" said Paul.

I didn't quite know, but nodded to find out more.

"I mean," he went on. "No one would think Susie would be insecure about her looks, right?"

I nodded again, that was easy to agree with, but also raised ugly pangs of envy that I wished I was above—but simply wasn't. I would have to remember not to badmouth my butt in front of Paul. Or my hips. Or thighs. Etc. Etc.

"But she was so insecure," Paul continued. "She needed constant reassurance. And it hardly changed from Year One to Year Ten of our relationship, no matter what I said to try to convince her otherwise, or how much I tried to emphasize her other gifts."

Other gifts? What other gifts? I wondered, unhelpful jealousy plaguing me around the topic of Susie. Did she have gifts like being a good teacher, making a yummy chicken pot pie, remembering birthdays? Or gifts like being great in bed? What gifts, exactly?! I wondered if I had gifts. This was another bad habit of mine, and surely was a sign of horrible egotism that my first instinct was to apply everything he said to me. I really thought I might be a self-absorbed wretch.

"It was like she needed those things to worry about, to

obsess about. So she didn't have to deal with bigger things. It kept her world small. It got so tiring." He paused to accept the second round of drinks from our waiter and sip into the foam of his Guinness. "But more than that," Paul continued, licking his lips. "It's hard to see someone every day missing their potential and feeling bad all the time. It's just depressing."

"Oh, I know," I said. "I have a bad habit of falling for potential. Of thinking the guy will grow into his true possibility, which I can see so clearly and he has never considered or even begun to recognize. I have since learned it tends not to work. Ever."

Paul smiled at me. "Annie, you deserve to fall for someone who's fully realized. None of these maybe types."

I would like to fall for you.

He smiled again and picked up and chewed one of my cold French fries. I loved that he felt comfortable enough to eat off my plate.

The effects of two big beers were hitting me. In my pleasant alcohol-infused haze I felt my inhibitions wane and I touched his arm for emphasis. "Paul, I think you deserve someone as great as you."

It had no discernible impact. He chomped another cold fry and glanced around the bar. "Thanks, Annie. I think it will be a little while before I'm ready to really think about other women."

On my ride home I thought about the time two years ago when I'd first laid eyes on Paul Dennison. He was just hot enough and just tall enough to get noticed by a significant percentage of the few hundred women in our business school class. Having nearly tripped over him on the steps of Baker Library while trying to simultaneously walk and read a case study the day before classes began, I was smitten from the start. And I thought I had some special claim, having spotted him so early, but the lust and hope that distracted me for a few solid days in the beginning disappeared just as quickly as it came when I discovered a major obstacle to my affection—his wife.

In those first weeks of school, my suitemates and I would gather in the common area between our dorm rooms at night to read our cases, drink a glass of wine, and scan the Prospectus, our facebook, for cute guys. We'd all noticed Paul as soon as he walked into our classroom that first day and were oohing over him that night—that is, until we found his Prospectus entry. His picture was perfect—handsome, casual. His hometown was Newton, Massachusetts. The rest of his description was indistinguishable from half of the guys in our class—Dartmouth undergrad in economics, several years of investment banking at Morgan Stanley, part of the time in Hong Kong. He liked skiing, chess and travel. All good. But then at the bottom, in italics, was the indisputable evidence that my fantasy was not going to work out. Susan Blanchard Dennison. His partner. With the same last name. He was already married. We learned quickly that there was a significant difference between a same-last-name partner and just-a-girlfriend partner. Many of the latter would be gone by Thanksgiving, we'd heard.

How had I not noticed his ring? We looked up Susan Blanchard Dennison's entry in the back, in the "Partners" section. Her photo—looking suspiciously like a Glamour Shot—was absurdly beautiful, like a sexed-up Meg Ryan. She went by Susie. She had attended SUNY Albany and studied history, and from her graduation date we figured she was Paul's age, which was a couple of years older than I was. She was a schoolteacher, which probably meant she was selfless and kind, and liked aerobics, travel and cooking. Ugh.

Naturally, the simple revelation of a wife brought a speedy

and complete end to my romantic hopes with her husband—feelings that were cemented upon meeting Susie in person, since she turned out to be as nice as she was pretty, with the aforementioned *Playboy* body, and she and Paul were the beautiful, popular and fun couple everyone loved and everyone wanted to be around.

In the benign comfort of our platonic status, Paul and I became fast friends. We had good friendship chemistry—the effortless kind where it just worked. We laughed at the same things and developed an easy rapport. Since we were in the same section, we had all of our classes together for the entire first year of our MBA program. We chatted before class, traded notes about Finance and Marketing, and loaned each other quarters for the vending machine to secure the essential caffeine. Paul sought me out for lunch at least once a week. Over salad bar fixings and iced tea in Kresge, the cafeteria, he would ask me about my occasional dates and soothe my ego when things went poorly—which was most of the time. I'd long since lost my dating mojo. Before business school, I'd spent the majority of my late teens and early twenties as someone's girlfriend, and my identity had been inexorably tied to that of whatever boyfriend I had at the time. The problem was, I never chose very well, ending up in a series of imbalanced relationships with dashing but unfaithful men where I was generally underappreciated and routinely hurt. To recover, there was a period where I turned the tables and was hell-bent on only dating men I didn't care about and could use up and toss aside when done. That was not a pretty time for anyone. Then I stumbled upon a psychology course in my senior year of college called Power in Relationships and was paired with a particularly insightful grad student advisor, and through conversations with her I started to recognize the pattern in my attraction to certain men and vowed to date only good guys with a brain. My strategy worked, in a way, ushering in a period of singledom that lasted until my second year in New York when I met Jonathan, a charming, short, slightly pudgy scientist who played jazz on the side—precisely the type I'd never have given the time of day before my vow to notice the nice guys. Jonathan was sweet and attentive and I was secure and happy, until he turned out to be the smarmiest and most crushing of them all, carrying on an affair with the married singer of his jazz band for nearly the entire year and a half we were together. My confidence in my ability to distinguish a good guy from the rest was permanently shaken, and I became far more comfortable steering clear of any entanglements, pouring myself into work instead.

It was only when I arrived at Harvard that I started dipping my toe back in the dating pool. It was hard not to—there were eager men everywhere. But I was still cautious and insecure. Paul talked about setting me up with his college friends and, even though it never happened, I came to believe he thought of me as a catch for someone, and that he really liked me—as a friend, of course. Perhaps because she knew Paul and I were buddies, and because I wasn't any sort of threat, Susie was warm and welcoming to me, too. She always invited me to their fun dinner parties and holiday events that stood out because they had real shrimp cocktail and sometimes a bartender—an extravagance unheard of for most of us, buried as we were up to our eyeballs in student loans and credit-card debt. There were murmurs then of family money, but no details were ever discussed. I was dying to discuss the details. Since I'd never had any money to speak of I found the topic endlessly fascinating and was not so repulsed by the crassness of dwelling on it. I didn't dare betray my ignorance by asking questions, though I'd have killed for more information.

By our second year Paul and I were only in one class together—Entrepreneurial Management—and by virtue of logistics and class schedules saw each other less frequently. But we still had beers on the occasional Wednesday and bumped into each other in the gym, and I was happy when he and Susie decided to stay in Boston after graduation. Then we all got busy starting Internet companies and never seemed to see each other, until Paul called me at the last minute for dinner one random Thursday night and dropped the Susie/Tree Guy bomb, then declared me his listener of choice, and everything changed.

CHAPTER 4

I got home from the Thirsty past midnight, exhausted. Crawling into bed and under my duvet, I heard Stephen come home and slam the door below, then take the stairs two at a time before peeking into my room. "Hey, you awake?"

Left alone I would sleep like a rock-climber—arms and legs sprawled at opposing right angles. But on the nights that Stephen strolled in and collapsed on my bed, I welcomed his company enough to curl up and keep on "my side" of the bed. I wriggled over to make room for him while he kicked off his shoes, and we settled in for our ritual late-night talk.

"Where'd you disappear to tonight?" Stephen asked.

"I met Paul Dennison for a late dinner," I answered tentatively.

"Oh, yeah? How is he?" Stephen and Paul were friends from school and intramural basketball. Paul had given me the okay to let our mutual friends know what was happening with him and Susie—he thought it would be easier if people heard about it indirectly.

"Well, it's a bit upsetting and it isn't very public yet, but he and Susie are getting divorced." I gave him the gist of the story, leaving out any details that I was pretty sure Paul wouldn't want shared, and by the end of it, Stephen was shaking his head in amazement.

"This is really unbelievable," said Stephen. "That is one

couple I never would have pictured breaking up."

"No kidding. It's quite sad, but it really seems to be inevitable that they're going to split up." We stayed silent for a few moments before I asked, "So how was the rest of your day?"

"Good. Busy." He tucked his hands behind his head and yawned.

"I meant to tell you," I said, "I'm just about done with the marketing section of the business plan. I think it's coming together well."

Stephen looked at the ceiling. "Great. We can pull it all together tomorrow. I'm still working the venture capital front. I think the DNGI meeting is going to happen next Tuesday."

DNGI was emerging as the leading venture capital, or VC, firm for start-ups like ours on the East Coast. Scoring a meeting with them was no small feat. Venture capital firms invested money in new companies that they believed had novel technology or a hot concept that could grow quickly into a big business and eventually go public on the stock market or be sold to a bigger company, and the idea was that everyone would then make a lot of money. But if you involved venture capitalists too early, they could end up owning most of your company, and then they could call the shots and the founders could lose control of the vision. It was all a bit of a catch-22, because at the end of the day you needed capital—cold hard cash—to get and keep things going. Computer hardware was unbelievably expensive—a single server could cost twenty-five thousand dollars—and it took a lot of programmer time to write the code we needed because most of it had never been done before, so cash flow, especially having the money in hand precisely when you needed it, was a critical part of a start-up company.

"That's such good news!" I said, thrilled that Stephen was able to get DNGI's attention.

"You're telling me," Stephen mumbled, beginning to doze off. "We need cash. Soon."

He wasn't kidding. We did need cash. I needed cash. We'd been "paid" mostly in equity for the past month and I couldn't make rent on that. My collection of credit cards was faltering under the mounting weight of my expenses, which were modest and unavoidable things only—like food and tampons. There hadn't been a clothes shopping splurge in months.

"Speaking of cash," I said, "rent is due next week and we need to find our new roommate. I only have one possibility left. She's a German med student and she's coming by tomorrow. I hope she likes this place."

Our place was typical of the converted old houses a few blocks from Harvard Yard, divided and repurposed to serve multiple roommates, usually grad students crowding together to keep the rent down. Stephen and I had been looking for a third roommate for weeks, ever since Mallory left in a huff that I still didn't understand and Stephen didn't seem to notice.

"Das klingt vollkommen," Stephen said.

"What does that mean?" I asked.

"Sounds perfect. I can practice my Deutsch. But really, as long as she can pay the rent, that's all I care about."

"I don't know how you can be so casual about someone you have to share a bathroom with." I felt Stephen shrug beside me.

"I'm a guy."

"You can say that again," I said.

"Ich bin ein Kerl."

Stephen's eyes were closing and he was starting to snore. First softly, then really loudly. This was an inevitable part of our routine—the snoring—which sometimes took twenty minutes to start, sometimes two hours, and was a highly reliable gauge for how tired Stephen was on any given night. I put up with the noise for as long as I could, and then I would surprise myself by insistently pushing him out of my bed and toward his own. This was progress. A younger, less tired me would have suffered through his racket, worried on some level if I made him leave he might not come back, and I loved our nightly time together. But no more. These days I needed sleep just slightly more than I needed company.

BZZZZP, BZZZZP! I jumped at the jarring sound of the doorbell. It was nearly eleven a.m.; it had to be the prospective roommate. I descended the big winding staircase. Dr. Elke Hermann was standing on the other side of the huge wood front door, which was painted red, with the "3" hand drawn on the window in red nail polish to distinguish it from the six other scattered front doors of each unit in the dilapidated house converted to an apartment building. A new roommate would not be sold on this place from the outside, so I had to get her inside quickly, where it was a little more charming and bright.

"Hi, you must be Elke."

"Yes, and you Anna?"

"Yes. Call me—yes, Anna. Please come on in."

Hmmm. Dr. Hermann looked awfully proper. I made a mental inspection of the basics. Tall. Really tall, close to six feet. Statuesque even. Tailored blue coat and severe rectangular glasses. Long, straight blonde hair tied neatly at the nape of her neck. German-English dictionary tucked in her pocket. The reserved German pulled ever so tightly together. Would she be any fun at all? Once I read that you could make an accurate assessment of a person within thirty seconds of meeting them. My snap judgment of Elke was "serious and boring." When I started the roommate search process three weeks before, visions of *Friends* filled my head. I imagined expanding my and Stephen's little surrogate family to welcome a new sister or brother, someone fun and lively and interesting and hip. Like Mallory had been. And someone else to help shoulder the minor but annoying household burdens of collecting rent, buying dishwasher detergent, sweeping the floor once in a while. Yes, a Monica Geller, that would be the right type of Friend. Stephen had always been a sleep-and-shower roommate. He didn't spend much time at home; the office claimed sixteen or eighteen or twenty hours most days. He managed to make it home most nights, though, for our roommate chats and the occasional dinner or weekend brunch. And he loved to repair a broken toilet or an unhinged door, but you couldn't expect him to remember to buy toilet paper or toss expired milk.

After a ten-day parade of un-Friendlike characters checking out the apartment and with the beginning of the month looming, I was starting to think "serious and boring" might be just the ticket.

Elke stepped in to join me in the foyer and looked around in silence. Luckily I had thought to organize the scattered slips of junk mail that normally dotted the corners of the small landing.

"Come upstairs and I'll show you around." I was seeing our apartment through Elke's eyes. A cleaning lady would've been good right about then. I pointed out the nicer details and highlighted the selling features of the place, hoping Elke didn't mind the shared bathroom. Please, please don't mind, I thought to myself. We need you. There's no one else. I've met all the freaks and creeps and otherwise inappropriate candidates, like the patchouli-wearing Reiki master who needed more space to meditate, a bike messenger who didn't seem to shower and a rich girl who couldn't tolerate the minimal closet space (and whom I couldn't tolerate, period).

On the positive side, the apartment was comfortable and

fully furnished with decent hand-me-downs bequeathed to Stephen and me (my grandmother's sofa, his old roommate's chair) draped in matching off-white cotton slipcovers. Best of all, with Mallory's hasty departure, we still had possession of a substantial collection of her original art, much of it created as part of her graduate work. We predicted that she'd appear one day to claim it, as she'd indicated in her parting note, but in the meantime the walls of the narrow hallway and open living room featured beautifully rendered abstract panels and realistic oil paintings of such a scale and thoughtful arrangement and lush palette that it felt like a private gallery. The art was complemented by plain eggshell walls, oak wood floors and ample natural light streaming through a pair of tall windows on the far side. And it was cheap. Relatively. For Cambridge, anyway.

"So this is it. The kitchen is through here." I led Elke through the dining area and into the narrow galley kitchen space, positioning myself in front of the refrigerator, hoping Elke didn't want to peek inside—it was not pretty in there. Same was true of the pantry, a corner closet that was filled with an assortment of household junk. There had been an aborted clean-up project, when I couldn't deal with the mishmash of stuff and decided instead just never to open the pantry door again.

Elke returned to the bedroom that would be hers.

"And the rent is four hundred per month?" she asked.

"Yes." I was trying to read her expression. When I looked at Elke's mouth, all I could think was "pursed."

"It is quite a bit much, yes?" Elke continued. "And the other roommate? She is nice?"

"It's a he." I'd written that on the card that I posted at the Harvard real estate office. "Stephen. He isn't here all that much, just at night and sometimes on the weekends. But he's a great guy. Really. Really fun . . . and he speaks German fluently!" I had to chill out; no one would want to enter a situation where they're wanted too much.

Elke asked a number of other basic questions—how much do utilities run, how does the single bathroom work out, was the neighborhood safe? When could she move in if it all worked out?

"As soon as you'd like. Mallory's been gone for weeks," I said.

"Where did she go?"

I wished I had an answer. I was still smarting from her sudden departure. Even though we'd been only roommate-friends who probably wouldn't have met or become close without the coincidence of apartment sharing, we'd really bonded in the short time we lived together and I missed her and wondered how she was, where she was, why she left. "You know, we don't exactly know. We think it had something to do with a guy. One day she told us she was moving to Europe for a year, and the next weekend her brother came and packed her stuff and she was gone, except for her art."

"She is the artist of this work belongs?" Elke scanned the paintings surrounding us in the living room.

"Yes, much of it. She's so talented. Most are hers and a few of the pieces were done by friends of hers."

"It is beautiful work. I hope she does not come back for it too soon." Elke smiled. She had a sweet smile, I realized, and a teensy dimple in her right cheek. Elke poked around some more in the apartment, looking into spaces and out of windows without expression. I noticed that she seemed uncommonly comfortable with silence, or maybe it was just the language thing.

After ten minutes or so of exploration, she turned to me. "May I call you in some hours and we can decide what to do? Do I have some think time?"

"Sure. I'm headed to the office, you can call me there." I wrote down the number on the back of a Bread and Circus receipt and walked her to the door. "Did you want to meet Stephen?"

"No, that is okay."

Really? Did that mean she wasn't really serious? I couldn't imagine moving into an apartment where I hadn't met all of the roommates.

"I will call you," she promised.

I waved her off and watched her perfect posture carry her down the walkway, wondering if she was born like that. I was forever intending to improve my posture and carry myself with more confidence, more poise, but I kept procrastinating. I suspected Elke didn't have to give it a moment's thought.

My mobile phone rang in my pocket. As I pulled it out I saw PAUL DENNISON on the caller ID. My heart jumped to the corner of my chest, instant tension caused by his name appearing on my phone, signaling his presence—right there! On the other end of the line!

"Hel-loo." I mustered my most carefree tone, which came out a little high-pitched but probably not too noticeable over the tinny connection.

"Hi Annie, it's me." His voice had always been so familiar and comfortable to me. Now when I heard it I felt an exhilarated rush. He had called to say hello, and to share some big news, and to see if I'd like to have dinner again later in the week, maybe Friday night?

"What's your big news?" Hadn't he had enough of that for a while?

"We just closed our second round of funding. Ten million. So we have something to celebrate."

"Ten million! Shut the front door!" My shock was that of mild envy. This was exciting for Paul, yes. And I wanted ten million dollars for our company, too.

Paul had started his company, RedDot.com, with a former boss. It was a clothing and accessories website that collected overstock from popular major retailers and managed the discounted sale online. Paul had been involved in the retail business as a banker, and had a ton of experience working with direct marketers—which is how he made the J. Crew connection—and used those contacts to build their initial partnerships. He started working on the business idea during our second year of school as a field study, so he was a full five or six months ahead of Stephen, but this money-raising was fantastic news, because if Paul could do it then, yes, I did believe Stephen could, too.

"So how does dinner sound?" he asked again.

Dinner wasn't in my budget, but I'd have to finagle it somehow because I couldn't miss an opportunity to have hours of uninterrupted time with Paul. "Friday is good, if we can meet on the later side, even better." I hoped that didn't complicate things.

"How about eight thirty, at the Blue Room?" said Paul.

The Blue Room was located in the same complex as my office. It couldn't have been more convenient, and I gushed agreement and started planning my outfit.

"Alright then, I'll meet you there."

Four hours later, Elke called me at the office and asked if she could take the room. She would move in that weekend. I went to find Stephen, who was plugging away at his keyboard, a frustrated expression on his face, looking a little sweaty like he'd just come back from a run.

"Hey," I said. "Good news. I found us a roommate. Elke. She's the German."

"El-kah. Is she cute?" he asked. I tried to hide my annoyance at his first impulse as he reached over to retrieve a can of Coke from the cube fridge next to his desk. He passed a Diet Coke to me, and I accepted it like any addict would.

"I wouldn't say cute," I said. "She's kind of serious. But she looks like she'll be neat and clean. You know — the type of person who makes her bed every day."

"Well then, she'll fit right in with us," Stephen said, with unselfconscious sarcasm.

"I make my bed! Most of the time," I said. It was Stephen who just skipped bed-making altogether.

"She sounds fine," Stephen amended. "Thanks for finding her. I don't think I'll be home much for the next couple of months anyway. So much to do to get the site launched and the money raised."

"Speaking of money," I continued. "I'm having dinner with Paul Dennison tomorrow night. He's had some major VC success lately. He just told me he raised ten million."

"Really? I should get in touch with him. See if he can make any introductions." Stephen sounded like his normal confident self but with just the slightest hint of competitive anxiety.

"When I see him I'll mention it," I said.

"How's he doing?" Stephen asked.

"Eh, he seems okay," I said. "Not great. But I think the money's helping. At least one thing in his life is working out." I glanced out at the office beyond the glass behind Stephen's head and watched people buzzing about. "Isn't there something strange about the fact that we actually know someone who has just raised ten million dollars? And that we think we can do the same thing?"

Stephen's mouth formed into a wry grin, his expression conveying just a touch of trepidation that only someone who lived and worked side by side with him might notice. "Yes,

Annie," he said. "It seems nuts, but I think this could be huge. And it will all be worth it."

"I know. I really believe that." And I did. One thing I trusted when it came to people was my gut. And my gut told me that Stephen was worth betting on; there was something about him, the kind of thing we'd studied in our leadership class. Certain charismatic leaders had this hard-to-pin-down quality that drew people to follow them, to believe in them, to support them. To hopefully give them money. And Stephen had it. Paul did, too. I thought I might have some of it, but not all that was necessary for a gamble like this. I didn't have the same magical ability to get people to do things for me at enormous personal sacrifice that Stephen did, with his employees or the women in his life, for example. And with Stephen, people did it willingly. I certainly did. It was fun and exhilarating and felt right.

"I know you do, Annie," Stephen replied.

I was pretty sure he appreciated my dedication. In many ways I was more comfortable as a cheerleader for other people's ideas than my own, operating in the safe spaces behind the scenes. Every once in a while I'd feel the urge to break out, to be on stage myself, driving and pushing for my own ideas. But so far the urge was never strong enough to overcome my lack of confidence and the crushing amount of work I'd piled up on my literal and figurative desk. It was the someday phenomenon. Someday I'd get on top of it all, and someday I'd pursue my own dreams. But for now I had too much to do.

CHAPTER 5

On Friday night before dinner with Paul, I wanted to dash home to change and freshen up but ran out of time. In general, I struggled mightily against the tyranny of the clock. I always felt a quiet desperation to get more done and that kept me going and going until the last second, squeezing out every possible drop of productivity. "You're a human being, not a human doer," my sister Jodie liked to say. But that wasn't how my brain worked; it was more complicated than that. With a five-page single-spaced to-do list, I believed on some unconscious level that as long as I kept producing, that was evidence of my worth. And who didn't need tangible evidence that her existence mattered? I'd been comforted by my business school experience, surrounded by so many other people who believed their personal value could be measured by their contribution to the GDP that it felt normal and right, and for months now I hadn't questioned that logic.

Earlier in the day I'd run into a few snags with the website, and the delay had left me with precious few minutes to myself before my date with Paul. *Stop it! It is not a date!* I needed to think about this as two friends getting together for dinner and conversation while one of them was going through a particularly rough and lonely patch. And the other one was getting divorced.

The time crunch prevented me from changing out of the really silly-looking outfit of mis-matched blacks that I'd thrown on that morning—a boxy cotton sweater and a flippy skirt in a waffle-weave fabric with thick tights and clog-like shoes. I didn't have time to change because my planned outfit required ironing. The boxy black patchwork waffle-weave outfit was not my sexiest but would have to do.

I scooted into the ladies' restroom and scrubbed my face clean of the day's makeup before realizing in horror that I'd left my cosmetics bag at home and had no fresh product to replace what I'd just washed down the sink. *Shit shit shit*. It would've been much better if I'd realized that three minutes sooner, as I paused to take a deep breath, arms braced against each side of the sink. This type of thing had been happening all the time lately. I was moving so fast I made small mistakes ten times a day. I could hear my mother now, tossing out a comment like "haste makes waste" with a *tsk, tsk* undercurrent, which was rooted in concern but came across as judgmental and crazy-making, like I was doing it all wrong despite hardcore effort and major sleep deprivation.

I glanced into the mirror at my pale skin, blotchy from the vigorous wash. It really could've used my usual layering of foundation and powder and blush, and I couldn't imagine going anywhere without lipstick. I often had an extra tube squirreled away in a pocket or corner of my bag. I plunged into my backpack in search of stray items that could provide relief and enhancement. *Aha!* I found a lipstick, albeit one worn down to the casing, and a compact with about enough powder for two applications. No mascara, no concealer, no blush, but I'd have to make do. I patted my face dry and applied the powder, creating an effect that was a bit more ghostlike than I was hoping for but better than nothing. The sharp plastic edges of the depleted tube of lipstick bruised my lips a little when applied directly, which turned them a darker pink, so that worked out all in all pretty well. Without eye makeup on it was hard for me not to look tired or age ten, but there was nothing to be done about it by that point. I'd never feel completely ready under such circumstances, and my tendency to keep trying to get a better look going until the last second before a date (or non-date) was now fully hampered by the lack of implements and supplies. I never understood women who actually finished getting ready. My feeling was you kept going and going and trying to improve and fix and smooth and enhance until your date showed up at the door or the taxi beeped.

When I arrived at the Blue Room Paul was already there and seated; I could see the back of his head and shoulders through the wall of windows, across the room. As I pushed through the door, the host greeted me from behind Elvis Costello glasses and his podium and immediately guessed me to be Paul's dinner partner. A guess based on what? How did he know that before I said a word? I imagined how Paul might have described me. How anyone might. "Average height, average weight, average brown-blonde hair, prettyish face if you don't mind dark under-eye circles..."

Elvis escorted me and two menus over to where Paul sat. I slid into my seat across the table as Paul did that half-stand thing to welcome me. He looked as handsome as ever, though perhaps less rested and more rumpled. We exchanged hellos and small talk while Paul ordered two glasses of Veuve Clicquot.

"How does it feel?" I wondered, and tried to maintain concentration on the conversation and not just on his teeth, so straight, so white, so close to those kissable lips.

"Well, Annie, I'm not going to lie to you. It feels pretty good. I highly recommend being flush with cash. Now we just have to do something with it." Paul had told me that the bulk of their funding would be used to further develop the website, secure partnerships with retailers, and marketing—lots of marketing and promotion. Then he turned to the topic of Susie, updating me on recent events. Susie seemed to be pushing ahead with the divorce, and Paul was reeling.

"I don't think I've fully accepted it yet. But it's getting harder to deny."

He was looking like his new self again, which was essentially his old self with a topping of sad and vulnerable. It made my heart ache and race at the same time. Now that I was getting used to this sensitive version of Paul, who talked about feelings and relationships, I was hooked.

While I sat and paid close attention and murmured supportive sounds and felt genuine sympathy and concern about Paul's ability to deal with the train wreck that was his marriage, I also found myself unable to forget that he was changed. He was now single. Unattached. Practically available. It made him different, and even if he wasn't sending any signals—yet—of being ready to move on, it didn't alter the fact that the energy was different. The tension and possibility that hung between us, even if I was the only one aware of it, was real. And distracting. I couldn't explain this intense emotional pull that I felt, that drew me into his world and made what he said and thought and felt so compelling and important. I felt like a sponge, willingly sopping up all of his emotions and soothing his nerves and reactions. And I felt the first twinge of relationship confidence. I knew Paul was a good guy, and I knew he cared about me deeply as a friend, and the only open question was whether there could be something more.

We talked for hours, a little about work, a lot about Susie—him and Susie, him and being single, him and his pain.

"Annie, I'm sorry to be so obsessive and needy. I've completely monopolized our conversation. Tell me what is happening with you," he said.

I smiled through my unspeakable thoughts. What? What was happening with me? Can't you tell? I'm falling in love, or at least lust, with you, you idiot. And then I tried to answer the question and realized I had almost nothing to say, unless I wanted to talk about work, which I didn't. I made a mental note to be more prepared for that inquiry next time—it was alarming to realize I had absolutely nothing of interest happening in my entire life! At least nothing I could say out loud to the secret object of my potentially misguided affection. I remembered the one thing new in my life was my roommate, but something made me hesitate to mention the tall German with the cute-sounding name. I thought she seemed more sexually appealing in description than in person, but nonetheless I didn't speak of her.

After Paul paid the check, he walked me to the door and through it, then paused outside and picked up both of my hands in his, sending a ridiculous tingle down my spine. Okay, continuing on from my spine and connecting with all of my parts. All parts a-tingle at that point. I hoped my hands felt soft and smooth and not too neglected. I wasn't a particularly accomplished girly girl and I often went for weeks without moisturizing anything.

"Annie," Paul began. "You are the greatest. The sweetest. I can't thank you enough for being here and listening. I don't know what I'd do without you to talk to." Then he leaned over and kissed my cheek and I could feel the wet of his lips on my skin—and this was no peck, but a lingering pause of lips on cheek—and I was tempted to turn my face and lock lips or stick my tongue down his throat, right then and there, but instead I stood frozen and prayed the moment wouldn't end. He was appreciating me for my friendship, not for kissing. *Damn.* Why was that always the way? Darn respect coming at the most inopportune moments.

After dinner, I headed back to my office, intending to attack my to-do list for as long as I could keep my eyes open. The office was abuzz, about half-staff at eleven thirty p.m., despite it being a Friday night.

"Hey Annie, how was dinner?" Stephen asked, standing over the copier, wrestling with a toner cartridge.

"Good. It was good. Things are looking good for Red Dot."

"Sounds good. Good, good." Stephen smiled, distracted by the directions on the toner package.

I made my way over to the copier and leaned my head on Stephen's shoulder. "I'm buzzed," I said softly.

Stephen replied without moving, going along for now with the clandestine confession. "Too much wine?"

Hardly. Too much unrequited lust. I was drunk with my desire for Paul Dennison. "Oh yeah." It was easier to blame the champagne than try to explain, because any sane person would judge me inept at falling in lust.

Jeet appeared from behind and took the toner from Stephen. "Lemme take care of that, boss." After handing off the toner task, Stephen disappeared to his office. He was expressing less interest in my time with Paul than I was hoping for. I checked my watch, and went to my desk to dial my sister Jodie, who answered the phone with sleep in her voice.

"Hey, Jodie, it's me. Am I waking you up?"

"Huh, what? No, I'm watching TV. What's up?" Jodie asked through a poorly stifled yawn.

I didn't feel like I could launch into the whole Paul thing without some backstory, and yet it was late, she was clearly sleeping, and I felt acutely stupid. I was the older sister, after all. I was the one accustomed to doling out advice and comfort. "Oh, nothing."

"You never call here. What's going on?"

With that small invitation to divulge, I spilled. "Well, do you remember my friend Paul Dennison, from my section in business school?" I provided the necessary context as quickly as I could and updated her on the latest developments, including the affair and his pending divorce and my uncontested role as ear-lending confidante. "I had dinner with him tonight," I said.

"Oh, how was it?"

"Dinner was nice. He held my hands and appreciated my friendship. I thought for a fleeting moment that maybe he was interested, you know. But turns out he needs a shoulder to cry on, ear to bend . . . story of my life."

"He probably does need a friend. It's a big deal that he's turning to you, don't you think?"

"I just thought, maybe, maybe. I am so attracted to him. It's quite distracting."

Jodie sounded unfazed. "Well, Annie, you wouldn't want to be with a guy this close to a breakup like that. Trust me." Jodie was younger, but more successful in long-term relationships than I was; she'd been with her current boyfriend, Christopher, for more than four years now. She was one of those women who was sufficiently confident, fun and pretty that she could be a world-class bitch and still get the sweet, hunky, brainy guys to fall hard and fast all over her.

"I know, but there aren't many guys like Paul or Christopher out there anymore. There probably never were. It's hard not to get a little excited when one frees up." Really hard. I was struggling to get a handle on my initial hopes about Paul, but if I was truly honest with myself, he had been pretty clear from the get-go that he was just trying to get over the shock of Susie's leaving him, not looking for someone else. But it was extraordinarily easy to forget that logic when I was sitting across from him at a candlelit restaurant drinking fancy champagne looking at his handsome face, or lying in bed feeling totally alone and like he might be the one person I could imagine myself with. "So how do you plan for that exact moment when he's had enough time to grieve and is ready to move on?"

"I don't think you want to be the first after a ten-year relationship," said Jodie. "Try being second—or better, third or fourth."

"It's much harder to orchestrate that."

"I know, but you can't control this. When he's ready, he's ready. Not a minute before."

"You're right. I know. I know."

"I believe you that you know this in your grown-up, Harvard-MBA brain, but you have to convince your stupid-girl brain to stop being distracted and find an available guy or be more patient and wait. You have no choice."

"I know. I know."

CHAPTER 6

Sleeping in any day of the week was a perk I'd left behind when I joined Stephen's company, along with hopes for a steady paycheck, manageable stress and vacation days. But it was Saturday, Elke's moving-in day, and I was committed to greeting her and making her feel welcome, so I stayed home from the office and relished the morning quiet and light.

Elke showed up with nothing more than two tidy suitcases, her laptop computer and a box of miscellaneous items—lamp, toiletries, linens, pens, paper. She reminded me of Stephen, who'd arrived with two pairs of jeans, some T-shirts and a blender.

Setting her belongings down in the center of her new bedroom, Elke started to unpack. She was wearing slim jeans and a navy blazer. Her hair was tied back in a bun, her face free of makeup, wearing her serious glasses. I helped with the least personal things, organizing Elke's computer and office supplies on the makeshift desk that Stephen helped rig last night with some filing cabinets and an old wood door.

"You can use one of the dining chairs for your desk if you'd like," I offered. "I can't remember the last time we had four people try to eat dinner at the same time." I had always loved hosting dinner parties, but there was no time for it these days.

"Danke, that would be good. Thank you for the desk and these other things." Luckily, Mallory had left behind a few items that Elke needed, including a futon mattress and a small chest of drawers. It was all working out well, I thought.

I noticed that everything of Elke's was immaculately kept. As she unpacked, jeans and jackets and skirts and tops were neatly folded and tucked away or hung in the closet near her door. Then we set about creating a makeshift bed. "I'm sorry Stephen's not here to welcome you," I said. I gathered the smooth excess of Elke's queen-sized sheet and tucked it under the corner of the futon mattress. That was some serious thread count. The cotton felt like silk. I resisted the urge to wrap myself in it.

"Ah, is not a problem. We have months to know each other," Elke replied. She was arranging a pale blue duvet at the end of the bed. "You two are not an article?"

"What? Me and Stephen? Oh, no. No no no. I love Stephen but I would never date him."

"Oh? Is he awful?"

"Oh no, not that." Stephen was hardly awful. He was one of my favorite people, one of my best friends. But I did have some innate sense that it would be a massive disaster to think of him as anything but, and, having made the decision in my head, it stuck and was never revisited. "He's quite popular with the opposite sex. But that is exactly my point. No, we're very much just friends." Elke nodded her understanding, and pulled the world's smallest pillow, flat and hard-looking, from her larger suitcase and completed her new bed with it. It didn't look too cozy to me, as someone who had come to rely on a collection of extra-soft pillows for all sorts of substitute comfort. Maybe I'd loan one to Elke. Maybe.

"Do you have a, what do you call it, significant other?"

"Not really, no." It was too soon to share Paul with someone I barely knew. And the polite thing would be to reciprocate the question but I didn't want to have that conversation.

I moved on to the kitchen to find a replacement lightbulb for

Elke's lamp, which had blown dark with a "pop" when we plugged it in. I opened the scary pantry door and sifted through the disorganization—old paint cans and cleaning supplies, the 1993 Cambridge/Arlington Yellow Pages, empty wine bottles we always intended to recycle, dusty bottles of liquor we never drank, Alka-Seltzer, and at least ten cans of Chicken & Stars soup—Stephen's favorite. Among the piles I spotted a four-pack of sixty-watt Soft White with one bulb left. I shook it to make sure the filament was intact and returned to Elke, who was moving around T-shirts and folded navy blue socks.

"So, you said you were living in Providence, but your school is here. What would make you commute that far?"

"Hmmmm. Love. Or so I thought. He did not appreciate my ongoing contact with my previous German lover."

"Oh. Well, I guess I can understand that," I said.

"Ja, ja. But it proved impossible to tolerate his jealousy. He asked me to leave. So here I am. I hope perhaps I may sort some things out if I am apart from both of them. So hard to choose, you know?"

I nodded with feigned understanding. The last time I had to choose was eleventh grade, when I was caught in a rare stretch without a boyfriend, and Teddy Leighton and Joey O'Brien both asked me to the junior prom. I'd picked Joey because he had a car, and lived to regret it when he drank himself into a puddle in the parking lot with half a bottle of Southern Comfort and barely made it into Stanek's Function Hall.

Elke stepped into the hallway between the living room and bathroom and surveyed a two-foot-by-three-foot oil painting that hung in the narrow corridor. It was a piece done by a former boyfriend of Mallory's.

"And who is this?"

"That's Anthony," I answered, following her appreciative

gaze to the self-portrait of Anthony standing naked to the waist, wearing nothing but a towel and brushing his teeth, looking through us as if at a mirror.

"Is this what he looks like in real life?" asked Elke. I glanced at Anthony's well-muscled and absurdly sexy take on himself.

"Um, yeah, actually. He's pretty hot." And sweet, and funny, and I never fully understood why Mallory let him go.

"Hmmmm. Does he ever come to visit?"

"He lives in Chicago."

"Maybe he deserves a more prominent location?"

Elke was indicating the painting, and checking out a more visible place in the living room where Anthony might be moved. I hesitated before reaching up to help her—Mallory would've hated this, but Mallory was gone.

"That's a great idea. I love it."

We moved Anthony above the sofa, where his hotness could be seen from all angles, including from Elke's bedroom if her door were ajar. I felt encouraged. Maybe Elke would be more fun than I originally thought.

We flopped on either end of the couch and fell into easy conversation, collecting bits of each other's lives and families and backgrounds. Elke was one of two sisters. Her parents still lived in her hometown of Hamburg, in Germany. She was here on a six-month fellowship with Harvard Medical School, working with faculty in the dermatology department studying wrinkles. At the end of her fellowship, she planned to return to Germany and join a dermatology practice. I was excited to have a wrinkle expert in the house. Maybe she could help me with mine. I shared some innocuous details of my family with Elke, such as my brother and sister and my sprawling and connected extended family.

Eventually we retired to our respective bedrooms: Elke

wanted to write some letters home, I needed to gather my laundry together. I liked having roommates. I wasn't sure if it was growing up in a noisy household, or just that I enjoyed people generally, but I liked having others around, even if we were all just doing our own thing. It created a sense of vitality and connection. Like family.

I'd gathered my laundry into two big bags and hauled it into the hallway, then backtracked. "Bye Elke . . . I'll see you later. I'm going to my parents' house." I poked my head into Elke's room. She was sitting on the floor sorting CDs.

"Alright, yes. Are they close by?"

"Yup. A half hour or so without traffic."

"Ah, do you go forth and back often?"

"Forth and back? Oh, yes. That's funny. We would typically say 'back and forth.' But forth and back actually makes more sense. I like it. I spend most of my life going forth and back from somewhere, it seems."

CHAPTER 7

I was willing to do a lot to save a buck, and traipsing seventeen miles on the Southeast Expressway to my parents' house to do laundry was one of those things. I never calculated the straight costs, because surely the driving time and the gas would add up and make me wonder if I should just suck it up and hang out at the laundromat like the rest of the Cantabridgians without washers or dryers. I did it for the priceless moments of quiet in my car, the couple of hours of feeling like someone (usually my mother, sometimes my sister Jodie) was taking care of me instead of me taking care of the world, and a small, blissful feeling of escape from start-up life.

I pulled up into the driveway of my childhood home, a compact Cape with a purple front door, my mother's favorite color. When I was growing up, we'd had several phases of purple-themed decor, from the lavender bathroom, to the plum-colored sofa, to the purple bedrooms. At this point my father, Parker, had gotten my mother to relinquish color selection to him, and over time he'd attempted, with some success, to convert the walls and floors to subtle beiges and off-whites that everyone but Mom preferred.

I dragged my two overstuffed bags up the stairs of the back porch and was met by my father, who stood at the threshold.

"Elizabeth, she's back! And, surprise, she has her laundry." He liked being king of his castle, pretending I was trespassing. I thought he was kidding, but couldn't be positive.

"Hi, Dad. You know it's the only way I find time to visit, if I'm multi-tasking."

Once I had brought my laundry to my grandmother's house during a Mother's Day get-together and my family still teased me about it, but I maintained it was better than being late for the party or going another week without clean clothes.

My father held open the door and took one of my bags. I entered the family room and was overcome by the latest change—wall-to-wall carpet in a sickly sweet shade of mauve.

"Oh my God!" I felt besieged by the color of black-raspberry ice cream. "When did you do this?"

"Do you love it?" My mother entered the family room, wiping her hands on a dish towel.

"Oh, Mom. So much purple!"

"I know. I LOVE it. We're doing the living room and the dining room next, as soon as we get our taxes back."

Holy moly. More mauve? At least it wouldn't happen for a couple of months, when their refund arrived. My parents were the type that would rather systematically overpay on taxes to be guaranteed a refund than take any risk they might owe money to the government. They'd do their Form 1040 by February 1 and use the refund to treat themselves to something they were sure they couldn't afford otherwise. Once, I tried to point out the fallacy of that thinking and was shut up quickly. It's the way we do it, the way we've always done it, they said.

"As long as you love it," I said.

"I do! Don't you, Annie? I think it's beautiful." My mother smiled and looked around proudly. I thought it was dreadful and that I would be nauseous if I had to look at it for too long.

"I love that you love it, Mom."

A couple of hours later I had freshly washed and dried

clothes and settled on the couch next to Jodie, who'd arrived home during the dryer cycle. She had moved home after college, anticipating that she and Christopher would marry and that saving for the wedding should be a priority. But, since she wasn't actually engaged yet and since she tended to dip into her wedding fund whenever there was a sale at Banana Republic or the Gap, I was betting it would have a negative balance by the time it was needed.

My mother sat nearby in her cotton housecoat, reading the latest Judith McNaught novel. I tried to create space for my folded clothes among my mother's collectibles—if you could call them that—covering half of the available surfaces. There were small items of minimal function all around—on shelves, countertops, tables and walls.

"Mom, don't all these knickknacks bug you?" I asked absently, moderately aware that I was being critical, unable to help myself.

"No, we like them."

I paused and held up a crocheted duck covering a bar of soap that belonged, if anywhere, in the bathroom. Its yarn body was rust colored, with a knitted golden beak and stick-on googly-eyes. "But really now, don't tell me you like this."

"We won that at Bingo last year. We had a lot of fun that night. That duck has good memories," my mother retorted. My father emerged from an adjacent room where he'd been fiddling with his new computer since I arrived.

"That's right. And we like it." He took the duck from me, dusted it off, and put it back on the shelf where it came from.

"What about this fake Fabergé egg?" asked Jodie.

"That's genuine porcelain," my mother answered.

"Yes, Mom, and so is your toilet," Jodie smiled.

My mother laughed easily and headed into the kitchen. I

was reloading my clothes into my laundry bags. The mass seemed to have grown considerably. "Okay, I gotta get back," I said to no one in particular.

My mother reemerged from the kitchen carrying a large Cool Whip container, and crossed the room to hand it to me. "I made you some of the Toll House cookies that Stephen likes, too."

"Thanks Mom. That's so nice of you." My father immediately appeared at the mention of cookies, and my mother wordlessly pointed to the remainder of the batch, cooling on the kitchen counter. "Hey, Dad, I forgot to ask if you could take a look at my car. It was making a funny noise when I drove here."

He cracked a smile. "Elizabeth, her carrrrr is making noise. What's a carrrr? I know what a cah is, what's a carrrr? Carrr. Carrrr. Carrr."

My mother defended me by shooting him a look, but I thought she was laughing under the surface. "Parker."

My father couldn't let go of the fact that I'd let go of my extreme Boston accent when I went to college, where in my first week an Indian classmate, finding it impossible to decipher my dialect, asked a mutual friend if I spoke English. I'd worked for years to retrieve my Rs and not sound like a townie, and he hated it. "Daaad."

My father always got aggravated when I wouldn't joke with him, which usually happened when he thought something was hysterically funny and I did not.

"Fine. Ya know, you women can't be trusted with cahs, I'm telling ya. I'll take a look in a minute." He bit into his second cookie. "Now, what's going on with ya job. How's Stephen. Have yahs made millions yet?"

I hated when he would go there. I tried not to lose my temper because that would get us nowhere. "Not millions, Dad. Not yet."

"You should be the president of Ford by now. Hurry up, will ya? I'm still waitin for you to buy me a boat. A yacht. You promised, you know."

"Dad, I was fifteen when I said that."

My mother piped in. "And he's never forgotten."

Of course not. He really wanted that boat. And he had more fanciful visions of my future success than I did. Perhaps from him is where I learned my lottery mentality, the one that led me to a risky start-up instead of a sober job at some consulting firm.

My father followed me to my car in the driveway and listened to it run. The noise was inexplicably gone now, but he tinkered around a bit anyway.

"Annie—" My mother had come outside to say goodbye. "Don't forget about your cousin's wedding."

My cousin Barbara was getting married in a couple of weeks, on the same day as my twenty-ninth birthday, and I'd completely forgotten. "Mom, how could I forget Barbara's wedding?" How in the world had I let that slip my mind? I'd had the poufy dress in my closet for months.

"Well, it's just that you're so busy these days."

"Don't forget about my birthday, either," I smiled. My mother never forgot a birthday.

"Okay," my father piped in, tapping the hood of my car, as though he'd done something to fix it. Either way, if it was problem-free, that was a relief. "You should be all set."

"Oh, good. I'll see you all soon. Bye . . ."

My father murmured goodbye and my mother waved. I climbed back into my car, self-consciously backed out of the driveway, and headed toward the highway. I managed to down half a dozen of my mother's cookies between Chester and Cambridge while trying, now that I was out of the bubble of my parents' world, to keep at bay the creeping feeling of being overwhelmed with things to do and worry about—a crazy, demanding job without a reliable paycheck, a new roommate I wanted to be happy, my cousin's nearly forgotten wedding where I was expected to be a bright and shiny bridesmaid. And none of it even as remotely captivating as my highly inappropriate and growing crush on Paul Dennison.

CHAPTER 8

I'd always thought generosity was a strong suit of mine—I tended to share willingly and usually without regret. Both to give things like time and attention, and to open my heart and my world and invite people in. Unconsciously I expected that this behavior would somehow get rewarded. If nothing else it was a prize in itself to feel like a fine and selfless person (if not a bit smug), and at best it could mean excellent karma for future generations of my soul. But the dark side of my giving nature was that I expected things of people, sometimes without telling them. Sometimes without realizing it.

Stephen was lying on his back on my bed, munching on Toll House cookies straight from the Cool Whip container resting on his chest and drinking a glass of Guinness that was sweating circles on my nightstand. It was dark outside, the shades were drawn and the room was lit with soft light from my nightstand and the desk lamp across the room. I finished putting my laundry away in the dresser next to my bed, and collapsed beside my roommate.

"Your mom's the best," he said between bites. "This is dinner, you know."

"I'll remind you of this moment of nutritional sacrifice after you've made your millions," I said. "Hey, watch it. Don't snarf all the cookies and leave all the crumbs between my sheets."

Stephen brushed crumbs off his chest onto the floor. I shot him a look.

"Sorry. Hey, can you give me the details from dinner last night with Paul?"

I knew he meant the VC money, but I wanted to talk about Paul the Romantic Prospect. I hesitated because I knew Stephen would be among the least tolerant of my misplaced lust. Or at least mistimed lust. He was nothing if not practical in matters of the heart.

"Well, I told him we're going to raise a round," I said. "He said he's happy to talk. It took them a while to put the deal together, and I think he learned a lot that could be helpful to us. So, maybe I could invite him over, make dinner or something."

"Or I can just meet him for a beer."

"Well, yes, but then I might not have a reason to be there," I said coyly. "And I want to be there."

"Hmmmm?"

"I just thought, with his pending divorce and everything, maybe I'll be able to help pick up the pieces. When the time is right." I was afraid that Stephen would think I was crazy to picture myself with Paul, not to mention the folly of the timing of it all, and felt that panicky feeling that comes when saying something really important out loud for the first time, knowing that it could backfire.

"Pick up the pieces? Or sift through the rubble? That sounds messy to me. Plus, I never knew you liked Paul."

"What do you mean? I always liked him as a friend. But he was married! Of course I didn't like him like that." I couldn't help but raise my voice.

"Like what? You're either attracted to someone or you're not. Has nothing to do with marriage." Stephen was smiling.

"Of course it does! If something is off-limits, you just don't go there," I responded, feeling quite certain in my position, wondering if our opposing views were a guy-girl, Mars-Venus interpretation thing.

Elke must've tuned into our voices from down the hall, because a minute later she poked her head in the doorway and I caught sight of her in my peripheral vision.

"Oh, hey Elke! Come join us." As our new roommate stepped into the room, I did a double take. A literal double take, like in the cartoons when the head snaps back and the eyes bug out in disbelief. Somehow my serious, studious, boring new roommate had transformed into a total hottie, with her mile-long legs descending from silky shorts, and long flax-colored hair— released from its proper tortoise clip—falling in waves over her shoulders, landing just above her perfect small breasts with nipples pressing ever so slightly against the cotton of her baby tee. *Whoa, whoa, wait just a sec!* Where'd those legs come from? And the nipples? What was happening? Who kidnapped Librarian Barbie and replaced her with Sexpot Barbie?

"Okay!" Elke said. She padded across the room and nonchalantly crawled into bed between me and Stephen. He and I exchanged looks—perplexed (me) and good-humored (him)—as Elke positioned herself smack dab in the middle of us. Once we'd shifted and settled, three roommates in a row, Stephen fell back into conversation as if it were nothing to have this six-foot-tall Germanic babe newly in the mix. I set aside my stupefaction and followed suit. This was the second time that Elke had surprised me by being more fun and social and laid-back than I expected.

"Elke," Stephen began. "Do you think your attraction to someone is dictated by whether or not that someone is married?"

"Oh, absolutely no," Elke replied. "I have been attracted to both."

"So you have been attracted to married men?" asked

Stephen.

"Oh yes, of course. I would hesitate to act, but yes, I have been attracted."

Stephen looked across Elke to me. "See, my point exactly."

I rolled my eyes as Stephen put the Cool Whip container in front of Elke. "Cookie?"

"Mmmmm. Danke."

Stephen passed Elke the glass of Guinness. She sipped, and then licked the foam off her lips—rather unnecessarily, I thought.

"Elke, I told you that Stephen speaks German, right?"

Stephen answered. "Yeah, we established that earlier tonight."

Earlier tonight? When earlier? I talked myself quickly out of feeling left out and changed the subject. "We're having a launch party for Stephen's company, when we get closer to the launch," I said. "It would give you a chance to meet some people, so you should definitely come."

Elke perked up. "That would be great. All I have done before now is work."

"Well, you'll fit right in with us, then." Stephen was munching on about his tenth cookie.

My eyes were closing; sleep deprivation was catching up with me. Three or four hours last night was just not enough, but I didn't regret my dinner with Paul. Hardly! I tried to suppress a yawn. I wanted to stay awake. I loved roommate bonding. I loved having my surrogate family all around me.

"But we will be taking off at least this one night for a party," I said. "We have to squeeze in a little fun now and then." I turned on my side away from Elke and Stephen and continued to mumble about the importance of having some fun once in a while, trying to keep myself in the conversation even though I couldn't keep my eyes open. My roommates talked easily, moving in and out of English and German. Lack of comprehension of half the conversation made it easy to zone out, and I dozed off with the happy, if squished, feeling that our household trio was complete again.

CHAPTER 9

The next morning, I woke up alone and rolled over to check my alarm clock, which I'd never set the night before, and felt the scratchy remnants of Toll House cookies sticking to my arms. 7:13 a.m. Ugh.

Maybe I'd walk to the office. A little exercise would do me some good. But it felt like it might be raining. I'll walk tomorrow. The procrastinator in me seemed to be at her best when the subject was exercise. Especially now, it seemed highly unlikely that I'd take that much time out of a day—any day—for something other than work. But if I could just get myself to start walking to and from work, that would be something. Yes, maybe I'd start tomorrow.

Stumbling my way to the kitchen, I entered the living room and tiptoed past Elke's bedroom. OUCH, ouch, ouch. I stubbed my toe on one of Stephen's hiking boots abandoned right there in the natural path toward the kitchen. Why were his shoes all over the house? I felt aggravated but willed it away. Stephen was there so infrequently, I didn't want him to feel nagged for a few items of abandoned footwear.

In search of something cool and wet and preferably caffeinated, I yanked on the refrigerator door. It smelled better inside than I was prepared for, and seemed to have been cleared of all expired items. Huh. That was puzzling. I was glad I didn't have to confront the milk (so disgusting) or the spaghetti sauce

Stephen's mom sent two months ago, but felt a little bad if Elke spent her first day in the apartment tackling our chilled cemetery of forgotten foods. In the past we would hit a breaking point together, buy a six-pack of beer, and team up to purge the contents while holding our noses, groaning and laughing and dumping cartons and bottles and bags of dripping and unidentifiable produce into the trash, then scrubbing the inside of the Frigidaire until it shined. It was a strangely bonding ritual, a result of busy people who forgot about food and could go weeks at a time without looking inside the fridge.

There was nothing to drink except water. So healthy, so boring. Where was a good Diet Coke when you needed one? I settled for the Poland Spring and felt my stomach growl. Too many cookies late at night left me with an insistent gurgling in my tummy. I needed something healthy. Shocking—it was always a serious sign when I actually craved the good stuff.

Turning on my heel, I noticed that Elke had created individual recycling boxes and lined them up along the far wall. One each for glass, plastic, paper, metal and the last for composting materials, indicated by hand-written signs surely meant to help the less environmentally aware Americans to distinguish what was what. That was serious. We'd hardly been able to separate the recycling from the trash, period, never mind subdivide the recyclables with any accuracy. It would do us good to be a little more conscientious.

I decided to walk myself to the office after all.

CHAPTER 10

My decision to walk was almost instantly and blissfully rewarded when, passing by the City Girl Cafe in Inman Square, I bumped into the one and only Paul Dennison, who was emerging from the small storefront restaurant with a cup of coffee in one hand and a carryout bag in the other. What were the chances?! Was the universe throwing us together, sending a message? We exchanged surprise and pleasantries and lingered on the sidewalk. I could feel the pink rise in my cheeks and took a deep breath to avoid betraying my racing heart. It was ridiculous how excited I felt when I was around him now. My head could not keep up with my heart—a heart with no regard for time or circumstance or propriety, a heart that just wanted its intense affection returned.

"Are you walking to work?" Paul asked, adjusting his messenger bag, with its wide strap slung across his chest, the bag itself hidden from view. It was terrible for the health of one's back, but God I loved that look.

"I am indeed. It's my new leaf, turning over," I said.

"I'm headed to MIT. I'll walk with you, if you don't mind the company."

I giggled in a really stupid way at the thought that I would *mind* Paul's company. Did I *mind*? How about *constantly crave*? *Yearn. Pine for.*

"So, what's with the new leaf?"

If I answered honestly I'd have to bring up my new roommate and her positive influence on me, and now that she'd emerged as a supervixen, I was doubly hesitant to create any knowledge of or curiosity about her. It was my sixth sense about certain women—the kind who could capture a man's imagination without even meeting them. I was sure to be overpowered by Elke's foreign intrigue—her name alone could do it—if I mentioned her. Even though it was possible Elke and Paul would meet eventually, I wanted to delay it for as long as I could.

"I just thought a little exercise would do me some good. Since my schedule and my finances make joining a gym impossible," I said.

"I haven't worked out in months. It's pathetic." Paul patted his stomach as if to suggest he was something other than perfectly fit. I didn't buy it. He looked as fine as ever to me. "But, I did find out that alumni can rent a racquetball court at Shad for five bucks. You wanna play some time?"

Racquetball? I think I'd tried to play precisely once in my two years at HBS, and was caught off guard that Paul considered me athletic enough to even suggest a matchup with his tall self. At this point I was uncertain of: 1) the sufficiency of my hand-eye coordination, 2) whether I could rustle up a racquet, and 3) how I would look from behind in gym shorts, not to mention while hurling myself around the claustrophobically enclosed court chasing after a hard, fast and potentially painful racquetball. But who was I kidding? I wasn't about to turn him down, and would quickly convince myself that this must mean Paul was interested in spending time with me, despite my obvious unsuitability for the sport. I'd simply have to strategize how to make it work, and agreed to join him the next week.

"Great. I'll reserve the court for us."

It felt good to me to relinquish the role of organizer, my

typical function in all relationships—personal and professional. "So what's up at MIT?"

"I'm meeting with some grad students who have a new technology that might have some online retail applications." Paul proceeded to describe the potential breakthroughs that would allow an unprecedented amount of personalization on the Red Dot site, and I was intrigued. It was challenging to stay on top of all of the technological developments—they were coming at such a rapid rate. Especially being near MIT, one felt constantly surrounded by new inventions and progress. It was exciting to be a part of it, even though my own insights were less about the technology itself and more about how people might react to it.

The rest of the walk to my office turned out to be far shorter than I'd expected, distracted as I was by Paul's presence, and the sense of possibility that filled me up every time I glanced beside me and saw his handsome face, his kind eyes, his half-smile.

CHAPTER 11

I'd always been intrigued by money. On the one hand, I could see it as a simple commodity, a stand-in for accessing other things that held real value. But in my reality, it held much more meaning and weight than that. Professionally, I had to deal with it, every day. The mechanics were not the issue—I was good enough at math. No, it was the emotional life of money—getting it, having it, asking for it—that I struggled with. The idea of putting a price tag on something—you, your time, your ideas, your plans—that's what had always felt so harsh. And yet cold hard cash was an essential fuel to keep a young company going, so I needed to suck it up and do my part.

I was in the office, working on a partnership agreement and our initial launch plan, when Stephen called me over. He pointed in the direction of his computer screen. "Here's a message from Paul," he said. "We're going to meet for drinks tonight to talk about financing."

"Oh?" I replied, stopped in my tracks.

"Yeah, he's going to make some introductions for us to VCs, but he's also talking about doing some personal investing. Possibly to help us with the bridge until we bring in institutional money."

"Oh?" I said again. "How does Paul have money for that?"

"Family money. They have a pool of money that they invest, and he runs it."

"Oh. What is the time frame for the bridge versus the full first round?" I asked.

I knew from our late-night discussions that Stephen wanted to try to carefully manage the timing of the first full round of institutional money. Rather than take that investment immediately, he wanted it to coincide with the period immediately after the launch. He believed if we waited until we were an official site with actual subscribers, a network of partners, and a good rate of sign-ups from new members, we'd get a much better financing deal than if we took the money before we had anything real to show for ourselves. This was because the venture capitalists were trying to assess how successful the company would be so they could, in essence, put a price tag on it. This was all assuming we could, in fact, attract the venture capitalists. If we failed to do that, we were sunk before we started.

Regardless, waiting until post-launch to bring in real money meant that we'd need some cash in the short term to tide us over—a much smaller amount, but still well beyond the limits of Stephen's credit cards. It was commonly called bridge financing, and in our case we were looking to angel investors—not professional investors, but rather individuals or small groups who were investing their own money, and would often invest smaller amounts and could generally move faster than big firms. It was a bold move, and I respected Stephen for it.

"We need to secure the bridge by year-end," Stephen said. "And we need to court the venture guys so that they're ready to invest and able to close the round within sixty days after the launch. That should tide us over, but we have to have the real money by then to build out the team and to do the big marketing push."

"Yeah, we do," I said, and meant it, even though I felt more comfortable operating on the shoestring budget we had during those pre-launch days, where my resourcefulness and innate cheapness were big plusses. We'd managed to run a marketing function on a few dollars and lots of late nights and goodwill, and were set to launch on time and on budget. But I fully understood that underinvesting in strategic and tactical marketing once the GoodMatch.com service was up and running would hurt us terribly in the long run. We had to establish brand recognition and attract a critical mass of subscribers quickly in order to be viable. It was all a self-reinforcing cycle—the more people we had in the database, the more likely we were to create good experiences for people—good matches. So we were experimenting with a number of trial models that allowed people to test the service for free and then convert if they wanted to keep using it. It was a delicate balance, and on top of it all we absolutely had to have the technology worked out. A buggy, slow or otherwise frustrating experience would be unacceptable. All the parts had to work together.

At around seven p.m. Elke appeared unexpectedly in the doorway of our office, which was propped open to help the air circulate. Wearing her hip, severe glasses and her hair loose around her shoulders, she stood silently, unencumbered by awkwardness, waiting to be seen. It took about three seconds for the first of the developers to take notice. Then, like popcorn, their heads bobbed up above their monitors to check her out. I spotted Elke from across the room but couldn't get off of my call with the team at Whisper, so Jeet was the first to invite her in.

"Hey there, can I help you?" Jeet said, and flashed his winning smile.

"Thank you. I see Anna." Elke gestured toward me with a hand that was both elegant and strong and I waved. Seeing me on the phone, she waited until I finished, soaking in glances from the tech contingent.

"Hi Elke, what a surprise," I said.

"I was walking to view a movie at the Kendall Theater and thought I would see if you or Stephen would like to join me."

I glanced at my watch and practically guffawed at the idea of leaving the office at seven p.m. "I'd love to but I can't get away," I said, indicating the activity around me.

"What about Stephen?" she asked, and I suppressed a smirk.

"I haven't seen Stephen go to the movies once since he started the company!" I answered.

"Oh." She looked disappointed and I felt bad. It would be nice to take a break, but I couldn't imagine it. We'd never catch up.

"Well," Elke continued, "maybe I'll just say hello to Stephen before I go."

"Sure," I answered. "He's in his office, around the corner." I pointed and she left. A little while later she reemerged and came to say goodbye.

"I'll see you at home, then?" Elke asked.

I felt guilty. "I'll meet you there later, after your movie. We can have tea."

Elke smiled and flashed her dimple, then waved goodbye and left, at which point the developers sunk a little in their chairs and half the energy left the room. It was amazing the impact that one stunning six-foot blonde could have on a room of sex-starved computer geeks.

I turned to tackle my to-do list with renewed vigor. It was written this week on a yellow legal pad with curled up corners from where I'd shoved it in my backpack. I used my to-do list like a child used a security blanket, soothing me in moments of upset and reassuring me that everything would be okay, so long as I could write it down and see it in plain ink. My list always started strong with big strategic issues like "Create incentive system for offline partners" or "Redesign look and feel of website" but then by about line eight, degenerated into the screechingly tactical, like "buy more Post-its." The current mess of a list had three different colors of ink, a dozen or more cross-outs, and too few check marks and was generally intolerable for its sabotaging of my desire to feel organized. I decided I couldn't do another thing until I'd rewritten the list entirely from scratch. So, if the list was my security blanket, rewriting it was thumb-sucking. Just the act of naming the tasks, organizing them, putting boxes next to things requiring action, writing down then checking off things I'd already done, was intoxicating and better than a stiff drink for calming my nerves.

A few hours later I left the office, bringing along my freshly transcribed list and more than a few tasks that I could do from home so that I could spend some time with Elke having tea and seeming present. Once home I slipped into my favorite pj's and curled up on the sofa under Anthony's gaze, reviewing the launch plan for GoodMatch.com before I turned it over to the PR team the next day. Elke hadn't arrived home from the movie yet, which surprised and annoyed me since I'd come home specifically to be with her. Ever since Elke moved in, and sort of without realizing it, I'd been spending more time than ever before at home. Usually I was working, but I thought physically being there was important. I felt an obligation on the part of America in general and Cambridge in particular to make sure Elke had a good time. I didn't want her to feel abandoned by me and Stephen, and definitely didn't want her going back to Germany next summer thinking Americans were inhospitable. Plus I liked her. She was cool and smart and interesting, and much more fun than I'd originally thought.

I heard the door open downstairs and Elke stepped in. She

was talking to someone, but I couldn't tell who from my place on the sofa. A minute later she poked her head into the living room and I looked up from my pages as she said "Guten Abend"— good evening.

"Hey," I said. I looked at my watch. "Were you at the movies this whole time?"

"Sort of. Then I had coffee. With a guy I met," Elke said, disappearing into her room to change.

"Really? How'd you meet him?" I called after her.

"At the popcorn stand. My preference was for the butter kind, by the way," Elke answered.

"Are you going to see him again?"

"Huh? Am I what?" Elke called out from behind her door.

"The guy. Popcorn Stand Coffee Guy," I asked.

In my entire history of movie-going that had never happened to me, or anyone I knew for that matter. The supermarket, sure. The laundromat, maybe. But the movies? Where every normal person is on a date or with friends? How did that happen, exactly? Not only did this guy see Elke, want to meet her, etc., but he was also willing to ditch his friends to do so? I recognized a pang of envy that Elke could so easily attract men without trying. I'd always secretly wanted to be one of those women who wandered through the world gathering attention and affection from strangers and acquaintances just by *being*. Instead I lived by the notion that it required a whole lot more effort on my part to make up for with tenacity what I lacked in natural appeal, or that magical quality that people like Elke and Stephen had.

Elke poked her head out of her room. "Eh, him. I don't know. Maybe. He would like to see me again, that is clear."

Of course he would, I thought. It seemed to be true for most guys who met Elke, and I was still marveling at the fact that I'd pegged her so incorrectly at the beginning. I didn't see this vixen, this heartbreaker coming from behind the blue coat and the harsh glasses. But here she was, my roommate. Confronting me daily with her long hair and long legs plus that brilliant, accomplished mind. That last part was the thing that really threw me. I could handle the fact that men found her beautiful but it was going to take some getting used to that she was also a real smarty-pants—I mean, she was a doctor studying at Harvard. No slouch.

At various points in my life I dutifully—happily, even—played the sidekick role to the real beauties who were my friends. With them I was the smart one. The nice one. The reliable one. The good listener. The ego soother. The one who took care of the drunk one, unless I was the drunk one, and then I took care of myself. In any case, I was more likely invisible than not. But the truth was, I craved being seen. I wanted to be noticed, loved, adored, respected, appreciated, desired. I wanted what everyone else wanted. *To matter.*

Elke reappeared in the doorway of her bedroom, across the living room, resting her back against the doorjamb. "Will you be having this party you mentioned last week? Is this true?" asked Elke, snapping me out of my musings.

"Yes, absolutely. We're launching the company to everyone, including investors. So the more people mixing and mingling, the better," I said.

Elke brightened, I think at the mention of mingling. "Ja! And I will wear my sock dress!"

I dropped my papers into my lap. "Your sock dress? What is a sock dress?"

"I will show you," Elke criss-crossed her arms and in one seamless move grabbed the bottom edges of her sweater and pulled it over her head while disappearing back inside her room. She emerged in a skintight, short-to-the-point-of-indecent dress in the color of espresso that looked incredible on her. She raised her arms in a "ta-da" fashion.

"Wallah! You see—fits like a sock!"

"Wow. It sure does. It's . . . perfect." My oh my. With her wardrobe selection Elke had just raised the bar more than a few notches for this party. And while I really wanted to be the kind of woman who could look at a sexy, beautiful other woman with appreciation and calm, and not comparison, right then I couldn't. Sorry, no way. Wasn't there yet. Instead I got that sinking, sucky feeling of total inadequacy and let my head fill up with inane questions like, Why can't I be six feet tall?

Elke smiled and her dimple showed and she looked pleased at the compliment and slid off in search of her killer heels. Like she needed any more height!

Wouldn't *I* like to have my outfit planned weeks in advance. But no, I could see it now . . . I'd probably end up throwing something entirely random together five minutes before I needed to get to the event, and settle for half-done hair and the wrong shoes and barely a slap of makeup.

I tried to refocus on my launch plan and couldn't concentrate. Arggh. I would have much preferred to stay comfortably immersed in estimating the market size of North American Internet users from 1995 to 2000 instead of being forced to contemplate how I was going to deal with dressing for this big party. Yes, I could do my usual straight black, fade-into-the-woodwork outfit. I'd grown incredibly, dangerously comfortable in the safe space behind the scenes. Complacent and still. Invisible.

I gave up on work for the night. It was close to midnight anyway. "I'm going to hit the hay," I said. Elke was absorbed by her closet, pulling together the rest of her outfit, sure to include the perfect accessories. She peeked out at me, looking puzzled.

"It means I'm going to bed."

"Ah, good night, Anna." Elke smiled and waved me off.

I wandered into my bedroom and collapsed on the bed, pathetic envy seeping into my bones. How had I let this happen? It was entirely unintentional that I'd allowed this stunning, statuesque, brilliant, worldly woman into my home, a daily reminder of all the things I wasn't and wanted to be. I knew better. I knew I didn't have the reservoir of self-esteem for such constant tweaking of these feelings of inadequacy.

I pulled myself vertical and opened my closet, spying the purple bridesmaid dress for my cousin Barbara's wedding in a hanging bag at the far end. I absently snapped molded plastic hangers across the wood rod, confronted with article after article of tedious black and brown clothing, things my mother would approve of, or even wear. Certainly nothing that would be suitable next to a Sock Dress. Except maybe one thing. Tucked in the back, covered in protective plastic, was my splurge purchase made during a trip to Filene's Basement last year. I drew out an elegant Prada top in a deep burgundy color paired with a pencil skirt, slit down the side with skinny ribbons crisscrossing to hold it together. Both pieces still had the tags on. I held them to my body, matching curves to curves against the cotton of my pajamas. A stitch of regret hit me then—this was a case of dramatic overspending on something I'd never worn. Even at 90 percent off, in an impressive playing of the Basement's Automatic Markdown scheme, my Prada binge had consumed hundreds of dollars of the credit limit on my Visa. I hung the ensemble on the outside of my closet door and crawled into bed, staring hard at the indisputably kickass outfit. My rest lasted for three seconds before anxiety pushed me out of bed, and I dropped to the floor and into a set of push-ups. Surely every little bit would help if I was even going to consider wearing the Prada to the launch party, and it couldn't hurt to prepare for my racquetball match with Paul. Concentrating on the trembling in my squishy biceps, I didn't hear Stephen come into my room.

"Annie, what are you doing?" he asked and I could feel the smile in his tone, catching me by surprise. I looked up without making eye contact and fell to my knees, flipping up my duvet and spontaneously initiating a search for whatever might be under there. Dust bunnies, a section of *The New York Times*, a single sock . . .

"Oh, hey. Nothing. Looking for my, my sock." I emerged with a dusty sock as Stephen fell onto the bed.

"What's that?" Stephen pointed to my outfit, hanging conspicuously nearby. I felt caught.

"That's my, um, aspiration. What I want to wear to the launch party." Don't tease me, please don't tease me.

"Nice."

I climbed into bed next to Stephen and we caught up on the day. A few minutes later Elke came in, still in her sock dress, and curled herself up along the foot of the bed. The three of us chatted for a while, with Stephen teasing Elke about getting settled in Cambridge, and had she found anyone interesting to hang around with, had she met any nice guys? I thought Elke enjoyed the playful attention. We agreed we should have a roommate dinner at least once a month, and planned the first one for the following weekend. I reminded them both that I had the wedding on Saturday so that wasn't a great day for me. I failed to mention my birthday. So, the roommate dinner would be on Sunday, it was settled.

CHAPTER 12

Start-up life was full of highs and lows, and thankfully they came in rapid enough spurts that they usually offset each other. It was like riding a wave, with the threat of it crashing onto your head hovering at all times, and sometimes it did. But then you'd have a lull after the battering, and time to catch your breath before doing it again, with the occasional successful run and rush that made it all worth it.

When I arrived at work the next day, Jeet cornered me before I could even sit down. "Annie, we've got a big issue to deal with," he said. Not given to overreaction, Jeet's obvious upset triggered my own nerves before I even knew what the issue was. He waved me over to his bullpen and pushed some printouts in front of me, a detailed report on the results of our usability tests from the prior week, and it was ugly. The data suggested that people found the site confusing, frustrating and non-intuitive. To say this was a problem was like saying the Titanic had some navigation troubles. The first rule in marketing was to have a product that worked—no amount of promotion and slick advertising would prevail over people having a bad experience once they got to our website. The problem seemed to rest in the interface—it wasn't easy enough to figure out what to do or how to sign up, how to find people, how to invite your friends so that you could build your personal network and help your people find people to date or socialize with. This was the innovation we were really excited about. We knew that traditional matchmaking had a one-to-one or a one-to-many construct. We thought that a many-to-many model would work best online. And we thought that friends encouraging friends to join their circles would be a great way to drive traffic and build the population of the site. At any rate, if it wasn't easy to maneuver around the site we had a huge problem on our hands. Jeet and I spent a tense morning diagnosing and prioritizing the issues, brainstorming solutions and coming up with a plan that I'd bring to Stephen when he freed up later in the day.

It wasn't until lunchtime that I even made my way to my own desk, but when I got there I found a flat package covering the entire surface, about four feet square, wrapped in plain brown paper and tied with twine like a massive—albeit flat—bakery cake. The routing slip stuck to the front indicated it was sent by courier. Was this what I thought it was?! After pulling at the knot and tearing away the paper in strips and eliminating a layer of bubble wrap, the glossy letters of our new name and logo—a stylized image of two puzzle pieces, which, if you looked closely, resembled two people connecting—emerged on a three-foot-by-four-foot sign that splashed www.GoodMatch.com across the bottom. I was stunned at the impact of seeing our brand presented with such polish and decisiveness, even though I'd worked side by side with Stephen and the graphic design student, a friend of Jeet's, through days and nights of drafts and revisions before finalizing it. It was much harder than we expected to come up with a single name and image that could capture the essence of our company and everything about our vision and the spirit of the service in essentially one glance. We realized that we'd have to drive toward an image that was completely consistent with the underlying philosophy *and* enticing enough to get people to be willing to discover more, to visit the website and learn about our approach and important features like trustworthiness, quality and good matches. We'd settled on a logo that conveyed a combination of fun and sophistication and used tones of periwinkle and charcoal grey and accents of bright orange, rejecting anything predictable or too feminine like red or pink.

I moved to sit on my chair and instead bumped into a second, smaller package that contained our business cards and stationery. I combed over the individual boxes within the carton to find my own cards and pulled a sample out to inspect. On one side of each individual card was the GoodMatch.com logo. On the opposite side, my name, title and contact information populated the four corners of the card. Anna C. Thompson. Chief Marketing Officer. *Chief Marketing Officer*. I felt both proud and silly to have such a pretentious title. Because the truth was, while I was certainly in charge of marketing, I was chief to no one. My staff consisted of several unpaid interns who showed up for work only sporadically. As a matter of (hopefully temporary) necessity, we kept our paid staff to a minimum. I did get to work with our great PR agency, Whisper, which was doing GoodMatch.com's promotions and public relations work—for a small equity stake. Charlotte was the partner in the agency who loved the GoodMatch.com concept and believed Whisper's PR efforts could make a big enough difference that working for equity was a smart move for them. But despite a great partnership with Whisper, the rest of the time I was pretty much on my own, and the start-up life forced me into a constant exercise in prioritization and sequencing. Since the only thing I was 100 percent sure of was that there wasn't enough time to do everything, the things I chose to do had to be the most important ones, and in the right order. In addition to working with the agency on the PR and launch plans, my focus was on the site itself and on structuring partnership deals that would allow us to link to other websites in order to generate traffic to GoodMatch.com. It was excruciating at times, because my preference was to do everything perfectly. And perfection simply wasn't an option in this line of work. Stephen and I spent many a night over bottles of Sam Adams discussing what "good enough" looked like, and Stephen had to coax me off the ledge more than once when something blew up that I could have prevented, in theory, if I'd had more time. "Annie, yes, maybe we could've seen that coming, but then something else would've fallen through the cracks," Stephen would say. Then he'd add his new motto: "Fast is more important than perfect."

"Drum roll, please," I said. Stephen looked up from his desk as I revealed the placard.

"Awesome. It looks terrific. Nice work, Annie." He agreed it was a bold and sophisticated look that should appeal to our target market and allow us to coordinate a guerilla branding effort that would make GoodMatch.com a household name.

"This will really help us with the look and feel of the site," I said. "And now I can start thinking about the details for our launch party. You'll need to start putting together the names of the VCs you want to invite."

Stephen responded with the same veiled anxious look that came up whenever fundraising and venture capitalists were mentioned.

"Yeah, I have a draft of it here."

I looked over the list. I recognized a few names, but for the most part it was a foreign world to me. I had figured out, though, that the venture capital world was as much about networking and selling as it was about finance. The deal was one thing, but it would never happen if the VCs couldn't be convinced there was a real business opportunity involved and, perhaps most important, that you had the management team to make it happen. Added to the challenge was the fact that the Internet was such a new thing, and while some deals were getting done, by no means was the VC world yet fully convinced that the Internet could be turned into a business. The number of people with Internet access was growing like crazy; even my father had gone out and bought a desktop, got himself online, and spent most evenings checking out postings and auctions for model cars from the 1950s and 1960s. But the base of people with dial-up connections was still relatively small, and consumers' willingness to pay for anything online almost entirely unproven, except in the case of Amazon.com, which was starting to take off in book and CD sales, and eBay, in auctions.

"We've got to convince these guys that people will actually use this service," said Stephen.

"I know. I do think people will eventually want the service. But I've got some—concerns. About the website. There's something you need to know about."

"Yeah, lay it on me." Stephen tended to stay calm until he knew he had something to worry about.

"Jeet got the interface and usability tests back," I said. "And you know how you're fond of saying 'average sucks'?"

Stephen nodded.

"Well, we don't even suck. We're so far below average it's wrenching. And we have got to fix it before we can start to build the database and be ready to launch."

"Shit. That's not okay. What do we think is going on?"

"I think I know exactly what's going on. Stephen, we've got a fraternity full of nineteen- and twenty-year-old MIT engineers working here—and I love 'em, I really do—but most of them don't know the first thing about the dating process. It's a completely foreign world to most of them. They're out of their element with what we're asking them to do. We're expecting them to understand how singles want to navigate a site like ours and they have no personal instincts about it because most of them have never been on a date—and I say that with affection, but it's true, and we've given them relatively little data to fill in their own blanks."

"Okay, let's think about what we can do here. We can't afford to buy any expertise." Stephen was right. We didn't have the resources to launch a big research effort. We needed to be cleverer than that.

"Right now they've got this mindset that all that matters is the functionality, you know, does the database work, can people technically register, will the pictures post if you can figure out which buttons to push. They don't get why it matters so much what the site looks and feels like, as long as it works. I need to convince them that the look and feel is just as important as the guts of the code. We've got to make it more real."

"And you've got an idea for how to do this?" Stephen asked. He knew I tried not to bring problems to him without having generated at least one possible course of action.

"Yes, I do. Give me twenty-four hours."

CHAPTER 13

I'd come to love the challenge of solving problems with massive constraints like no money and no time. It was exhilarating and sparked a creative burst in me that must have released large quantities of dopamine into my brain because it felt better than sex, assuming of course that I was remembering accurately what that felt like. And the rush of it all made me forget for a few minutes that I hadn't talked to Paul in days.

I began at my desk making phone calls to hatch my plan, and then decided to continue while driving to Chester, as I deemed it a more efficient use of time. A while later, I pulled into my parents' driveway, attempting to talk on my cell phone while referencing my Day-Timer for numbers. I'd managed to reach almost all of the people I needed to make my Band-Aid solution come together.

"Yup, seven o'clock sharp at our offices. It will be fun. Okay, see you then." Clicking off the phone, I headed into my parents' house. My father was predictably at his computer and watching CNBC at the same time, tracking his retirement portfolio.

"Hi, Dad." He looked up to see who was distracting him from his online car-collecting community.

"Hi, Annie, what are you doing here?"

"I called Mom to borrow the digital camcorder. For a few weeks." My mother came in from the kitchen.

"I told her I thought you wouldn't mind," she said.

"That's my camcorder," my father said to me. "She can't tell you that you can take it."

Parker Thompson was generous to a point, but he occasionally liked to assert his ownership rights and familial authority. It annoyed me because he did it unpredictably.

"Are you kidding, Dad? Mom has to ask your permission? She gave it to you!" It was his big present from the Christmas before last.

"Annie, it's an expensive piece of equipment. Do you even know how to use it? No, I'm sure you don't. You women aren't good with mechanical things." He shook his head and let out a sigh and turned his attention back to the computer.

I sighed and ignored him. I didn't have the energy to argue. I put my cell phone and Day-Timer on the coffee table to free my hands for other tasks. "Mom, can I get the party stuff while I'm here?"

"It's in the dining room, in the sideboard." My mother led me past the kitchen and into the dining room to retrieve the items, dropping to her knees to start pulling party supplies out of the wood cabinet. Elizabeth Thompson was a masterful bargain shopper, with a stash of deeply discounted party supplies on hand at all times, and an exceptional recycler. She was the type of person who washed the plastic forks and knives instead of throwing them away and had amassed a collection of four or five hundred sets. I found that having her genes was a godsend when it came to work; I could easily budget and plan and scheme and save, just like she did.

I wasn't sure of the last time I'd been in our family dining room. I noticed that the coffee mugs I'd given my parents for Christmas—one said *Harvard Mom*, the other *Harvard Dad*—were now displayed on a new, small shelf stained to match the sideboard and table and screwed into the wood paneling.

"Hey Mom, I meant for you to drink coffee out of these," I said.

My mother looked back and up at me. "Huh? What? Oh, no. We like them there. But Jodie says she wants a *Harvard Sister* mug, and then we'll need another shelf."

I smiled, certain Jodie's wish was merely to tease. Within a few minutes there was a hefty stack of plastic and paper on the table, and I loaded up both arms and carried two stacks of miscellaneous supplies back to the family room, where I heard my father saying "Bye" into my cell phone and clicking it off.

"Dad, what are you doing?" I asked in the calmest voice I could produce.

"Your phone rang. I yelled for you."

"Did you let it go to voicemail?" I asked, alarm rising in my temples.

"Voicemail? I didn't know it had voicemail. I answered it for you."

Oh, shit. Who knew what kind of conversation my father could get into? And with whom? "You answered it for me? Dad, that's, that's for work. Who was it?"

"It was a guy named Paul. Paul something."

Of course it was Paul something. Couldn't have been Stephen something, who knew my father and found him funny. Or Elke. Or any single other person in my life. *Had* to be Paul.

"Paul Dennison? Was it Paul *Dennison*?" I asked, a feeling of alarm squeezing the space between my eyes.

He nodded. "Yes, that's who it was."

"Dad, I can't believe you did that. What did you say?!" My anxiety was contributing the exclamation point to my sentence; my annoyance registered clearly in the pitch of my voice.

"I told him you were, ah, busy." He looked irritated. In the Thompson family the discipline and disappointment went only one way—from father to child. "What's the big problem?"

I took a breath to stay calm.

"Dad, well, Paul is a potential investor. I'm just anxious about making a good impression. We're trying to raise ten million dollars in the next few months, and I don't want our investors to think we're in any way—um, unprofessional."

"Well, he just asked for you to call him back."

"Okay, I will. Thank you. I know you were just helping me out. Sorry to overreact. It's just a tense time."

"I hope this is all worth it. You look terrible. Have you slept at all?"

"Some," I responded. "This Internet-pioneer thing can be exhausting."

My father looked at me with a mix of concern and skepticism and possibly a hint of pride. Jodie walked in and we nodded hello as she flopped on the sofa, wearing workout clothes and eating fat-free ice cream out of the container.

"Ten million dollars?" he continued. "I don't know where you came from, Annie. You're not like the rest of us."

I thought this was a compliment, but couldn't be sure, and my family survival instincts told me that willingly accepting this "not like the rest of us" label was a mistake. "Yes I am," I shrugged.

"No, you're not," he continued. "You're different. Your brother and your sister, they don't have what you have. They don't want what you want."

"They don't want the camcorder?" I tried to ease the tension I'd created. My father half smiled and left to retrieve the device.

"He's right," Jodie said between mouthfuls of Breyers Gourmet Chocolate. "You're totally not like us. Mom and Dad didn't even go to college, and the rest of us, we're all just happy to have made it through undergrad. You and your friends are all like . . . overgrad."

I laughed. "It remains to be seen what I will make of my overeducation."

My father returned without the camcorder. "I don't know where it is. Where's your mother? She'll know." He hollered in the direction of the bedrooms. "'Lizabeth, where's the camcahda?"

My mother came back into the family room. "In the antique."

"The what?" I asked while my father departed, apparently headed toward "the antique."

"It's the dresser you gave us from your old apartment," my mother explained. "You told us it was an antique. So that's what we call it."

My father returned with the camcorder in a black carrying case. I quickly realized I must have been the butt of an ongoing joke about "the antique." My parents were the kind of people who prized newness above all else. Antiques made no sense. They, for example, would rather buy a new cheap couch every few years than invest in one high-quality piece that they'd have to live with forever.

"Well, it is technically an antique," I explained. "But I paid forty dollars for it at a flea market in Vermont, so I hardly think you need to call it 'the antique.'"

Jodie giggled silently and ate more ice cream.

"Well, that's what we named it. Can't change it now," said my mother.

"Like it's a pet," Jodie laughed.

It occurred to me that I'd better not show my family my business cards. They'd have a field day laughing at me for the chief marketing officer thing.

My father handed the camcorder to me. "Here. Now make

sure you read the instructions before you use it."

As soon as I got into my car I tried to call Paul back, to see what he wanted and to repair any damage.

"Hi, it's Annie."

"Oh, hey Annie. That was quick."

"Yeah, so sorry about that, before."

"Huh? So sorry about what?" Paul answered.

"I mean, sorry I wasn't available when you called."

"Oh, no problem. I was just seeing what you're up to. My buddy needs the apartment to himself tonight, he's hosting a book club or something like that, so I was thinking about swinging by your place, maybe hanging out, if you're around."

"Oh, really, yeah, well, I'm not there right now." In fact, the only person there was probably the supervixen. Warning bells filled my head. As much as I would love-love-love to hang out in my apartment with Paul, I just couldn't risk it. Plus, when I glanced in the rearview mirror I could see nothing but dark under-eye circles and messy hair. Not to mention I had a mere twenty-four hours to fix our wretched interface problem.

"Yeah, sounds like you're driving," Paul said.

"I am. Hey, my apartment is kind of a wreck and we have this thing blowing up at work and I have to get back there. I think I'll have to catch up with you another time." I couldn't believe the words were coming out of my mouth, but circumstances were extreme.

"Ah, sure, no problem." Paul had the flat tone of someone unused to being turned down, for anything. "I'll go catch a movie or something."

"My roomm—um, someone said *Mighty Aphrodite* is good, you know, the Woody Allen movie?" Elke had liked it when she saw it, the night she'd met Popcorn Stand Coffee Guy.

"Yeah, I think I'll head over to the Kendall and see what's

playing. Maybe I'll bring you some Twizzlers afterward."

My office was located close to the movie theater, so it would hardly be inconvenient for Paul to stop by, but it was not lost on me that the tiniest hint of unavailability, even in a relationship that sat squarely in the friendship realm, worked like magic. Not that I was trying to work it, but still.

CHAPTER 14

The next day at the office, all of GoodMatch.com's Web developers sat in the developer pit, a configuration of computer stations positioned to allow both privacy and collaboration. By moving chairs slightly, almost everyone could see everyone else, but they also could rearrange themselves to minimize distractions.

I walked into the room and unconsciously scrunched my nose. I turned to one of my more reliable interns named Polly, a perky marketing major from Boston College with a crush on Jeet.

"Okay, we need some scented candles, and some lamps in here. I want tape recorders at all computers, and I borrowed two digital cameras, so let's set them up." Polly took off to handle her tasks. I spotted Jeet and waved him over.

"Jeet, can we get all of the guys to go home for a couple of hours, take a shower, and be back by seven? They can stay on the clock, but the shower is non-negotiable."

"You got it." Jeet took off to inform the boys they were getting paid to fumigate.

When the office clock said seven fifteen p.m. all of the developers were back at work, newly clean, and standing around the mini-fridge where I had gathered them and handed out half a case of Rolling Rock. It was not entirely uncommon to have a beer at work but rarely did the entire team pause all at once.

"Okay guys," I began. "I mentioned we'd be doing some of

our own customer experience labs tonight. I wanted to make sure we gave you a chance to spend time directly with people that will be using our website. I've already instructed the customer group. So all I want you to do is sit with them and listen as they go through the site. The tape recorders and video recorders will track specific comments, so you need to just concentrate on what you're hearing and try to understand our site and our service from the customer's point of view. For tonight, you're not a programmer. You're a listener. Any questions?"

The developers were all polite young men, mostly students from MIT and BU and Northeastern, with a few recent graduates thrown in. They were not particularly interested in or enthused about this project until I ushered in a dozen extremely attractive, outgoing young women, friends and friends of friends of mine, including Elke, who had become excited about the possibilities that GoodMatch.com represented if only it was launched before she left to go back to Germany. Each of the prospective customers took a seat in front of the dozen or so computers in the room with instructions to go through the sign-up process and to fill out a profile. The developers were supposed to listen to the thought process and the questions that popped up for the customers, including places where the site was confusing or unfriendly. The room was instantly abuzz with chatter and laughter. A few minutes into the lab, Stephen popped his head in and surveyed the scene, and gave me the thumbs-up.

"I decided we had to make it more real," I said to Stephen. "Get them out of their heads and a little more into their . . . you know, guts."

By nine p.m., the beer was gone, the developers had received an engrossing narration and first-hand account of what it felt like to be a consumer of their programming efforts, ideas for improving the GoodMatch.com experience flowed, and one developer had a date for Thursday night. GoodMatch.com had twelve gorgeous women as our initial pool of possible matches. Not exactly enough, but a start. I asked Jeet, who was a talented photographer, to take digital photos of each of the women to post to their profiles, and I'd done brief interviews on video to capture their initial experiences for PR purposes. With some careful editing, they could be used as testimonials on the website or to show initial enthusiasm for GoodMatch.com to prospective investors. I asked each of the women to suggest at least two friends to participate in the next round of tests, women or men. I'd do another couple of rounds with just women, and then the all-male development team would have to listen to the guys, too.

I was so filled with ideas and excitement that I worked without stopping until well past two a.m., writing down and typing up everything we'd learned so I didn't forget it. The ideas multiplied and I faced the ongoing challenge to accept that everything couldn't be done at once. We needed to prioritize and sequence. Jeet and I would meet in the morning to figure out a smart way to make the most important changes quickly, and a longer-term plan to make the other improvements over time.

I hit a wall at two thirty a.m. and went to check on Stephen, who was alternately sipping a Coke and hammering at his keyboard. It seemed that the later it got the harder you had to type, the jarring motion helping to keep you conscious.

"Hey. I'm going home. Do you want a ride?" I asked, not expecting a yes but wanting to check anyway.

"No thanks, I'll ride my bike, or I might crash here."

Once home, as I headed up the walkway to my apartment, I was surprised to see the living room lights shining through the tall windows. Elke was über-responsible with energy—she never let a lightbulb burn in a room she wasn't using—and it was nearly three a.m. I found my house keys on my crowded key chain and was ascending the back steps when the big wood door opened unexpectedly, startling me to the point of speechlessness, especially when I realized the tall figure leaving the apartment was not Elke but one of our developers named Tommy, a shy MIT grad student with jet black hair and a charming space between his teeth.

"Oh, ah, hey, hi, Annie," Tommy stammered, looking caught.

"Hi . . . Tommy, what are you . . ." I started to ask, and then stopped myself.

"That was cool tonight, the customer labs."

"Yeah, it was, thanks for doing it." I remembered that Tommy and Elke had been paired together for the second round of tests earlier that evening.

"You and Elke—must have hit it off . . . ?" Tommy's face collapsed into the dreamy, gushing grin of a twenty-something who hadn't been with many women, never mind a temptress like Elke.

"Yeah, she's amazing . . ." His thoughts seemed to drift with his eyes toward the door where he'd just left Elke, bearing the smile of someone feeling unbelievably lucky. He looked lost in it and I felt embarrassed for him—and me. I didn't want the details, couldn't stand the intimate reflections here on my doorstep, or the probable outcome of Tommy's heart and hopes getting broken. It was possible, but highly unlikely, that Elke would ever see him again, and looking at him now, he hadn't a clue.

"It's so late, we both better get some sleep," I said, sounding like a mother hen. He glanced at his watch, registering the time with pride, and I could just imagine the retelling of the night to his guy friends.

"G'night Annie." He turned slowly, reluctant to leave.

"Bye, Tommy. See you tomorrow," I responded, and headed

inside. Some of the lights were now off.

At the top of the stairs I saw Elke emerging from the bathroom, drying her face on a towel.

"Anna, you're home."

"Hi Elke. You're up late . . ." I smiled, one eyebrow raised in a question.

"Ja, I am," she agreed nonchalantly. This was a normal pattern, for Elke to have her hookups and not make a big deal of them. To not bother to share details or even disclose they happened. She was so different from my other friends, who would gossip about all of the details all of the time. It was refreshing.

"I can't find sleep," Elke said. "Would you like some chamomile tea? I've turned on the kettle."

We gathered our steaming mugs and ourselves onto opposite ends of the sofa under Anthony's portrait, gently dunking teabags and sipping in silence. In the time since Elke had arrived I'd come to enjoy our roommate time. We had long, winding conversations about life and love and being single and yet I surprised myself by never confiding about Paul to her. It wasn't that I didn't trust her or value her opinion—the opposite was true. It was just that she had such a calm maturity about her when it came to men, and I sensed two things. First, that she would think I was wasting my time if I wasn't getting what I wanted from Paul. She herself would never waste time in a situation that was so imbalanced, so unsatisfying. She would also not hesitate, I suspected, to make a move to find out if there was any reciprocal interest. I couldn't quite handle the contrast with my own approach—one so marked by fear of losing access to him. Second, I had this nagging fear about having these two parts of my life—the Paul part and the Elke part—intersect. I was increasingly of the mind that Elke was possibly the coolest woman I'd ever met. I'd never known a woman like her—so stunningly casual about men while also being a brilliant doctor, and though I liked her enormously, I felt alternately inadequate and judgmental toward her. Part of me wanted to be more like her, part of me couldn't imagine being anything like her.

Elke was quizzing me about my work schedule. She did this occasionally—called into question my choices about how I spent my time. (She seemed to have mastered work-life balance. I guess there weren't too many dermatology emergencies and she always seemed to be out of work by seven.) Particularly concerning to her was my apparent lack of attention to my love life. Lately Elke was tapping economic theory to help persuade me to reconsider my preoccupation with my career and procrastination around relationships. "There's a new body of research that shows that more money doesn't make us happy."

"That's not new, is it?" I wasn't sure I believed it anyway. I agreed with my mother, who always said, "Money doesn't buy happiness, but it sure does help."

"Well," Elke went on, "what they're saying is that most of us adapt quickly to financial improvements—we just covet a higher class of goods."

"Expenses rise to meet income." It was true for me. When I had more money, I got a seventy-dollar haircut every six or seven weeks. When I had less, like in these early start-up days, I'd let my hair grow and grow until in a fit of desperation I cut it myself. It was the one blessing of having long hair unhampered by any real aspirations of style—kitchen scissors and a hair tie could suffice for months at a time. But that didn't seem to be Elke's point.

"Right. But what's interesting is that marriage does seem to induce happiness that lasts and lasts. May I read you something?"

"Sure."

I sipped my tea as Elke retrieved a printout and began reading. This was commonplace—she was always sharing advice. I liked it.

"According to a paper by two University of Zurich economists, getting married provides 'basic insurance against adverse life events and allows gains from economies of scale and specialization within the family.'"

"That's so romantic, I might cry." To me it was academic-speak for having someone to listen when you bitch, split the cost of cable and do the dishes after you cooked dinner. And it was surprising to me that Elke would advocate marriage.

"But what it says is that you'd need to make a lot more money to be as happy as a married couple in love."

"How much?" I asked, stifling a yawn.

"Well, precise numbers are not so much available," Elke said. "But these economists Blanchflower and Oswald have estimated a happy marriage is worth one hundred thousand dollars a year."

"That's it? I could be making that now if I worked for a big company," I said. It was true. Many of my classmates took jobs making six figures, and I had offers in that range. And my family did not entirely understand my choice to turn them down to go into debt on an Internet pipe dream.

"Well, Anna, that's not really the point."

"Why can't I have both marriage and money?" I was glib. Elke did a head tilt, and decided, as she was sometimes wont to do, that if she couldn't reach me with the rational facts then she'd bop me over the head with the hard cold truth.

"You can have both," said Elke. "But you don't have both. You have neither. One single solitary thing in your life, Anna. A job that pays you nothing."

Okày, technically she was right. But I had stock options, the possibility of making real money some day from this sweat and hard work. And then there was Paul.

CHAPTER 15

Paul made good on his proposal to reserve us a racquetball court at Shad, the gym on the business school campus. I had borrowed a racquet and ball from Jeet and spent more time than I cared to admit scouring my wardrobe for an ensemble that looked effortless and casual and—if at all possible—cute. I searched on Yahoo! to find the rules of the game, and I continued with my evening push-ups and added sit-ups to my routine—simultaneously certain it wouldn't make a difference and feeling better all the same. I went down to the basement of our apartment building for ten minutes and practiced hitting the ball against the wall, just to be sure I could make contact reliably. When the day came, I was kind of excited for it.

Stepping back onto campus with Paul was strange, and I was proud to be seen with him. Many of the now-second-year students were people we recognized, since we'd been on campus together last year, and I caught more than a couple of women noticing Paul, trying to remember who he was, where they'd seen him before, probably confused by his companion, me, who didn't look quite right next to him.

The gym was ridiculously high-end, like any fine Manhattan boutique health club, and we picked up towels at the front desk and put away our things in our respective locker rooms before meeting by the racquet courts. The courts were completely enclosed, the door flush to the back wall, with bright white walls and ceiling, a sleek wood floor, and a certain surreal air to the setting. Once we stepped inside, it was like a secluded bubble for just the two of us. As I stretched my legs a bit, across the court, Paul seemed most concerned with getting his game on, bouncing the blue ball and swinging his racquet. I was most concerned with him seeing me in shorts.

I decided quickly that the most disconcerting thing for me in a racquetball court was that, while there is a front and a back wall, the state of play could take you in any direction, rendering it impossible to control the viewing angle that another player would have of, say, your ass. This was concerning to me only in the first few minutes of our game, after which the hollow rubber ball was bouncing so quickly and uncontrollably around us that all thoughts—other than avoiding being hit by said fast-moving ball—melted completely away. Since the court's walls, floor and ceiling were legal playing surfaces, with nothing out-of-bounds, it was a total free-for-all—exhilarating and fun. At first I was focused on just hitting the ball. Once I was steadily making contact, I realized that the name of the game was placement, and Paul was much better at making me run, scramble and dive (okay, I never actually dove, but could have) to keep up with his shots. I was sweating and out of breath, but it was a blast, and once I started getting the hang of it, I was able to place more shots where Paul wasn't, and he actually had to start working a little for some of his many, many points.

In the speed of the action, and given the cursory nature of my glance over the rules on Yahoo!, I committed two types of faults multiple times before Paul paused to coach me on proper use of walls. Once, in my newfound enthusiasm for the game, I overdid it on one of my serves and sent the ball flying to the back wall and screaming on the rebound toward Paul, hitting him hard on his backside.

"Owwwwww!!!!"

Although I should have immediately launched into an apology, since I was clearly a rule breaker, seeing Paul bounce around rubbing his butt was just too funny, and I collapsed into hysterics. It was also a chance to pause and catch my breath.

"What are you laughing at? This really hurts!" Paul was smiling through his pain.

"I'm sorry, I'm sorry, I've just never seen a grown man rubbing his butt cheek and crying out in pain."

"Well, if you don't stop laughing that'll be grounds for making *you* rub my butt cheek." I giggled a bit more and smiled at the thought. I probably paused a little too long and it was possible Paul could read my mind then, but I was happy and exhausted and I didn't care if he knew that I would willingly, gladly, lustfully volunteer to take care of his sore butt, any day of the week.

"C'mon, I'll buy you a Gatorade," I said.

"Hmmm, I think I'd rather have a beer. Can you spare the time?"

The honest answer was no, I had a load of work to do and should've gone back to the office as soon as possible. But twenty minutes later, after the world's fastest shower, we were sitting in the lounge with two Amstel Lights and a bowl of pretzels, relaxed and laughing. Paul was telling me a funny story about adapting to life with a roommate after having a wife for so long.

"He's better than a wife, because he's neat and clean but doesn't bitch about me not being."

"I forget, how did you find this roommate?"

"He's a buddy from high school, actually. You know, the kind of friend you might not talk to all the time but always feel you can rely on. Good guy. You should meet him some time."

We finished our beer and, as much as I wanted to stay

longer, I felt the pull of GoodMatch.com, which needed me to figure out how to reach ten thousand members by the date of our launch. I was working on a geographic strategy: starting with major cities with high rates of singledom.

I walked back to my car with Paul. "Thank you—that was really fun," I said, reaching for my keys.

"It was. We should do it again. Good for your heart." *You don't say.*

"If not your butt." In an unguarded moment, I reached around and patted Paul's rear in the spot where my ball had hit him and smiled, and he looked a little shocked but smiled back. Then we hugged goodbye and I breathed in the scent of the locker-room soap on his neck, the same soap I smelled on my own skin.

CHAPTER 16

Sometimes it was astonishing to realize just how separate my worlds were—the one I lived and worked in on a daily basis, and the other one, my family, where I did the periodic laundry drive-by and visited occasionally, quite literally, as there tended to be lots of occasions like birthdays, christenings, weddings and other celebrations that beckoned for an appearance. Lately I'd been missing more than my share of occasions, and trying to keep the guilt at bay.

It was Saturday morning. And my twenty-ninth birthday. And my cousin Barbara's wedding, which justified an absence from work in a way the other two things couldn't. Few things were just cause for missing work at the height of our start-up frenzy, when we were trying to raise the venture capital to keep the business going. So if I had to be away from the office, I appreciated the combo birthday-wedding gig because it merged two separate obligations to eat cake with my family into one. And I always got a bit of a rush from a well-timed and efficient coincidence.

Stephen seemed not to have come home the night before. He was staying at the office more and more. Elke was missing, too. I had breakfast, flipped through some mail, and took a shower. I had an hour before I needed to leave for the wedding—an unprecedented window for primping. Clean and made up and padding around in my shaggy slippers, I answered the telephone while negotiating an increasingly desperate search for hole-free panty hose. *Why didn't I just buy a new pair?* It was my mother on the line.

"Hi. I'm just checking in to make sure you're all set," she said.

And not running too late, that's what she was really concerned about. Her monitoring irked me, but I was defenseless because I *was* always running late. "Yup, I'll see you in, in, an hour. Okay?"

"Don't forget to check your oil."

Ever since I had confessed that my oil leaked a bit, my mother was vigilant about it. "I will check the oil, Mother."

"And don't forget your shoes."

Ugh. One time I forgot the dyed shoes for another cousin's wedding. "No Mother, I won't forget my shoes!" Damn, the shoes! Where had I put the shoes?

I spent the next twenty minutes searching for the pumps that nearly matched the bright lavender but otherwise not-the-worst-ever bridesmaid dress selected by The Bride. The shoes were there somewhere, I was certain of it. Why was I not more organized?! I berated myself as I scanned the room. Eventually I located the pumps, unaccountably tucked into a shopping bag under a putty-colored Gap sweater (bought on sale). Ultimately I failed in the hole-free hose mission, and instead picked the best of the lot, with the smallest of runs. I pulled and twisted the holey part like I was closing the end of a plastic bread bag, tucking it under my toes, and carefully slipped into the pumps, clicking toward the stairs with my arms loaded with presents and makeup and extra shoes.

Stephen arrived home, presumably to shower, and bounded up the stairs as I was leaving. We chatted for a few minutes until a glance at my watch incited mild panic. "I gotta go."

"I'll try to hold down the fort. The VCs are coming Monday, you know," Stephen said.

I felt apologetic. Why did I always feel so guilty? So responsible? "It's a wedding, Stephen. I can miss a lot of things. But not a wedding."

"I know, I know. Have fun. Say hi to everyone for me."

Once outside, I realized that Stephen hadn't mentioned my birthday, conjuring a strange satisfaction at being forgotten, akin to relief. What was that about? I clicked down the narrow path toward my car, and caught sight of Elke, walking beside her bike up the path.

"Oh hello, Anna." She surveyed my dress. "You look . . . nice."

"I'm puffy, and purple."

"Well, yes, I suppose so." She smiled as I passed and waved goodbye, calling behind me, "Have fun at the wedding!"

As I approached my car, I spotted a pink square and a single hand-picked flower on the windshield. I retrieved both, tossing my things on the passenger seat, and started the car while tearing open the envelope with my free hand and my teeth.

The birthday card made a stupid women-and-chocolate joke but it also made me smile, and was signed "Love, Stephen," which made me smile more. My delight in the flower was undiminished when I realized it was picked from our neighbor's garden.

Finally, I was on the road. I'd mastered the mid-Cambridge side streets and found what I affectionately called the "wiggle way" to get from my apartment to the Massachusetts Turnpike in five minutes. From the Mass Pike, heading east, I could pick up the Southeast Expressway and be in my hometown in thirty minutes. So close, I thought. It was a mere twenty miles away, and approximately a world apart.

CHAPTER 17

Hustling toward the church, I felt fresh dissatisfaction that my family parish was the rare Catholic church with a modern design. Chester St. Mary's was a late 1950s-era brick and wood structure, all angles with only the slightest amount of disappointingly pale stained glass. Sometime in the 1980s the caretakers and Monsignor McLoften got the idea to paint the interior of the whole thing—walls, ceiling, doors—a mauvy-pink. As I entered the building, I realized my dress clashed perfectly.

Thankfully the wedding didn't start for another two hours. I made my way to the makeshift dressing room, since I had promised to help my cousin Barbara, The Bride, with her makeup. I pushed through the door and was shocked to see dozens of people swarming around Barb, who was perched on a stool in front of a foggy mirror, wearing a slip, a plaid work shirt and exceedingly pale and blotchy skin. The Bride looked uncharacteristically nervous, which dredged up a pang of guilt in me.

Try as I did to enter discreetly, everyone turned as I moved into the crowd and let up a cheer. The Bride was flanked by her mother—my Aunt Belle—as well as her sister Liz, who was matron of honor, and Liz's two daughters, nine-year-old April and her little sister Melody, who was six. The girls could barely contain the excitement of being flower girls, dressed in ankle-length lavender dresses, smiling and jumping in their white patent-leather Mary Janes. They wore wide brimmed hats, probably chosen to hide the bald evidence of little April's chemotherapy treatments, which had thankfully ended before the wedding, but not in time for her to grow her hair back.

Barbara hugged me really tight.

"You made it."

"And only sixteen minutes late!" I offered a tacit apology. "I always make it for the important things, don't I?"

"Okay, here are a couple of other important things."

Barbara handed me a glass of champagne and a bag of brand new makeup, much of it still in original packaging.

"Help."

My cousin always hated girly things like makeup and completely lacked the vanity gene. Barbara would have avoided a photographer and pictures altogether if she could have, but seeing as it was her wedding, she acquiesced and decided that if she was going to memorialize the day on film, she should call in reinforcements. I was deemed the most makeup savvy but planned to fake my way through, because, truth be told, my cosmetics confidence wasn't all that great.

At this point Jodie and my mother and even more girl cousins and nieces arrived to watch. Barbara didn't seem to mind the racket. I would have freaked! There was always a certain amount of *volume* in everything associated with our family. It turned out Barbara just assumed every bride had a pre-party in her dressing room and invited them all along. I marveled at her ability to let go of control. Bless her. Bless her laid-back soul.

April stepped up toward me, and I noticed that her eyes were the color of Elke's—a brilliant blue.

"Can I help?" she asked earnestly. She liked to keep herself busy, to be involved in everything, and I welcomed the extra pair of hands and the sharing of makeover responsibility.

"Sure, honey. Will you open these packages, and hand me the brushes when I need them?"

April concentrated on removing the blush and powder and eye shadow and lipstick from the packaging, then she carefully selected and handed over brushes and tissues to me, or placed them gently on a towel in the order she expected I would need them. Her skinny fingers worked away at organizing the tools of Barbara's makeover so that I could find what I needed. Of all the little girls, she took this wedding business the most seriously.

About halfway through the makeup application I realized, with great excitement—*it was working!* The sales lady at the Filene's Clinique counter had done us right. A light foundation and powder evened Barbara's skin tone, the blush was a perfect shade of tawny pink and, once applied as instructed in the latest issue of *Glamour*, actually did highlight her cheekbones. Who knew? The eye makeup illuminated a stunning surprise— Barbara's eyes turned a unique and gorgeous chocolate brown flecked with gold next to the right eyeliner and mascara. With the Sweet Mocha Pink lip liner and lipstick smoothed on, with a touch of Pure Gloss for shine, Barbara was fully transformed. This helped solidify my theory that the primary difference between stunning people and plain people was not genes, but packaging.

Liz helped me slip on Barbara's gown and veil, which we stuck firmly to the back of her head with sixteen bobby pins and a few combs. The simple long rectangle of tulle magically completed the look so that when Barbara spun around to face the roomful of clucking female relatives, Aunt Belle went speechless and was about to start crying, while all of the little girls clapped and jumped.

Melody let out an "Ooooh!"

April squealed. "Oh Auntie Barbara, you look so so so

beautiful!"

I shared the delight in Barb's new look, but suddenly felt inescapably ugly. Where was my makeup bag? My lipstick and powder? My B Str8 Frizz Control serum?

Liz smiled. "Oh, Barb. This is good."

Barbara hesitated but then looked at her reflection with some admiration, and laughed nervously. "Except of course that my fiancé may not recognize me." She peeked again in the mirror and smiled broadly.

I snuck off to a corner to reapply my lipstick and check on my powder. Barbara and I had in common pale skin and chocolate brown eyes and brown-blonde hair, though mine was more getting to be just brown lately since I hadn't been in the sun and couldn't afford highlighting. While I was reapplying lip liner sans mirror in the corner and the rest of the crowd was polishing off the champagne, the photographer busted in and joined in the reverie. He was not a tall man, and was dressed entirely in black, carrying his camera and a cardboard box covered in aluminum foil, which he handed over to Liz, and asked for her help. "Hold this for me, will ya, darlin. We gotta get the light. Gotta get the light on her face, ya know what I'm saying?"

"Sure. Got it. The light," Liz said and held the tin-foil-covered box to reflect the sunlight from a single tiny window onto Barbara's face.

I looked over at Barbara, puzzled.

She spoke out of the corner of her Sweet Mocha smile. "He works with Jimmy."

"At the Marshfield Police Department?"

Liz replied in a loud whisper. "Barbara didn't want a photographer but Jimmy's mother made her. We didn't have much time. Pete's the official homicide photographer, he just does weddings on the side."

Abetted by a second glass of champagne, I laughed while Jodie laid down on the ground and faked her death and asked someone to chalk her outline "so that the photographer would feel more at home, more comfortable in his surroundings." Barbara was glamming for the camera and Pete did his best to capture the chaos, including a group toast with our family's favorite Callatore champagne, just $5.99 a bottle if you got it on sale.

"Pete, can you get one of us?" I wrapped my arms around April and Pete snapped our photo. When I started to walk away I could feel a tugging on my dress.

"Annie, can I have some makeup please?" April pleaded in a quiet but determined voice.

I glanced down at her sweet face, freckles skipping across her button nose, blue eyes hopeful. "Sweetie, you look perfect just as you are! You don't need a thing on your face."

"Yes I do. I do. I really do." She was jumping a little with anticipation.

I was about to give in, but called to Liz across the room first. "Liz, can April have a little blush and powder?"

Liz nodded yes.

"Lipstick too!" April whispered.

CHAPTER 18

The ceremony was pleasant and tearful and familiar and long, like full-on Catholic masses always are. Boring and repetitive for the most part. Punctuated by rote vows and the same "Love is Patient" reading and a hit-or-miss homily, depending on the priest. The organist was marginal at best, the trumpets too loud and strangely ostentatious. But none of that mattered—it was a wedding, and I loved it. Loved the pomp, the reverence, the seriousness and romance of the public display of commitment.

The soloist was amazing, and when she sang the Ave Maria during communion I was sure it made my father cry. I couldn't see him from my position at the front of the church, but I was willing to make a bet. Monsignor McLoften himself said the Mass, and his homily was the rare hit, in my opinion, the highlight of the entire ceremony. I couldn't remember his exact words, but something about love being a verb, a choice. Not a thing that happens to you, but something you decide to do and then you do. And then he encouraged us all to be love, to choose love, to do love. My inner control freak soaked in that message, that love wasn't something that just happened, that you had no control over, it was something you could influence. Romantic proactivity blessed by the church, no less.

Later, after the ceremony and inside the reception hall, the best man wrapped up his toast and asked everyone to raise their glasses. The groom looked a bit stunned. He'd sought out something stronger than the pink sparkling wine, and downed his scotch in response to the well-wishes of the crowd. All one hundred and twenty guests murmured "cheers" and clinked their glasses. I glanced around and saw a sea of faces flush with happiness and tradition. These were big moments, these weddings. A rare opportunity to safely express an emotion or two, or at least to comment on the prettiness of the bride, the luck of the groom, and how nice the place looked. "The place" was a Sons of Italy hall adorned with pink and purple linens, carnations and baby's breath, and cute photos of the bride and groom as children to mark the table numbers (age five equaled table five, age seven equaled table seven, and so on).

I loved our family weddings. I would get a little tipsy (okay, sometimes a lot) with my sister and brother and cousins, eat too much cake, dance like a fool, and laugh at my father's attempts to do the Electric Slide and my brother's Sinatra renditions. I relished family events like weddings because they contained a certain sanctuary from the rest of my life, where I could never slow down enough to enjoy much of anything. Here I just got to be myself, and no one cared or noticed.

What would happen if I brought Paul to a wedding like this? I couldn't imagine, really, especially when I spotted my father across the room, looking handsome in a snug suit, visiting several nearby tables and consolidating into one glass the champagne that had been abandoned once the toast was over. My father hated waste, but didn't, it appeared, mind backwash.

I was standing nearby, amused and a little stunned, with my brother Andy. "What is Dad doing?"

My younger brother laughed and looked at his watch. "Oh. The open bar's over." Andy observed his own half-empty drink. "Damn. I knew I should've gotten two."

After collecting enough champagne for two full glasses, my father sauntered across the dance floor to deliver one to my mother. Then he turned his attention to the cheese table, his champagne in one hand, and proceeded to eat directly from the serving plate without a pause between bites, making it awkward—no, impossible—for other guests to partake.

"Oh jeez. Now what's he doing? I'm going in." Andy headed over and deftly redirected Parker away from the cheese. Unless willing to risk a scene, we'd learned one could not correct our father's manners in too overt a way.

On the dance floor, the young DJ in a wrinkled tuxedo shirt and hook-on bowtie blasted Garth Brooks' "Friends in Low Places." April was pulling her aunts and cousins onto the dance floor. They knew the words by heart, and expertly balanced singing, dancing and drinking. A few minutes later April was doing a swing dance with a man I didn't recognize, looking on top of the world.

Liz appeared beside me and we watched April together.

"How's she doing?" I asked gently.

"So far so good. She's responding to the treatment, but we'll only know for sure in a couple of months."

"I'll say a prayer."

"Say two," smiled Liz, and then headed off to join her daughter.

CHAPTER 19

It was getting late, but the reception was still raging on. I was impressed by the staying power of my extended family, scattered across the dance floor, stoked by booze and a DJ with a bottomless supply of cheesy line dances and seventies disco. At the moment when it looked like things might wind down, he'd throw on the Village People. *Dah, dah, dah, dah dun dun dun dun dun dah* . . . which incited a rush to the center in time to claim props for "YMCA." My mother had the Indian headdress. Aunt Belle was in the police cap. Jodie scored the hardhat, someone else the biker cap. The DJ was trading the army cap for April's flower girl hat when I arrived too late. Damn, stuck with the tambourine again. The groom sat this one out, preferring his scotch to any type of disco.

Mid-Y, Jodie turned to Barbara and shouted, "How's it feel to be married?"

From under her cowboy hat, Barbara yelled back, "So far it's great. Hey Annie, have you met Eddie yet?" Barbara asked, looking toward the edge of the dance floor.

"Eddie?" Oh no. Who was Eddie and why did she want me to meet him?

Barbara was gesturing toward someone who turned out to be Eddie DiPietro, the same guy who'd been swing dancing with April earlier. Hmmm. I could smell a setup and I wasn't biting. Eddie looked like an average guy who might be attractive, were he not wedged in the mid-eighties, with his hair in a mullet (a mild one, but still), wearing a dark suit, a skinny tie and off-white shoes.

"Nope. He's a friend of Jimmy's?" I recommitted to forming my letters in hopes of ending this line of discussion. *YYYY. MM. C-A. It's fun to stay at the YYYY MM C-Aaaay.* It always felt dangerous when my family tried to involve themselves in my dating life.

"Well, yes, but he's also Bobby's cousin," explained Barbara.

Now that was a curious connection. The infamous Bobby.

"Really? But I've never seen him before." Bobby was ex-husband to Liz, who started out nice but after a series of personal setbacks became a big jerk and a bigger drinker, and Liz finally had enough and they split up, while she was pregnant with Melody. After that he really hit the bottle, and passed away from related complications a few years later.

Barbara continued, "Eddie didn't get along with Bobby. We only really met him after Bobby died. They're nothing alike. And Eddie really loves the kids."

I believed Barbara if she said Eddie was a nice guy, but the stigma of being biologically linked to a jerk like Bobby was a serious liability and left me suspicious.

"YMCA" was followed by "Chicken Dance" and "The Hustle," then Jodie leading a group in a dance I didn't recognize, but upon closer inspection I realized she'd combined our mother's trademark dance move—a slide shuffle with an arm dip done in a constant side to side motion, employed for every song, fast or slow—with Parker's more ambitious tendency to scamper-gallop back and forth across the dance floor while pumping his arms up and down, and created what appeared to the rest of the crowd to be a new line dance. Jodie, unaware that she had a group of people behind her copying the moves, was having a blast. Then the DJ played that brand new one, "Macarena," with the fancy hip shake and turning jump with a clap that I could only do with the aid of a few Amstel Lights. My mother had mastered the arm movements but was struggling with the turn because she was laughing so hard. Jodie seemed to get it the best of the Thompsons, though across the room April and Melody put us all to shame. Kids. So flexible. So cute-looking when they're bouncing. Unlike purple-clad bridesmaids with boobs. I tried to focus. Arms out, out; cross, cross; shoulder, shoulder.

Jodie interrupted my concentration. "Barbara and Liz want you to meet Eddie."

Mid-hip-shake I shot her a look. Jodie of all people should have known that I wouldn't be interested. Turn and claaaap.

"Please." And again—arms out, out . . .

"He seems very nice." That was my mother's two cents, from behind. Cross, cross . . .

I rolled my eyes. "*Mom.*" Shoulder, shoulder . . .

"What? I'm just saying, he seems like a nice young man." Waist, waist . . .

"Mother, do you realize he's related to Bobby?" Almost to the hip shake . . .

She shook her head. "I don't think Eddie is anything like Bobby."

Jodie agreed. "He's not. He's pretty cool." Turn and claaap!

When the song ended we retreated to our table in search of water, with my mother still carrying on. "You can't be so picky. Dismissing him so fast."

"So picky? Mom, I think the women in this family could stand to be a little pickier!" I said it with a smile but there was an unmistakable edge in my voice.

Jodie raised her eyebrows in protest. "I'm picky enough."

"Well, then maybe you're the first!" I looked at my mother.

"'Cause you're not, Mom."

Whoops. As soon as the words came out of my mouth I regretted it. I could tell by the look on my mother's face that she didn't appreciate the comment, and I had a deep aversion to hurting her feelings. But she was also accustomed to letting things roll off her back.

"Stop it. It's Barbara's wedding. And your father's not that bad."

"Okay, he's not *as* bad." I retreated, feeling guilty for being a disrespectful brat, not living up to my image of myself as nice.

"He's better than he used to be," said Jodie.

My mother looked innocently over at me. "Well, I thought for sure you would meet someone at Harvard."

Who said that? My mother? *My* mother? Her comment stung more than I wanted to admit, especially given my dramatically failed attempts to date successfully there, my broken heart, my wounded pride, the minor humiliations suffered in the dating fishbowl of Harvard Business School. My mother had never before admitted to having any hope or expectation for my love life, or worse, disappointment. The stinging sensation came from another place, though. It came from a place of familiarity, because I, too, imagined I'd meet someone in business school. Damn, what single woman there didn't? The ratio of men to women was three to one. The place was notorious for hookups and relationships and marriages. To emerge single seemed a statistically low probability, but I'd managed to do so. And now my mother was speaking entirely out of character, and admitting that she expected something different. I needed a drink.

"Well, I didn't, Mom. I didn't."

"She got her MBA not her M-R-S." Jodie cracked herself up.

I looked at my sister sideways. Then the DJ made another of his periodic announcements and we were all relieved at the distraction.

"Okay, we're winding down the evening. Can I have all the single ladies on the dance floor please."

"Oh no, you're kidding me. No one does this anymore!" I was genuinely horrified.

Jodie was undeterred, and a little tipsy. "We do! Come on." She pulled me toward the dance floor. I resisted until April grabbed my other arm and earnestly pulled me along.

There, in the middle of the removable parquet wood dance floor with the prerecorded drum roll and a patchy crowd of mostly drunk onlookers, Jodie and I were soon surrounded by our widowed aunt, eighty-one-year-old divorced grandmother, miscellaneous tipsy twenty-somethings, Liz, and many, many hopeful little girls. The Bride peered over her shoulder, smiled at me while I tried to hide my disinterest and tossed the bouquet. As if she had planned it this way (she did) the flower bouquet hit me high on the chest and landed in my hands. As much as I wanted to drop-kick or bat it away, I couldn't risk hurting Barb's feelings so I caught the damn thing and braced myself for the consequences. At that point I definitely knew I couldn't bring Paul to a place like this. Jodie teased me for taking the flowers that were rightfully hers but then refocused her attention on the male single contingent gathered in the center of the dance floor, while Jimmy the Groom elaborately executed the tossing of the garter. It flew through the air, past the swarm of drunkish single guys, and the ubiquitous Eddie reached up and caught it with just the slightest hint of effort.

I turned to Jodie. "You do realize this is mortifying."

"For you maybe. For me it's pretty fun. Let's go, Cinderella."

Eddie the garter catcher dutifully appeared to play his part. Wasn't it nifty that I could feed into my family's matchmaking conspiracy so seamlessly?

"Hi, I'm Eddie." He had a nice smile and was taller than he appeared from a distance.

"Hi Eddie, I'm Annie. Barbara's cousin."

"Nice to meet you. Having fun?"

"Well, can we see how this goes before I decide how to respond to that?" I smiled and sat on a magically appeared chair. April arrived at the opportune moment to help by taking off my shoe. I remembered my holes just in time and motioned to April "not that one!" and kicked off the shoe of my non-holey toe. The DJ continued to play his cheesy music.

In the moments that followed I felt particularly relieved that I'd taken the time to shave my legs. Eddie calmly inched the bride's garter onto my leg while the crowd clapped and whistled. He seemed rather unembarrassed by the whole charade, and I tried to follow suit. It was mostly family, and everyone was mostly sloshed at this point. There was really no reason for embarrassment. Eddie politely stopped the garter progression at a point just above my knee. Someone shouted for him to go higher—probably Jimmy—but I held my grapey poof down to prevent such a move and gave Eddie a forced smile. I shouldn't have worried, he was a total gentleman. Nearby, April and Melody jumped up and down, clapping and displaying colossal giddiness at what was to them a most exciting turn of events.

The DJ continued: "And now if Barbara and Jimmy would come up for their final dance . . ."

Eddie and I tried to move away, but the DJ had other ridiculous plans. "And if our new couple would remain on the dance floor, too . . ."

What?! What new couple? The last dance should be for the bride and groom only! Not some random pair of people brought together by a blatantly fixed throwing of things! Still, there was some pressure to comply, as Barbara and Jimmy smiled and nodded from across the parquet. Eddie saw them too and held out his arms to me and I swallowed my discomfort. Eddie put his hand on my back and I hoped it didn't feel too soft, but I didn't care much either way. Then he held my other hand in his and I was reminded yet again that I needed to do my nails. Why I couldn't get on a regular schedule of proper hand grooming was beyond me.

"So I don't think we've ever met before," I said. I placed my left hand on Eddie's shoulder like I'd learned in Ballroom Dance in college and we started to sway a little.

"Nah, I don't think so. I didn't see you at your grandmother's birthday party last month."

"You were at Grammie's birthday party?" Catholic guilt set in fast. I had intended to go, but got caught on a conference call with Stephen and Jeet and one of our advisors.

"Yup. She's quite the firecracker." Eddie did a little turn and pulled me with him—quite good form, actually—then went back to swaying.

"I had to work," I explained. "I'm involved in this start-up, it's crazy." Such excuses! Bad granddaughter. Bad.

"Barbara told me you went to Harvard Business School."

I could hear the DJ behind us. "We have a special treat . . ."

My brother Andy was holding the DJ's second microphone as something Sinatra-esque started playing.

"Oh, boy. Here goes my brother. The closet crooner."

"The summer wind . . ."

"He's not bad," offered Eddie.

"Comes blowin in . . ."

"No, I know," I agreed. "He's pretty good. He sings at all the family weddings and the occasional karaoke night." Andy was serenading the bride and groom while swaying guests gathered in a big circle. Eddie guided us to the perimeter so we could join in.

"So did you just graduate?" Eddie asked.

"Yup, this past June."

"You know," Eddie continued, "I think we have a mutual friend, who was in your class."

"Really. Who?" First Bobby, now an HBS classmate. Who else was this Eddie guy connected to? And as he formed the words and named his connection, my jaw dropped appropriately.

"Paul Dennison?"

Paul Dennison? *My* Paul Dennison? No way! Here I'd been thinking about Paul Dennison half the night, in between Amstels and line dances, and now here was someone who knew him, too? This was a sign, I thought, a definite sign about me and Paul. Coincidence? Or the universe at work? Needless to say, I was instantly, thoroughly intrigued. I tried not to betray my beyond-regular-friendship interest. "Paul Dennison is a good friend of mine. He was in my section. What a small world! How do you know Paul?" *And do you know his wife left him for the Tree Guy?*

"We were like best friends in high school. We lost touch for a while after college, but we've been spending a lot of time together lately."

"So you know . . ."

"About Susie? Yeah. Wasn't sure how public that news is."

"We've been hanging out a bit since it happened. It's unbelievable."

"He's been staying in my spare room."

"You're kidding. So you're the friend who lives in Cambridge?" And you have a spare room? No one I knew had a spare room. They were like me and Stephen and Elke, converting dining rooms and sharing bathrooms.

"Yup. Broadway and Ellery."

"Right, that's what Paul told me. I'm right around the corner.

We're practically neighbors," I said, trying not to sound too eager or excited.

"Well nice to meet you, neighbor."

"You, too, Eddie."

Moments later Barbara walked toward me holding a chocolate cupcake with a single candle in it, singing "Happy Birthday" and encouraging Jodie and the others nearby—my parents, my brother Andy, my Aunt Belle, April and Melody—to join her. I caught Barbara's eye, touched that she'd taken time out of her own wedding to arrange a birthday cupcake for me, and I was momentarily overwhelmed with the feeling of being loved, appreciated, *seen*.

CHAPTER 20

After the wedding I drove back to Cambridge with the radio off, allowing myself to think about the night and to dwell on the surprising connection between Eddie DiPietro and Paul Dennison. Usually I loved the unlikely coincidences that seemed to populate life, but this was less comfortable because it involved my family. I felt terrible about that, but having Eddie randomly connected to my relatives *and* to be good friends and temporary roommates with Paul left me feeling vulnerable and exposed. What if he mentioned our meeting, as he surely would? What would he say? Would he describe the wedding? Would he talk about my family? Exaggerate the garter toss? More likely he would simply tell the truth, and that was more than enough to show Paul that we were from different worlds, and that I wouldn't fit in his.

When I got to my street it was packed with cars, and I surmised that someone was having a party. It was past nine p.m. A few spins around the block and I eventually nabbed a parking spot a street away from mine. I would normally walk back via the most direct route but tonight I found myself going slightly out of my way to pass Broadway and Ellery. I went slowly through that intersection, wondering if Paul might be around, wanting to see him but half hoping I didn't, since I was in a rather unflattering getup. Eventually even my snail's pace got me home, and I noticed that our apartment lights were on.

I walked in and toward the back of the house, looking for Elke.

"No, wait there!" She yelled to me as I walked toward her in the kitchen, then stopped.

She emerged a few seconds later carrying something chocolate with a single candle in it. Then she sang "Happy Birthday" in German. I blew out the candle, which she probably found in the junk drawer, or perhaps she'd even ventured into the pantry. Her gesture was thoughtful and sweet.

"How did you know?" I asked.

"The little bird told me," Elke answered. "You know in Germany it is customary for the birthday girl or guy to throw a birthday party of their own. Everyone expects it." It seemed she was just sharing the information, not judging me. In the past I'd hosted elaborate birthday parties for friends and my sister but always felt strange throwing the self-party. More likely I'd organize the entire thing and then have Jodie or a friend send out the invitation. That was the control freak's modus operandi, yes.

I settled at the kitchen table while Elke cut the dense cake into bite-sized pieces and turned on the kettle. We compared notes on other German versus American customs. Elke told me how friends in Germany usually made up nicknames for each other, usually by adding extra vowels and the occasional consonant to the end of the names.

"Like I would call you Annika or Annalisa," Elke explained.

"Or Annie. It's funny that a nickname would make your name longer. Sweet, though." Elke started calling me Annika so I responded in kind and called her variations like Ellie and KeKe. I wasn't sure I was doing it right but I liked the affectionate custom anyway.

"Tell me about the wedding. Was it fun?"

I recapped the day's highlights, including the bouquet

catch—a tradition that required some explanation. I almost spilled Eddie's revelation of the Paul Dennison connection, but caught myself. Having mentioned Eddie at all, I told her about the garter scene and the dancing. She was amused by the customs, having never attended an American wedding. I regretted not inviting her; we could've easily had one more person there and it would've been a culturally eye-opening experience to the world outside of Cambridge and Harvard. I suspected Elke was getting a warped sense of America, having only spent time with the overeducated and relatively privileged. Her dermatology fellowship was with a high-end practice based out of Mass General.

"What was this Eddie like?"

"You sound like my mother. And my cousins. They all had elaborate designs on Eddie and me meeting. They even fixed the bouquet toss."

"And what's wrong with that?"

"It's just not right. A real injustice. There were hordes of twenty-somethings like my sister who actually wanted the thing."

"I meant what's wrong with Eddie."

"Oh. Him. Nice guy, but not for me. I have one word: mullet."

"Mullet? Is that bad?" Elke looked sympathetic but puzzled.

"A mullet? Hockey hair? Long in back, short in front?" Elke made a face and shrugged. "You'd know it if you saw it," I added.

Elke tilted her head to the side, squinted a little and pursed her lips as if in doubt.

"What?" I asked.

"Oh, I don't know. It's just that, well, it would be good for you to be with someone." Elke was being kind. Certainly in our time of living together she hadn't seen me with anyone, given the only relationship I had going was primarily in my head and behind her back.

The tea kettle was whistling and hurling a tight spray of steam, and Elke rose to shut off the gas. We relocated to the living room and collapsed on the sofa, steaming cups of peppermint tea in hand along with the birthday cake. Elke reached to the end table.

"I have a birthday gift for you."

"No you don't."

"It's just a little something." She retrieved a small Tiffany-blue box with white satin ribbon tied in a perfect bow. Wait, that didn't make sense. Elke was a grad student. She shouldn't be buying presents from Tiffany.

"A *little* something?"

"This is not actually from Tiffany. But, I think the box adds a little something special." I'd never owned a thing from Tiffany & Company. I pulled at the ends of the ribbon and the silky strips let go easily and puddled in my lap. I teased apart the package and found inside a small metal box, square with nine richly colored stones in shades of russet and plum and ruby and amber, evenly spaced all around it. It was lovely.

"I've been studying feng shui, which I have discovered is all about intention. And this, is a Relationship Box," said Elke.

"It's beautiful. What exactly does one do with a Relationship Box?"

"Well, you're supposed to fill it with your intentions—what you're looking for and intend to find in a relationship."

"Oh, you know. I'm not so great at relationships." What I was good at was setting my sights on the most emotionally unavailable of men, the hardest nuts to crack, the ones sure to break my heart. It was a pattern that had been true since college, when my first real boyfriend shattered my heart and I'd probably never recovered. But if the Relationship Box could help me with Paul, well then I might be interested.

Elke continued, undeterred. "As I was saying, you put this in your Relationship Corner."

"My what?"

"Yes, it would be, let me think, yes, your Relationship Corner is in your bedroom, by your desk."

"Ah. Okay. So I just think really hard and then put this in that corner and everything will fall into place?"

Elke was really serious about this feng intention stuff.

"Oh, not just thinking. You need to write down what your intentions are and put them inside. Then place in the corner."

"You mean you actually want me to commit something to paper?"

"Exactly."

I thought it all sounded a bit new-agey and weird, but I really wasn't in a position to reject anything designed to help me get the guy.

"Thank you for my present. I love it." And I really did. In fact I was a little overwhelmed by how sweet a gesture it was.

"You're welcome, Annika. Happy birthday. Happy year."

"Goodnight, Elketta." I headed off to my bedroom.

A half hour later I was freed from my puffy dress and tucked into my covers, when Stephen surprised me at my door.

"Hey, birthday girl."

I made room for him to flop on the bed beside me. He kicked off his shoes, which landed on the floor in their customary two thumps.

"How was the wedding?" Stephen asked.

I picked up the wilting flowers from my nightstand and put them in front of his face. "Caught the bouquet."

"Atta girl."

"Thank you for the birthday card. And flower. How was your day?"

"Good. Busy." Stephen tucked his hands behind his head and yawned.

"Did you miss me?" I asked.

"Of course," he answered, and then yawned, before dozing off and starting to snore. The rhythmic, if loud, sound of his breathing was comforting next to me, and sent my mind wandering. I wondered if Paul snored. I wondered if Paul would fit in my bed as nicely and comfortably as Stephen did. I wondered what he was doing, what he was thinking, was he by chance thinking of me? Had Eddie gone home after the wedding and mentioned me? What would he say? What would Paul say back?

It was official. I was feeling the full weight of my condition. My chest felt crushed with hope and longing. I really wanted something to happen, but I had to dig deep for reserves of patience. To wait until the time was right, and enjoy the companionship Paul offered in the meantime. I let the possibility play out in my mind of Paul getting over the shock of his divorce and opening up to the idea of something more with me. I replayed the scenes in my head of Paul finally realizing I was perfect for him. It was a wonderful thought, and I fell asleep to it playing over and over again.

CHAPTER 21

I woke up the next morning around seven to Stephen rolling out of my bed and toward the shower. It was the first time I'd made it through a night of his snoring without waking up and kicking him out.

We went through our morning routine in relative silence without waking Elke, and were the first to arrive in the office, by eight a.m. There was an unwritten rule that Sunday mornings were personal time and the developers would start rolling in by ten or eleven, depending on how hungover they were. Since I had taken the entire prior day off for the wedding, I was feeling eager to reconnect with my list and happy to use the quiet of the office to get organized.

I checked my email. There were dozens of work messages and a single personal one, but of the best kind—a message from Paul, sent at nine p.m. the night before.

Hey girl, happy birthday. I hope you had a wonderful day. See you soon. How about Friday? I'll take you for a belated birthday surprise. Be ready at 8?
—PJD

No wonder I slept so well last night! I must have cosmically known that this message waited for me. A birthday surprise? This sounded too good to be true. I emailed him back, adopting my determinedly casual tone.

> *PJD—*
> *Friday at 8 it is. I love surprises.*
> *A.*

Before hitting send I wondered aloud if my message was too coy.

"What?" Stephen asked.

"Oh, nothing. I'm just laboring over a one-line email. Such is the life of the perfectionist."

"Perfect is the enemy of the good. Or something like that." Stephen walked away and I returned to my keyboard. I decided coy was fine. Hadn't the priest told me not twenty-four hours ago that love is a verb? And verbs, being action words, required action. I was going to act. I was going to *do* love. Or at least send this damn email and see what Friday would bring. I hit send and felt instant relief at having acted, followed immediately by the discomforting sense of loss of control now that things were in his court. Oh shush, I told myself, control is an illusion. Just get back to work so it's Friday sooner.

And that is precisely what I did—immersed myself in the million boring and exciting things to do to get GoodMatch.com off the ground. At five p.m. my cell phone rang. It was Elke.

"Annika, it is me," Elke said.

"Hi Elke, what's up?"

"I'm checking on the plan for the roommate dinner. We didn't settle a time. How about eight o'clock? I have done the shopping and will make my famous Bavarian roasted ham, with Weisse Bohnesuppe, as well as Spargelgemüse and Kartoffelknödel, of course. Would you bring the wine?"

I had rarely heard Elke sound so animated. I'd completely

forgotten about the dinner and suspected Stephen had, too. Elke didn't know that we routinely made plans with the knowledge that work always came first, so the chance of something actually happening was fairly low.

"Oh, Ellika, you're so good to remember. I'd almost forgotten."

"Oh, no, we cannot forget. It's our first time," Elke said.

I didn't want to cut the work night short with dinner, preferring to press on, but guilt guided me differently. "Of course, you're right. I'll corral Stephen and be home at eight o'clock. About the wine—it's Sunday, so we won't be able to buy any. But we might have something here. I'll bring what I can."

"Okay. Red would be best, but whatever you can do," Elke said.

I hung up my phone and typed a quick email reminder to Stephen about the dinner, presenting it as a fait accompli. Then I checked the cabinets in the kitchenette and found two bottles of cheap wine—one red, one white. They would have to do. I peeled off the $3.99 price stickers.

At seven fifty p.m., I poked my head into Stephen's office.

"Ready, boss? Dinner's waiting for us."

Stephen looked up from his desk. He was planted there, like a potted fern, with no intention of being uprooted.

"I can't, Annie. Tell Elke sorry for me."

"Stephen! Elke's been shopping and cooking all day. We gave her the impression we were really going to do this."

"Can't you represent us?" Stephen asked.

"Sorry Stephen, I don't have your charm and wit. You're needed."

"Annie, I really don't think I can."

"It's two miles down the street. You have to eat. You can come back afterward."

He looked unconvinced. He didn't think he had any obligations that compared to his company, and he didn't feel bad about it.

"But she made her famous Bavarian roasted ham. And spargelgesomething." I saw a glimmer of reconsideration but he stood firm, or sat firm, and I left in silence because for reasons I didn't fully understand I was completely and totally pissed off at him for this.

"Elke, I'm home."

Elke emerged from the kitchen wearing one of the aprons that typically hung on a nail near the back door that we hadn't touched in years. Her skin looked flushed in a pretty way from the steam.

"Where is Stephen?"

"I'm sorry, I don't know if he's going to make it. Work stuff." I thought I saw a flash of disappointment in her face but then it was gone.

"Hmmmph. No matter. We'll have a good meal with or without our third roommate. Were you able to find wine?"

"Well . . . I found some, but it's not great stuff." I handed her the bottles and she looked at the label on the red.

"Actually, this is not bad. Inexpensive, yes, but smooth and quite nice. You'll like it."

I apologized again for Stephen.

"I believe that this roommate gathering is a nice idea," replied Elke. "We'll just start without Stephen and one of these days he'll join us."

So aside from that one momentary sign of disappointment, Elke seemed delighted to cook for just the two of us. Her talents in the kitchen were extraordinary. We started with the white bean soup and then progressed to the main course of roasted ham, fresh asparagus, and potato dumpling. The food was so good, the wine was fine, as Elke suggested, and our conversation flowed from work to school to books to movies to men. We forgot all about Stephen until he walked in halfway through the meal.

"Hi, sorry I'm so late. Can I still join?" He pulled out the third chair.

Elke had placed the fresh-cut flowers on his place setting, and now moved them back to the center of the table. She smiled but did not really speak to Stephen. She just went and got him some soup, then sat back down. We filled our wine glasses and toasted to our first roommate dinner and made glowing praises of Elke's cooking. We finished the meal and the wine and had apple strudel for dessert, then collapsed on the sofa with peppermint tea. Stephen got up as abruptly as he came and announced he had to go back to the office. We waved him goodbye and Elke and I remained on the couch, sipping our tea and surveying the scene.

"Stephen has interesting timing, I think," Elke said, observing the dishes to be cleaned, and we laughed. I thought for a second that I should probably have gone back to the office, too. Then Elke and I pulled ourselves vertical and tackled the mess. Some aspects of my job could make washing dishes seem like a guilty pleasure.

CHAPTER 22

By Friday morning—the day of my surprise date with Paul—I was barely able to keep the butterflies in check as I figured out my plan for the day. Having learned from painful recent experience, I was bringing *everything* I might possibly need to work. If by some miracle I had time to come home and shower that would be fine, but in the likely case I didn't I would have proper garments and undergarments, makeup and primping apparatus at hand.

The hours dragged on as I worked—or tried to—with Jeet most of the day on site-related issues, and he sensed something was up.

"You don't seem like yourself today, Annie," he said, flashing a smile worthy of a toothpaste commercial.

"Oh, I'm a little distracted. Nothing major."

"Annie T distracted? No way. Are you feeling okay?"

I decided I didn't want to have to answer to Jeet or anyone for being mildly off my game in the face of a bona fide crush.

"To tell you the truth, I have terrible stomachache. Just trying to get through the day," I lied through a weak smile. He raised his eyebrows sympathetically and got back to work without further comment. I was amazed at how guilt-free I felt in the wake of such a blatant but effective lie.

Paul had emailed me a couple more times that week to confirm our plan. He would pick me up at eight at my office. At seven fifteen I disappeared to the restroom and changed my clothes from casual, practical work attire to a short black skirt, opaque black tights and ridiculously high heels that I loved to look at but struggled to wear. They were the kind of shoes you put on only to arrive at your destination—and pose. Certainly not for walking. I knew it was a calculated risk since this was a birthday *surprise*, but I was willing to bet Paul was taking me to a nice restaurant for a late-ish dinner. I was pleased to discover that my skirt fit better than it had the last time I wore it and was sufficiently loose that it could spin around my waist without effort or getting hung up on a hip. I lined up the slit that was meant to be at the side and needed to stay there if I didn't want to be obscene. Pulling on a slim-fitting purple v-neck sweater with three-quarter sleeves, I had a momentary confidence lapse. My insecurity was sealed when Polly the intern came into the bathroom and whistled.

"Whoa, Annie. What's the occasion?" Polly asked.

"Oh, nothing, just a little birthday thing." I felt my face turn red.

"Oh, *happy* birthday. Have *fun*." She said it with all the confidence of a nineteen-year-old with a perfect body and disappeared into the stall, and I looked into the mirror again. I turned to the side. Yes, I'd dropped some weight but my stomach wasn't perfectly flat and the sweater was unforgiving. Plus with the deep cleavage-bearing V-neck I thought the whole ensemble screamed "take me now" and I wasn't sure I was ready to hit Paul with that.

It was seven fifty-five. I finished my makeup and when Polly left I stripped off the tight purple sweater and replaced it with the top I'd worn all day—a shapeless thing in a shade of gray that should match the cement of any parking garage, but at least I no longer felt absurd. I spritzed some perfume to freshen my top and headed out to meet Paul.

He was waiting in the front space of our office, chatting with Stephen. I tried to sashay in, attempting to look elegant in my impossible-to-wear shoes while dropping my backpack in the corner discreetly. Polly walked by me and did a double-take and started to talk but I shut her up with a look—possibly a glare, I'm not sure—and she kept moving.

Paul saw me and did his own double-take. He kissed me on the cheek and said "Happy birthday" again. We said goodbye to Stephen and left. In my super-tall shoes I noticed I had closed half the gap in my height difference with Paul as we walked toward his car.

"I hope you like my surprise," he said as he pulled keys out of his pocket.

"I'm sure I will," I replied.

"I probably should have given you a hint how to dress," he said, with a look that suggested I'd guessed wrong.

"Oh?"

"But it should be fine."

"Okay . . ."

We got into Paul's car and headed out of the garage. I liked the feeling of being next to him in the dark.

"So I heard you met my roommate," Paul said with a smile. I didn't answer him right away because I was busy trying to decipher his face.

"Yeah, what a small world, huh?"

"It really is. We should all go out some time. He's a great guy."

"He seems like it. My family loves him." Why, why, *why* did I bring up my family?!

"He says they're great. Down to earth." Down to earth? Damn, that was rich person's code for simple and white-trashy, wasn't it?

Twenty minutes of chit-chat later we pulled up to the Milky Way in Jamaica Plain, a restaurant and bowling alley famous for its old-fashioned lanes that were difficult to reserve on a weekend night. Apparently Paul had done so.

"Wow. The Milky Way. I've never been here," I said, truthfully.

"Do you like to bowl?" Paul asked. "I thought it would be fun. Like a throwback to when we were kids."

"Yes, I love bowling," I lied. "But I'm not that good." That was the truth. I tended to get competitive and lose control of my ball and vacillate between howling gutter balls and the occasional strike. I certainly wasn't dressed for it. "You're right, though. I should've worn my jeans." My itty bitty skirt was not going to look its best with bowling shoes.

We had some drinks and nibbles at the bar while we waited for our lane to open up, straining to hear each other over the din and crash of balls to pins, which I liked because it gave me cover in my timid attempts to put my face next to Paul's. He didn't mention Susie and I wondered if it was in honor of my birthday or a sign of his progress. I hoped both. He looked fantastic, leaning against his barstool in worn Levi's and a navy Polo shirt. Still more wrinkly than usual, but I was getting used to that.

Our name was called and we got our bowling shoes and settled into our lane, trying to appreciate that part of the charm of the Milky Way was that the lanes were crooked in some places, which did not appeal to my competitive side. But we sorted out the idiosyncrasies pretty quickly and got into the game. Paul won the first string—but only by ten points, which I felt was a credible showing on my part. I even forgot about how silly I must've looked in my skirt until the second string when Paul took a bathroom break and a woman from the next lane pulled me aside. She was tall and brunette and had gorgeous almond-shaped eyes and a Julia Roberts smile.

"Sweetie, can I help you out?" she asked.

"Sorry?"

"Your little skirt keeps shifting and your slit is showing your adorable butt to the rest of us." She was pointing to my tush.

"Omigod." I grabbed the back of my skirt and sure enough the slit was perfectly aligned with my ass. And who was she kidding? I did *not* have an adorable butt. *But thank goodness for dark tights.*

"Do you want to borrow my jacket to tie around your waist?" She handed me a thin cotton shirt thing with long sleeves.

"You're a lifesaver, thank you!" I whispered, blushing ten shades of red.

"I would've said something sooner but I couldn't figure out if it was on purpose," said the almond-eyed girl.

"Huh?"

"I thought maybe you were a couple and that was your thing," she smiled mischievously. Everything she said came out in a confident, casual tone despite the shaming insinuations.

"Oh, no. It was an accident. A surprise. I mean, I didn't know we were coming here or I would've, well, I would've dressed for it."

"We were trying to figure out if he's your date, or a friend, or maybe your brother? He's hot." The "we" seemed to refer to the almond-eyed woman and her equally pretty friends, who were half-heartedly bowling and glancing over at our conversation. And I started to get furious, furious that total strangers took the time to dissect my nonsensical relationship with Paul, to wonder what we were—friends, lovers, *siblings*?! They had no more insight from their objective viewpoint as to what the hell was going on with us than I did—which at least validated my own confusion.

"Yes, he is hot," I agreed. *And he's not available. To you, or unfortunately, to me. But definitely not to you.* "But sorry, he's married." It was my third lie of the day, my third remorseless fib after the fake stomach cramps and the claim to love bowling.

"Oh, shoot. Figures. He really should wear a ring."

I thanked Almond-Eyed Girl for the loan of the shirt and tied it around my waist. Paul returned a minute later carrying two plastic cups of beers for us.

"Here you go," he said.

"Hey, thanks," I said. He was looking at my waist. "My skirt's twisting around and that nice woman loaned me her jacket."

"Oh, cool." He looked past me to Almond-Eyed Girl and smiled. "She's pretty."

I ignored him.

"Ready?" I asked.

"Yup. You're up."

I managed to win the second string by a few points, perhaps fueled by the adrenaline rush embedded in my half-truths and the competitive energy in defense of my lust interest. We played a third string and Paul beat me handily, but by then my arm was spaghetti and I was ready to be done with the little balls and the crooked floors of our lane. But it had been more fun than I expected, and we laughed a lot and it was an excellent birthday surprise. I returned the shirt to Almond-Eyed Girl and thanked her. Even if she was after my man she saved me further embarrassment and for that I was grateful.

Back in the car, I felt the pleasant buzz of beer and endorphins and close proximity to Paul. I felt emboldened, and I wanted something to happen.

"You know, you probably should have told me I was baring

my butt to the entire place."

"Huh, what? I hadn't noticed."

"How could you not have noticed?! The woman who gave me her shirt said everyone noticed! Except me, of course." I pushed him playfully in the arm and he smiled.

"Okay, okay. Maybe I noticed a little, but I didn't think it was a problem. I thought it was cute."

"What was cute? Flashing my ass to a crowd of a hundred people? That's mortifying, not cute!"

"No, I meant your ass was cute."

"Oh." I paused for a second. I didn't believe that my ass was cute but I loved him for saying it anyway. "Well, please tell me the next time it's showing."

"Okay, birthday girl. I will do that." He smiled, and reached over and pinched my cheek. Why he pinched my cheek, I did not know, but that's what he did. And it tingled the entire ride home.

When he dropped me off at my car he got out and hugged me goodbye, pulling me into his body in a way I was sure he had never done before, because I literally felt like I was melting into him—his arms, his chest, his thighs. It was heavenly.

The weekend sailed by. It was all work, hardly any play, and I didn't care. The presence of Paul in my life in this way made everything better. Even though it was unclear what was happening, if anything, with us, and how he was really doing with the Susie stuff, he was in my life—on Saturday he called, he sent emails, he stopped by to grab coffee for ten minutes while we each slaved over our respective to-do lists. On Sunday he brought his laptop over to our office so we could get work done while we watched the Patriots game on TV and drank beer with Stephen and Jeet, and ran numbers and edited documents and talked business.

He was exciting and gorgeous and warm and he really cared

about me, that much I was sure of. He valued me as a friend, a confidante, even a professional. He asked my advice on marketing questions for his company, he talked through business challenges he was facing, he gave me thoughtful advice about my own projects.

After the Patriots won, we celebrated for five minutes then settled back into work. I admit it was harder to concentrate on my projects with Paul sitting across the makeshift lounge from me, but it was easier than if he wasn't there at all and left me wondering what he was up to. And after a while we all got into a state of flow that felt really productive and good. At ten p.m. Paul stood up and stretched and his shirt untucked from his pants, and I spotted his bare stomach. His skin was paler than I expected and his stomach was fleshier, but sexy nonetheless, and wildly distracting. I shook my head to free it of its inappropriate thoughts.

"Are you cold?" he asked.

"Huh?"

"You shivered."

"Oh, no, I'm fine." How funny. He saw me do that.

"I should probably go. I have early meetings."

I didn't want him to leave at all, but I couldn't *make* him stay. What was the point? We'd just keep working, and such close proximity without actual contact got unbearable after a while.

"Okay, I'll walk you out."

He stood at the door and I smiled at him.

"I'm glad you came over today. It's easier to work with friends around."

"Yeah, I know. I'm glad I came, too. Should we make a plan for this week sometime? Maybe grab drinks? Tuesday? Thirsty?" he asked.

"Sure, Tuesday at the Thirsty. Nine p.m.?"

"Sounds like a plan." He hugged me goodbye in an especially tight embrace that lifted me an inch off the ground. "You're the best, Annie." And then he kissed my cheek and left, and I floated back to my desk.

"Paul leave?" Stephen asked from behind and made me jump.

"Yeah, he just left."

"What's going on with him?"

"Going on?"

"Yeah, between you two."

"Nothing, really. Same old. Hanging out. Friends."

"Really?"

"What else would it be?"

"I don't know. Seems like he's with you a lot. A real lot."

"Are you jealous?" I teased.

"Of course. I don't want his broken heart interfering with my chief marketing officer's productivity." He smiled and was trying to sound like he was teasing, but I knew he was partly serious.

"Well, so far there's been no major interference. Just a little static. And that small matter of my innermost romantic hopes and dreams, but that's a different issue."

"Be careful, Annie-belle," Stephen said.

"I am, Stevie K. Always." That last part was a little untrue. I was actually careful in all parts of my life *except* my love life. In that arena I took ridiculous, unfounded risk and so far in my life it hadn't paid off. But maybe, just maybe, now was the time.

CHAPTER 23

Coping strategies being what they are—ways of dealing with things that are just shy of *actually* dealing with them—for better or worse, I was expert at redirecting anxiety and stress. Most often I spun my excess energy into some work project, but I had other techniques, too. I could daydream about a boy, or eat too much chocolate, or go shopping for stuff I couldn't afford or didn't need. And every once in a while my system would break down, and that usually occurred when something sufficiently big was happening and I simply couldn't deal. Couldn't take in one more thing, process one more complicated issue or set of feelings. And when that happened, I went into efficient, emotionless denial.

Starting Monday, the following week was a full-court press of activity to push the business along on multiple dimensions—refining the website, creating investor materials, executing the pre-launch marketing plan. Mid-week we did our second and third sets of user tests, and when they were finished on Thursday I drove to my parents' house to return their video camera. Normally I wouldn't feel like I could get away, but I was eager for some space to think and the drive to Chester and back would be just the ticket. I needed to sort out some big questions in my mind about the next few months as we began a more broad-scale testing of our site and prepared for the national launch. I was feeling overwhelmed by the workload and needed some space to think it all through.

When I arrived my parents were having dinner. Hamburger pie, a mash of meat and vegetables molded into a crust of Pillsbury dinner rolls. It was delicious in a store-bought kind of way and I loved it.

"Have something to eat?" my mother asked.

"Ah, maybe just a bite," I said. I dropped my things at the doorway to the kitchen and joined them at the table. The hamburger pie tasted particularly good to me, as I'd been subsisting on frozen bean and rice burritos—$1.19 at Bread and Circus—for the past month, punctuated only by the roommate dinner. The salad of lettuce and tomatoes and croutons was heavenly. I hadn't had vegetables in days. I helped myself to seconds of everything. I hadn't realized how hungry I was. I ate and let my parents talk.

After dinner we had small cups of chocolate pudding with Cool Whip. This had been a wonderful diversion indeed. I checked my watch. I'd been there for almost an hour. An hour longer than I'd meant to stay.

"Okay, I'd better scoot!" I said.

"So soon?" My mother asked.

"Yeah, sorry to eat and run but I have to get back. There's the camera. Do you want me to put it away? In the antique?" I smiled.

"No," my father answered. "I'll take care of that. You get going. Drive safely."

I kissed them goodbye then exited to the family room, and headed down the back steps to my car.

"Annie." My mother had come outside to talk to me. I turned to face her and she continued. "I wanted to let you know that Liz took April to Mass General this morning."

"What? Why didn't you tell me?" I dropped my backpack

onto the backseat. My mother had a habit of not sharing all highly relevant information with the family, and her sorting mechanism for what to tell and what to skip was indecipherable.

"I'm telling you now."

"What happened?"

"I don't really know the details, just that her chemo isn't working like they expected. She can have visitors starting Monday, they said." My mother presented this information without emotion, as though she were communicating the weather, albeit on a cloudy day. My first reaction was unspoken defiance—no, not now, I can't handle one more thing, especially something as big and important as April's health. And my second reaction was, well, that I'd just have to deal. To find a way to do it all, even if it seemed impossible at first glance. The truth was, we'd been here before with April—she'd been fighting the cancer for months, and it didn't make sense to catastrophize until we had more information about what was going on.

"Okay, I'll go and see her."

"Don't you have to work?"

"I'll go after work. Let me know if anything new happens, okay?"

"Of course," she answered, as though she never forgot to pass along news. And then I left and filed this information away with a prayer that everything would be fine, but with the anxiety that quite possibly it would not. Until I had more information, until I could see her and talk to Liz, I would try to put it out of my head.

CHAPTER 24

On Monday evening at seven p.m. I wandered across the office to see Stephen, to remind him that I was going to the hospital to visit April and Liz, and without so much as a question he waved me off. I don't know why I was surprised that he had no issue with my leaving, but it certainly seemed he didn't. It was my guilt and sense of responsibility to my job that made me drag my feet, but eventually I exited the building and tried to remember where I'd parked my car.

My Toyota made its way down Broadway, negotiating stop-and-start traffic across the Salt and Pepper Bridge and onto Cambridge Street. After my first loop around lower Beacon Hill failed to score a free meter spot, I took my place in Mass General's Fruit Street garage among the other evening parkers. As I made my way out of the damp maze of concrete ramps, I dug into my bag and realized that I didn't have the five dollars I'd need to get my car back out, and hoped my credit cards would come through.

After speed-walking to the hospital entrance, I made my way to the Wang elevator bank, and pressed the button. The lift arrived promptly and transported me and a few other stressed-out people headed for the pediatric oncology floor. Stepping off the elevator, I was surprised to see my parents waiting there.

"Oh, hi Annie. We didn't think we'd see you this late. We told Liz you had to work," my mother said.

"No, no, of course I'd come." My parents provided a quick update on April and then my father started tapping his foot on the linoleum floor.

"We have to go." He checked his gold Seiko watch, last Christmas's big gift from my mother.

"You know how your father hates driving in the city at night."

As they moved to leave, I remembered my cash situation.

"Dad, can I borrow a few dollars? I had to park in the garage."

He let out an exaggerated sigh. "Elizabeth, do you see this? What would she do if she didn't see me here?"

"I'll pay you back." I would have figured something out if I hadn't seen them, but even with the minor humiliation of an almost-thirty-year-old asking her parents for money, getting cash from my frugal father would be easier than from my ATM card.

He handed me a ten-dollar bill and said gently, "Don't be silly. Now you be careful when you leave here." He reached around me to press the down button.

"That nice Eddie is here. I'm sure he'd walk you to your car." My mother threw the idea over her shoulder as she let my father guide her by the elbow. I waved goodbye, surprised again that my mother would be pushing the Eddie thing. Was this a permanent change in her demeanor toward my dating life, or did she just like Eddie? I'd always appreciated that my mother was different from so many mothers, never bugging me about boyfriends, dating, getting married, having her grandchildren.

Eddie was here. Hmmmm. That would be okay. He was a nice guy. Quiet, but nice. And I was dying to talk to him about Paul, if I could find the right moment. It was always good to befriend the friend, so long as you weren't too obvious or insincere. Thankfully, I had liked Eddie the first time I met him, so I could be genuine in chatting him up.

April's hospital room was surprisingly cozy. Except for the equipment, it could be any sparse bedroom in a suburban home with soft lighting, plants and stuffed animals scattered around. I tiptoed in and April, covered in a pale yellow cotton blanket, attached to an IV tube, smiled. Liz dozed on a turquoise-colored vinyl chair that pulled out to a bed.

"Hey, April," I whispered. Chemo had left her sleepy, but she brightened with each new round of company and opened and closed her hand a few times in a wave, then put a finger to her lips.

"Shhhhh. My mother just got to sleep." April stretched and yawned and I nodded and began straightening things—a size 6X sweatshirt, a dozen books and games, a Fleece the Lamb Beanie Baby, several half-empty soda cups and a slew of "Get Well" cards that fell down in a domino effect as I tried to organize them.

Liz's eyes popped open, as if she were having a bad dream. She looked to April first, then smiled a hello to me, giving herself a minute to come out of her short sleep before speaking. Liz had just passed her thirty-second birthday, and wore each and every year on her face—around her hazel eyes, etched across her forehead, and tucked in the small lines by her mouth—lines earned equally from laughter and tears. She had a button nose and a spray of freckles, like her daughters. Volumes of chestnut-colored hair framed her face in chunky bangs that swept haphazardly to one side or the other, and the rest fell in a straight curtain down to the middle of her back, in need of a trim. Liz's favorite color was yellow, and she wore it in some form almost every day, in contrast to her circumstances. That day she was wearing a gold sweatshirt that said "Cape Cod" in colored embroidery across the chest.

In my view, Liz had about the best attitude you could ask a

mother with a sick child to have. If someone observed to Liz that her life was hard she'd just point out the dozens of families she'd met at Mass General who had it worse. She was tough and clear-headed in her pain and fear.

"Ask April who called her today." Liz smiled toward her daughter.

"Who called you today?" I asked.

April was smug. "Garth Brooks!"

"The real Garth Brooks? 'Friends in Low Places' Garth Brooks? You're kidding! What did he say?" I asked.

"He said he hopes I get better soon, and that I can come to his concert in the spring and sit in the front row."

"Wow. He called you himself? How did that happen?" I was intensely curious. This was especially cool because April loved country music and adored Garth Brooks.

Liz jumped in. "Through Cape 107.5. And she's taking me, so don't even ask."

"I'm jealous. But Andy will be even more jealous," I said to April. "He loves Garth Brooks almost as much as you do!" April smiled with self-satisfaction as the door swung open. Eddie and Melody strolled in together. Melody was grasping one of Eddie's hands while he tried to maintain a hold on a tray of French fries, soup, chocolate pudding and paper cups of soda with his other hand. When she saw me, she let go and leaped ahead of Eddie.

"Hi Annie Banannie!" Melody jumped into a big hug, tightening her arms around my neck and kissing my cheek with an exaggerated smacking sound and giggling into my ear. She was so affectionate and sweet, I could've hugged her all day. I smiled to Eddie over Melody's blond curls and he murmured hello, explaining I'd just missed Barbara and Jimmy, then claiming the corner seat and handing a soda to April. Liz accepted the tray of her supper. Melody climbed into bed with

April and cuddled sweetly with her sister and made me marvel at how easily and unselfconsciously she expressed her affection. Why couldn't I be more like that? If a six-year-old could be fearless like Melody, surely I could stop loving April from such a distance.

Eddie spoke up. "April, should we let Annie join in on our game?'

"What game?" I asked.

"Pretty Pretty Princess, what else?" said Eddie.

"Yes, but I get to be pink," said April.

"I'm green!" screeched Melody.

"Blue," added Eddie.

"I'm, I'm, what else is there?" I asked, trying to catch up.

At this point April was fully awake and smiling. "You can be purple. Come sit here."

I complied and followed Melody's lead and sat close to April so we and Eddie could settle in for a marathon of Pretty Pretty Princess while Liz stayed put and ate her chicken noodle soup. The object was to move around a game board while collecting various pieces of plastic jewelry. On the board, April advanced early and got a pink necklace, while Eddie won a bracelet of light blue beads. Melody and I each settled for a single dangling clip-on earring in green and purple, respectively. Within fifteen minutes Eddie was adorned with earrings and a necklace, too. I had landed on the evil black ring and slipped into fourth place, and April won the prized pink ring, to which we all offered the appropriate oohs and ahhs.

"Eddie, do you have a girlfriend?" asked April, rolling the dice.

"Nope, not anymore," he answered, continuing to study the board.

"Annie, do you have a boyfriend?" asked April.

"No, do you?" I asked and turned to Melody. "Do you?" I tickled them both and April and Melody giggled together (and I wished I really was as easygoing as I was pretending to be) and realized Eddie had just rolled a six, selected his final blue jewel and won the game. Next April wanted to play Go Fish, and the little girls thought it was hysterical that we were all still wearing our jewelry, especially Eddie, who carried a focused and serious expression along with his blue baubles, and the girls filled the room with their sweet peals of laughter.

A resident came in to check on April and then pulled Liz outside to talk. April squinted to see their faces but couldn't, and looked frustrated. She had a feisty streak, and it tended to come out whenever she was being discussed by other people and not told what was going on.

After another round of winning Go Fish, April was getting tired again. Before Liz got back, April was dozing in and out of sleep and Melody was curled into her side and snoring. The plastic earring was pressing little diamond shapes into Melody's cheek and April's bracelet was caught on one of her tubes. I gently pulled off the pieces they won during the game while Eddie packed the board away and put the Go Fish cards in their box. The sleeping children made it necessary to either be quiet or whisper, but I sensed that Eddie wouldn't have said much anyway. Liz reappeared.

"What did the doctor say?" I whispered.

"That we have to come up twice a week for platelets, but otherwise April can go home in two days," Liz said in a low voice, through a relieved and cautious half-smile.

"That's great. Other than the drive," observed Eddie. Liz and the kids lived on Cape Cod, easily a ninety-minute trip, not counting traffic.

"Do you think me and April can stay with you some of the

times?" Liz asked. "My mother will watch Melody."

"Of course! I would love that. Come anytime." I was still whispering but April stirred. I turned to her, speaking softly. "How does that sound to you sweetie? Sleepover at my place next time?"

April smiled behind her half-closed eyes. Then she was asleep again.

CHAPTER 25

I offered Eddie a ride home, and we walked in silence most of the way to the parking garage. Eddie had a nice presence about him, quiet and unassuming, but kind and confident. I liked that he hung back, wasn't in your face or overbearing in any way. I did wonder what made him spend so much time with this sick child. I would have to remember to ask Barbara and Liz about it.

As we approached the glassed-in section where the cashier sat, Eddie spoke up.

"Let me pay for the parking. You're saving me cab fare."

That was true, but I was bothered by the fact that cab fare wouldn't cost much more than five dollars so Eddie wasn't really saving anything except a speck of time.

On the short ride home we tried to figure out our relationship.

"Well, Liz is my first cousin . . ." I said. "And you're the first cousin of Liz's husband."

"I think we're second cousins-in-law once or twice removed, or something like that," offered Eddie, in between providing directions to his apartment. I knew exactly *exactly* where he lived but let him direct me anyway. For weeks now I'd been driving out of my way to go past his apartment on the off-chance I'd see Paul. I never had spotted him in this way, not once, despite dozens of unnecessary trips around the block.

"It's strange we never met before, though. When did you start hanging around, anyway?" I asked.

"Not until after Bobby died. When April first got sick. I never really got along with Bobby, and I had always assumed that Liz would be the same as him, you know? But Jimmy's a friend of mine, so I met Barbara and then Liz and the girls. I was glad I was wrong about Liz."

I was relieved to hear that Eddie wasn't a fan of Bobby's. "Yeah, she was just young and blind and thought she was in love. No one wanted her to marry Bobby."

"But they did have two great kids."

"That much is true," I agreed. We arrived at Eddie's place and I pulled in front of a hydrant, the only space available.

"How long have you lived here?" I asked. If Eddie would bear with me, we could sit here and talk for a while, increasing the chances that I'd "bump into" Paul.

"I've been here for almost ten years, actually. My parents used to own the place. I bought it from them once I got a real job."

"Your parents must've been smart about real estate," I said. Eddie's apartment was in a prime area of mid-Cambridge, in close proximity to Harvard Yard, and was surely worth three or four times what he'd paid for it.

"Yeah, I guess so. Or lucky. They've just been around for a while, so it's just home, you know? And it's convenient."

I also realized I had no idea what Eddie did for a living, and felt slightly embarrassed at my disinterest. "Where do you work?"

"In Somerville."

"Somerville?" There were no companies of any size located in Somerville, at least that I was aware of.

"Well, believe it or not I'm a used-car salesman," Eddie said with a smile. I was sure he was joking. Or maybe not. Shit. How many college-educated used-car salesmen could there be? Wait, was Eddie college educated? I didn't know that for certain either, but had just assumed so since he and Paul were friends. What happened to my natural and often overbearing curiosity about people? Why was it on hold with Eddie DiPietro?

"Why are you smiling like that?" I asked, dodging the need to convey whether I thought he was kidding or not.

"Because used-car salesmen are the lowest of the low in most people's eyes, rated just above trial lawyers in trustworthiness."

"But you're trustworthy." I felt certain of this, so I made it as a statement rather than a question. And it did seem incongruous, the idea that Eddie was a used-car salesman. But it did explain the mullet, and the white shoes . . .

"I like to think so."

"It must be hard to feel misjudged all the time," I said.

"It's fine. I don't mind being underestimated by people," Eddie said.

"Me either." It was true. I'd found in my career so far that people often miscalculated my abilities because I was female. And I liked it that people's guards were often down around me, expectations lowered, telling me things they shouldn't, feeling comfortable and unthreatened by me. "I like underdogs in general," I continued.

Eddie looked skeptical, even challenging. What? Why was he looking at me like that? I didn't understand his expression. I did like underdogs, I empathized with them. I was one, after all.

"It's great that you have your own place. I'd love to see it sometime." I hoped my motives weren't too see-through. While I would have loved to check out Eddie's place, it was seeing Paul that I really wanted.

"Anytime. Sort of. I'd have to make sure Paul hasn't left his stuff all over the place before letting anyone in. The place tends to go to hell whenever he's around." Eddie was smiling good-naturedly, like he meant it that Paul trashed the place but wasn't too perturbed by it. I tried to remain aloof and casual at the mention of Paul's name.

"Is he here now?" I asked, trying to sound laid-back.

"Nope. Or he's asleep." Eddie was looking up at his apartment window while I pictured Paul in slumber. Wearing drawstring pajama bottoms and no shirt, with the covers tossed aside revealing chiseled abs and the slightest tuft of hair under his well-muscled arms. I shook my head out of this short and possibly inaccurate fantasy. Paul could have love handles for all I knew. I'd never seen him even close to naked, except the other day when I'd spotted his tummy when he stretched, and it really wasn't all that chiseled.

"Well, say hi for me when you see him."

Eddie played with his keys and stared out the windshield, which was looking a little dirty, I noticed, trying to focus on the mundane instead of Paul's possible sleeping nakedness.

"Okay. Good night." Eddie opened his door.

"Good night, second-cousin-in-law." I smiled at the back of Eddie's mullet as he pulled himself out of my car, which was a bit small for his frame. He turned to look back in before shutting the door.

"Thanks for the ride."

"Anytime. Seriously."

"I'll probably see you tomorrow night at the hospital?" Eddie asked.

"I'll be there. And next Pretty Pretty Princess game, I want to be blue, by the way."

"Hmmm, not if I'm there first," Eddie said. I smiled and

waved across the seat.

"Good night, Eddie."

CHAPTER 26

I called Paul early in the day on Tuesday to change our meeting place to Harvard Gardens, a yuppie bar located across from Mass General in Beacon Hill. It was quite possibly a first for me — to take the risk of changing set plans with the object of my desire, to introduce the possibility of logistic complications that might interfere with me being with him. But my fears were for naught; he readily agreed to meet me there at nine.

The plan allowed me to visit April and still get to see Paul, and I was pleased at the efficiency of it all. When I got to the hospital, Eddie was there. We played another round of games and Eddie won, again, and April got a little perturbed about not being the princess, but Eddie seemed to think this was no time to start giving April special treatment — he evidently believed she needed to be treated as normally as possible, especially while in the hospital. And normal for him apparently meant being an able competitor. It was fun to see. Watching men with little kids, especially little girls, was quite an endearing thing.

At about ten to nine I started looking at my watch, planning to leave. Eddie followed my lead. I was aware that it would be perfectly normal to invite him to join me and Paul for a drink but I hesitated. My instincts to be inclusive were strong, but not so strong as the tug in my heart for time alone with Paul. If I brought Eddie along it would change everything — the conversation, the tone, the intimacy. We'd have to spend at least half the time telling stories about how Eddie and Paul met, they'd launch into old high school memories, and we'd bobble around in the unsatisfying world of small talk for a couple of hours and then go home. It wouldn't be bad to know more about Paul's younger years, for sure, but what I really craved was the chance for more private, revealing, connecting conversations like the kind we'd been having lately.

Eddie and I matched each other's steps down the corridor, to the elevator, out the revolving door. Naturally he'd expect me to offer him a ride, like I did last night. Of course he would. I was about to explain that I wasn't going home, but there was no need, because Eddie spoke first.

"Are you going to meet Paul?"

"Ah, yeah, I was going across the street. Do you want to come?"

"He mentioned it. Is that cool with you?"

"Of course, of course. That would be great."

We found Paul at the bar watching a Celtics game.

"Hey, man." Eddie held out his hand and Paul shook it. "What's the score?"

"Celts up by fifteen."

The Celtics were winning and all was well in Beantown. Paul leaned toward me and kissed me on the cheek hello. "Annie, how's everything?"

"It's okay. April's doing alright and we're hoping for the best."

"Such a great kid," Eddie added.

"It's kinda crazy that you two are practically related," Paul said, looking back and forth between me and Eddie.

"By marriage," Eddie said.

"We're second cousins twice removed, or something," I offered with a smile.

"Well, it's a pretty small world if you ask me," Paul said. He finished his beer and got up so we could relocate to a table. He was wearing jeans and a white button-down shirt with a missing button near the collar. When he stood next to Eddie I noticed they were almost the same height, though somehow Paul seemed taller to me, larger and more substantial, though objectively speaking he wasn't. No, Eddie was more broad-shouldered and solid, but with such an unimposing, quiet way about him, Eddie just didn't take up as much space as Paul.

Led by the hostess, we settled into a booth, and despite my attempts to maneuver the arrangement so I would naturally be sitting next to Paul, he placed himself in the middle of the bench on one side of the booth, while Eddie, on the opposite side, moved all the way in toward the wall to make room for me. Still, it meant I got to face Paul and that was nice, too. The hostess took away the extra place setting and I watched Paul gaze at the empty space for a few seconds. Eddie was scanning the menu.

"Hey, buddy, they have mac and cheese. Mac and cheese 'al forno,'" Eddie said. "It's not Kraft, but it's probably okay."

"*Nothing* beats Kraft," Paul countered.

"This is how Dennison rebelled in high school," Eddie said to me. "He'd pass up his mother's gourmet meals and come to my house for boxed pasta."

"That stuff was good, man. What are you having, Annie?"

I hadn't looked at the menu and didn't care what I ate, since I never seemed to have an appetite around Paul, what with longing and butterflies occupying all of the space in my midsection. I chose the asparagus ravioli—the English peas and wild mushrooms appealed to me, especially at just fourteen dollars, while Paul ordered the steak frites and Eddie settled on the oven-roasted salmon. We ordered wine and Paul initiated a toast.

"To a small world of good friends."

We clinked glasses and sipped and made eye contact and probably each had a slightly different take on the awkward comfort of our threesome. I felt special to be with them both, because to have another meaningful connection to Paul felt nice, and Eddie was easy to be with and just so kind. I wasn't sure yet if he was a little boring or maybe just shy, but it didn't matter, because he was a friend of Paul's and, even if that preoccupied my view of him in that moment at dinner, he was, more importantly, a friend to my family at a time of great stress, and that mattered more to me than I realized.

Paul and Eddie were predictably telling funny, embarrassing stories about each other in high school, about Eddie's failed attempts to make the football team and how he took up track instead and became the team captain as a sophomore; about how Paul's unsuccessful bid for freshman class president spurred him to extreme campaign tactics and led him to take the title for the next three years, even though he didn't want the job; how Eddie was always in the darkroom experimenting with photography while Paul was more interested in sports, and presumably cheerleaders, and how Eddie always befriended the hottest girls in school, who loved him—as a friend—but it seemed he never made a move.

"Seriously, Eddie, remember Lora Phillips?"

"Of course I remember her," Eddie replied. "I remember you taking her to the prom."

"Well, yeah, but . . ."

"I also remember Joanna Damon," Eddie said with a smile, taking a sip of his wine.

"Oh, that's a low blow. That was a rough time." Paul turned toward me. "Joanna Damon was my first crush, and let's just say she crushed me completely."

"You're leaving out some really important details," said Eddie.

"Fine. I wasn't a model boyfriend, and Eddie thought I deserved everything that happened and he told me so, and it pissed me off and we didn't speak for months until I realized he was right." Paul drank his wine and stared into his glass for a few seconds. "Though it didn't seem to have enough impact to prevent the same thing from happening again. What's up with that, Ed? Now that I think of it, I'm in one big déjà vu episode. Good thing I have Annie to talk to this time around."

"Good thing," said Eddie, smiling toward me.

CHAPTER 27

Liz and April arrived at my apartment the next week, and they would stay for two days while April was treated at Mass General as an outpatient. The evening they arrived, we ate slices of mushroom and pepperoni from Tommy's Pizza and watched television. Later we got ready to go to sleep for the night, and while Liz started to make a bed out of my small sofa, April wandered around my room, licking an orange Popsicle and looking at pictures.

"Where are your roommates?" she asked.

"Well, Stephen is at work . . ."

"But it's late."

"Well sometimes he even sleeps there."

"He sleeps at work?!"

"Sometimes I do, too," I said. April shook her head with incomprehension and the slightest bit of judgment. I continued, "And Elke must be, I think, out with a friend."

"A friend or a boyfriend?"

"Well, I think kind of a boyfriend, but more a friend."

Liz and I exchanged looks. Something occurred to me.

"You know, Liz, if Stephen's not coming home then you can sleep in his bed. It's much more comfortable than that." But my cousin had already kicked off her shoes and gone horizontal, burrowing into the layers of cotton encasing the sofa.

"Nope, this is totally fine. I am so tired I could fall on the floor and still sleep like a baby."

"If you say so."

"I do," Liz answered with a big, noisy, openmouthed yawn.

April nodded in agreement then faced me. "Annie, how old are you?" she asked.

"Twenty-nine."

"You're twenty-nine and you don't even have a boyfriend." April looked concerned. Deeply concerned. I looked to Liz for solidarity but she was already drifting off.

"Well, I've got some time, don't you think?" I asked.

"No, I think you better get a boyfriend." Then April crossed to my bookshelf and picked up the Relationship Box. "What's this?"

"It's funny you should ask. That is a Relationship Box."

"What is a Relationship Box?"

"It's a special box that you use to put your wishes for a boyfriend inside and it helps them come true."

April opened the box and looked inside, then held it up accusingly to me. "There's nothing in here."

"You're right. I haven't had time to fill it. Do you want to help me?"

April scowled a little. "Okay. Anything to help you get a boyfriend for crying out loud."

I retrieved a Post-it note and pens from my desk. April noticed that her mother had already fallen asleep, and covered her carefully with a blanket.

"She's tired," April whispered to me. "She doesn't sleep at night when I'm going to the hospital."

"We can be very quiet," I whispered back.

"That's okay. Once she's asleep she can sleep through anything. She'll start snoring soon." April joined me on my bed where I sat with pen in hand ready to make my list.

"Okay, let's think about what should be on this list. Should my future boyfriend be tall or short?"

"Tall," April offered with certainty.

"Dark and handsome?"

"Yes, handsome. Very handsome."

"Smart or dumb?"

April smirked. "Smart."

"Nice or mean?"

"Don't be stupid," April said. "Of course he should be nice."

"Bald or hair?"

April looked at me in exasperation. Her chemotherapy had left her bald. "What do you think?"

I patted the top of April's head, which was covered by a Boston Red Sox cap. "I think I know some very nice-looking bald people."

April shot me a look. She was not one to tolerate patronizing. But the truth was I did think she was adorable, with or without her hair. She had beautiful skin, purpley blue eyes, and freckles.

"What else?" I asked, returning to the inventory of characteristics for my fictional future boyfriend, which covered most of the pink Post-it note. "We're running out of room. We can put one more thing on this list. What should it be? Funny? Rich?" April shook her head no.

"Skinny? Strong?" April shook her head no to those, too.

"Okay, well what then?"

"Shhh. I'm thinking." April put a finger to her lips and pondered. She walked about the floor space at the end of my bed in a small circle, twice around, and then said "He should love you. More than anyone or anything."

"Whoa, that's a biggie. Okay," I wrote it down. "Done." I looked at the list and couldn't help but compare it to Paul. I stopped myself short of admitting he had every quality going for him—and me—except that critical last one about loving me more than anyone or anything. Drat.

CHAPTER 28

For the first time that I could remember, I resented the arrival of the holiday season with its excessive demands for time and money. There was hardly an opportunity to eat, drink and be merry with the dizzying pace of my job.

Once we safely passed into 1996, the first several weeks of the new year were a blur as we got ready for the launch party. RSVPs trickled in at first and then grew to a steady stream of "yesses" — and with one week to go we had more than two hundred and thirty people on the list. Of course the name that pleased me the most was Paul's. We needed him there for many reasons, but for me it heightened the excitement and the performance pressure — this would be a chance to really impress him, and I so wanted to stand out in his eyes.

I secretly hoped for three hundred guests; that seemed like the number that would create critical mass for the event as I'd designed it. The PR team at Whisper was a group of skilled professionals and superbly helpful partners in getting the event properly executed. Charlotte's brother worked with someone who was a silent partner in a new Internet café in Harvard Square called CyberSpace, and we'd reserved the entire four floors for the launch. With my interns, we'd designed an event meant to replicate the GoodMatch.com process. Anyone who was attending the party who was part of the target market for GoodMatch.com would be invited to participate in the experience; married or otherwise attached people, like many of the VCs, would be able to observe and join in the non-matching activities.

Jeet oversaw the development of a special, private GoodMatch.com site that included only the people who were coming to the launch party. As part of the invitation, we encouraged as many of the guests as possible to fill out profiles online before the party, and then we'd set up the hundreds of computers at CyberSpace to the GoodMatch.com site and invite anyone else who wanted to fill out a profile. We'd promote searching and matching for the first part of the evening, then split off into the meet-and-greet part. The Whisper team and I conceived of a party-within-a party, a structure of several parties within the overall launch event, where part of each floor of the CyberSpace venue was designated for some common set of interests—sports, music, reading, art, dancing, cooking, wine, etc. When guests came, they could use GoodMatch.com to search the party attendees and find out what shared interests they had, then have the chance to meet face-to-face in one of the areas of the party. There were pool tables, sports trivia games and sports on television in the sports area; a cooking class led by Terry Britain, a local celebrity chef who was a friend of Blake Hadley's; wine tasting organized by Milly Knight, a friend who owned a wine store in the South End; live music by Michael Nole, a singer-songwriter that Elke had recently discovered at Club Passim; a design exhibit hosted by B. Lee Ryan, a hot young architect; and a photography exhibit set up by Jeff Panns, a friend from New York. On the bottom floor a writer friend of mine and Stephen's named Chris Macadamia was reading his short story about blind dates set up by people like your boss and your sister, then giving tips on how to write the best personal profile on GoodMatch.com. The events happened at different start times over the course of the night so people could easily attend more than one. I would try to see everything. When I thought about the fun I'd had conceiving of the party and executing it, I'd never been professionally happier. It came so naturally to me to dream up the idea and sort out the special details, to network with friends to get the right people hosting each mini-party. From the beginning to those moments leading up to the event, I'd experienced the indescribable rush of feeling extremely competent and energized. I wished I could do it all the time.

A few weeks before Elke had approached me late at night, offering tea and some incredible lemon poppy seed cake she'd baked herself, and asked if she could help with the launch party. She'd grudgingly accepted that GoodMatch.com was consuming all of the time and attention Stephen and I had, and she wanted in. If nothing else so she could hang out with us instead of being home alone. I welcomed the extra pair of über-competent hands and assigned Elke to work on the cooking section of the evening. She would be the chef Terry Britain's liaison and make sure that everything came together during that portion of the event. I thought Elke would probably enjoy that, too, as Terry was exceedingly handsome and newly divorced.

By the night before the actual party, we had 273 RSVPs and 80 percent of the venture capitalists we wanted there had agreed to come for at least the first part of the evening. We'd temporarily moved GoodMatch.com headquarters to a room over at CyberSpace. Stephen and I were putting finishing touches on the kickoff presentation, balancing between a fun, sexy message appropriate for general guests and prospective GoodMatch.com users, and one that would convince the VCs to agree to further conversation about investing. When we finished that critical task, Stephen was once again on his cell phone and working on his laptop computer while I concentrated on deploying my small team of volunteers for the rest of the setup—putting out the party supplies, hanging the GoodMatch.com sign, changing the home page of each of the computers in the room to GoodMatch.com, arranging nametags. The last detail wasn't in place before 3 a.m., and the lateness of the hour practically guaranteed I would have dark circles under my eyes the next day. But I was excited, and knew my adrenaline would get me through.

I managed four-and-a-quarter hours of sleep, astonishing given the stakes of the launch party, and I actually *hopped* out of bed, feeling rested and eager. I surprised myself with my organization and general calm around the party. When it came to these events I could do something that was hard in other aspects of my work. I could prioritize with ease, I could delegate well, I could explain to others exactly what I wanted, and I had a never-ending supply of ideas for creative touches that made it truly special. And I had *fun*. It was still hectic and stressful, but I was pretty sure I could pull it off, dig down and find the energy and stamina to just do it, a delicious feeling to have, mere hours before such a critical test.

Once I was back in our makeshift office, the day flew by as we put the last details into place and answered my cell phone to accept another dozen or so RSVPs. In these final hours we'd become the hot ticket in town, and we were exceptionally close to my target three hundred guests, and I thought surely there'd be some party crashers to fill in the blanks.

Just as I'd predicted, my getting-ready time was squeezed by a few last-minute tasks, but I did manage to get home, slip into a hot shower, and steal a few minutes with the hairdryer and my makeup case. Before rushing out the door, I paused to glance in the mirror at my Prada outfit—unearthed, unbagged, strapped on. And it was stunning. Truly stunning, but in a bare-more-breast-than-you-meant-to way. I doubled back to my closet to grab a sweater—just in case.

By eight p.m. the GoodMatch.com launch party was in full swing. People had been streaming in steadily since around seven and I felt like the consummate hostess, remembering names, hugging and kissing and shaking hands, attending to everyone's needs. The only uncomfortable part had been the number of looks and comments on my outfit—mostly compliments, but the kind that told you they couldn't believe you were actually wearing such a thing. And yes, my inner wimp won out over my inner vamp. So I pulled on my cardigan just to shush the reaction—I didn't have time for the distraction of feeling self-conscious tonight.

Self-conscious was not how I would describe my supervixen of a roommate, however. She arrived promptly as "Party-Elke," dressed to kill in her sock dress, and without her severe glasses hiding her pretty face or masking her rather sunny disposition. She was a total knockout, and I wasn't the only one to notice. But she whisked on by with an air-kiss and something about finding Terry, and I went about my business of corralling people to hear the presentation, which Stephen delivered flawlessly except for a little minor sweating and a tiny snafu in the Web demo that showed how the matching worked. We'd had guests filling out profiles and inputting them into the private database all evening, assuming that only single, datable people would do so. When Stephen showed in real time how the matching worked, one of the married venture capitalists somehow ended up matched with Elke's profile, via Stephen as the connector. Stephen milked it for laughs and the VC shrugged it off with a smile. No major harm done, especially since his wife was at home with their four children.

Elke was easily the most-noticed woman at the party. Later, as Stephen and I moved from the main presentation area to circulate among the mini-parties, we bumped into Elke holding court with at least half a dozen men of different ages and types, over by the wine tasting. As we temporarily joined their conversation, the discussion seemed to be about New Year's resolutions. Someone mentioned running a marathon, another claimed to be learning German. A third had resolved to meet his wife by the end of 1996. Elke's resolution topped them all.

"I am here in the States for nine months only, and I want to have as many love affairs as possible." With her German accent, it came out sounding like *"I am here in zee States for seex months only, and I vant to have as many love affairs as poss-ee-bll."* Her men smiled and chuckled and stood a little taller and she smiled and tilted her head and looked every bit as comfortable as if she'd resolved to start going to church regularly. Stephen and I exchanged amused looks, then continued on. Glancing back at Elke, I tried not to let my dark side take hold. This was supposed to be a moment—an entire evening, ideally—of professional triumph for me and instead I was distracted and feeling jealous of my roommate. Jealous not just of her flowing blonde hair, her six feet of height, her scandalous sock dress wrapped snugly around every curve and line of her lithe and beautiful body. I was jealous because she had precisely the confidence I lacked, and the contrast was becoming harder to ignore. I couldn't pretend and hide any longer without noticing the reaction in myself, and the recognition was painful. Quite possibly the hardest part was that there was nothing about Elke I could totally dismiss—I really liked the woman, dammit.

I moved down to the next level of CyberSpace, signaling waiters to pick up cups and glasses, organizing tables, exchanging hellos, introducing everyone I knew to everyone else I knew. I moved through the crowd easily, having mastered the art of quick small talk, without allowing myself to pause too long.

It was much more comfortable to keep moving, with a sense of purpose and work, than to engage in a fuller conversation. As a result, I felt both like the heartbeat at the center of the party and fully isolated from its real pulse. Except when I spotted Paul—then my heartbeat and my pulse fully synchronized. But that only happened once that evening, in the sports section, where Paul was glued to the TV watching a basketball game.

"Hi, Paul. Whatcha doing?" I asked from behind his back. He turned and broke into a grin.

"Annie! This is a great party. I can't believe you have the game on. I was so bummed when I thought I was going to miss it."

"Glad we could accommodate! Have you seen any of the other party spaces?" I desperately wanted him to see what I'd done. I was hoping he'd be impressed with my creativity and resourcefulness.

"Not yet, but I'm planning to. At halftime. It all looks great." He put his arm over my shoulders and squeezed me.

I needed to break away from the sports area to check on the cooking demo, which was happening clear across the party, three floors up. It had been a conscious decision to assign spaces that way—knowing that Elke would be helping Terry, and Paul would most likely hole up near the sports corner and the beer, and I just liked the idea of them being separated. Not that I didn't want them ever to meet—of course they would, *eventually*. After Paul and I were, hopefully someday, maybe, actually an item. It was just that I didn't want my hottie roommate and my lust interest bumping into one another—and heaven forbid, hooking up—at my big party. That I couldn't have handled. Was that a reasonable fear? Was I being too paranoid? Too controlling? *No way.* I had lived with Elke for more than four months now and I knew what she was capable of falling into, seemingly without trying, and I wasn't going to create the kindling for that situation.

The cooking demo was arranged in a corner of the third floor that Elke had staked out during one of our visits earlier that week, and she'd brought all of her taste and talent to bear to create an intimate yet functional space that showed both Terry's cooking prowess and his chiseled cheekbones and strong chin and shiny dark hair. The setting was spare but with small touches like live plants, artfully displayed cookbooks and a row of colorful communal aprons, silkscreened with the GoodMatch.com logo, hanging on pegs against a side wall. As I arrived, Terry was sautéing something with one hand and gesturing wildly with the other, pausing to grab a torch of some kind to light his concoction on fire. I jumped and prayed we had the right insurance as the flame stretched toward the ceiling, but seconds later everything seemed under control. Terry then signaled to Elke, who started handing out aprons to a select few of the observers. I noticed that Elke was choosing an even mix of men and women, with a more than slight bias to the really good-looking ones. A half-dozen guests, now clad in their aprons and chef's hats, stepped up front to help with the demo. Flanked by dazzling Terry on one end and stunning Elke in her sock dress on the other, the cooking demo was hotter than Terry's flambé, so if the audience wasn't already captivated by the culinary wizardry, they had lots of pleasing people to look at. Brilliant. Just brilliant. Kudos to Elke. While I was surveying the scene, my eyes were drawn to one amateur chef in particular. He was the one standing closest to Elke, absorbed in his job rolling out small balls of dough, while Elke helped and flirted and he absorbed the attention. When the dough ball roller looked up, laughing at something Elke had whispered to him, I figured out who he was. Oh my. Ohhhh, my. It was Jefferson Taggert, a partner at DNGI, and one of our most important guests. As I watched Elke pour on the flirt all I could think was, *let's hope his wife isn't here.*

Convinced Elke had everything under control, I headed downstairs. I was happy to see that Jodie and Christopher had made it and were enjoying moving from floor to floor to check out the various goings-on. On the second floor Milly Knight was about to start her wine tasting, and I felt instantly thirsty, craving that soothing feeling that accompanied a smooth sip—or five—of wine. I adored this woman, with her effervescent personality, easy wit and sharp mind. She'd built a mini-chain of high-end wine stores around greater Boston and had hopes of developing a wine show for cable television, so any chance to be on stage in front of a crowd was a welcome one.

"Hi, Annie, doll. How are things going?" Milly asked while setting out glasses.

"So far, so good. Everyone seems to be having a good time. I myself am dying for a glass of wine."

"Oh! We can fix that." Milly moved to her display table and twisted off the top of a bottle. There were the damn screwtops again!

"Milly, what's with the screwtops?" I asked as quietly as possible.

"Oh, this is a New Zealand pinot gris from a great little vineyard over there. They use screwtops because they're young struggling winemakers, not pretentious fucks like the French, and they know screwcaps protect wine more reliably than cork. I promise you, in most cases, especially from New Zealand, it has nothing to do with the quality of the wine, just the philosophy of the winemakers, who don't want to risk ruining 10 or 15 percent of their wine to corkage. Taste this." She offered me a glass.

"It's white." I had a vague recollection of pinot being red. Shit, I'd never figure it out.

"The pinot grape is red, but they remove the skins, and

therefore the color. Taste."

I sipped and the crisp liquid soothed my throat and surrounded my taste buds, sending happy signals to my brain.

"Delicious."

"I'm glad you like it." Milly filled the rest of my glass. "Anytime you want to taste you let me know and I'll meet you at a store."

"Thanks Milly, that's so sweet."

"Really, anytime. And I think I'll add that little screwtop lesson to my demo." Milly looked past me to the gathering crowd of singles. "Now, tell me something. Is that Stephen Kanner single? He's hot."

Uh,oh. Here we go again. But, Milly wasn't a pushover. She just might be a match for Stephen.

"He is single, but proceed with caution. I love him love him love him, but he's fairly single-minded about work these days. Doing more of the casual dating thing, if you know what I mean."

"Know what you mean?! That's my mantra. Casual dating, casual sex, too busy for messy relationships." Milly was scanning the crowd. "If I don't see him again tonight, you'll give him my number, won't you?" Milly handed me her business card and I glanced at it before tucking it into my pocket.

"Sure. So long as you go in with all eyes open." There, I had delivered encouragement with appropriate warnings. Plus, I suspected Milly could hold her own.

Since I was deliberately moving from floor to floor all evening, Paul, who was still glued to the TV, was out of my line of sight for much of the time. Not so Eddie, who seemed to be everywhere that I was. At the cooking demo, then the wine tasting, and then as I arrived at the photography exhibit on the top floor, there he was again.

"Hi, Annie. This is such a great party."

"Thanks, Eddie. Are you having a good time?"

"Yeah. I love all this stuff." He did? I was struck by Eddie's quiet enthusiasm, so genuine. We walked through the photo exhibit and Eddie had many more insights and opinions about what we saw than I did, distracted as I was by responsibility for pulling the whole thing off. I parted ways with Eddie as he engaged in a long discussion about Sally Mann with the exhibit curator Jeff Panns, my friend from New York, whom I cheek-kissed on my way out and promised to catch up with later.

I was planning to check on the Chris Macadamia reading downstairs, but first needed to find my bag and my lipstick. I passed the waiters as I slipped into the small makeshift kitchen on the third floor, trying to remember where in the mass of furniture and trays and pots and pans I tucked my backpack. It was hours before that I'd left it there, and I needed my lipstick to feel pulled together. I moved behind the massive assembly table where Terry Britain had prepped and pulled together his cooking lesson. The party was raging outside the kitchen, but behind the scenes no one was around. Still, I could hear an undecipherable noise—a conversation? An argument, whispered?—coming from the darkened hallway behind the kitchen space. Curious, I peeked around the corner. I couldn't see well. But the noises continued, quiet at first then gaining volume. As I moved past a door that was ajar, I saw through the crack that Terry Britain was standing a few paces away, passionately kissing Elke, hands tangled in her hair. I knew I should leave, but I was frozen there, and luckily hidden. I regained my composure and retreated, smoothing my hair and tiptoeing out of the kitchen, dying to kiss someone.

A few minutes later, I was sipping water with my still-pale lips when Terry exited the kitchen area, followed by Elke, who was smoothing her sock dress over her ridiculously long legs. *Let's see . . . love affair number*—oh, I'd lost count.

Later, with the party rocking, Stephen joined me on a balcony overlooking a crowd of people who were mixing and mingling and swaying and flirting.

"See, Stephen—this is the last mile of online matchmaking, making it easy to meet people in person. That's where the chemistry happens. Before this it's all in your head. We gotta do this. And there's money in it—I ran the numbers."

"Yeah, but first we have to raise ten million dollars. And that means staying focused and getting oodles of subscribers . . . and the margins online are better, and there's only so much we can do at once."

"I know. I know. But eventually." I turned to look at him. "Did you just say 'oodles'?"

The party lasted until CyberSpace closed after one a.m. Stephen and I were picking up remnants with one hand and drinking celebratory drinks in the other.

"I gotta hand it to you, Annie. This was a huge success," he said.

"It really was. And so fun! This is a good sign, Stephen." We clinked glasses and downed the last bit of champagne.

CHAPTER 29

The next day, Paul and I were having coffee at the Starbucks on Broadway. We'd snagged the two overstuffed chairs and our knees occasionally touched, especially if I moved mine slightly to the left every chance I could.

"Annie, that was a phenomenal turnout. You must be so happy with the party. Everyone I talked to had a great time."

"Ha! You stayed in the sports bar the entire night!" I was trying to tease, but I had been deeply disappointed by the fact that Paul didn't venture past the basketball game, and I probably didn't completely hide the annoyance in my voice.

"But plenty of people came by there, and they were all raving. You have a real knack, Annie. I need to get you to do my promotions."

"Oh, no, no time for that." *Did I really just turn down an opportunity to help Paul?* "But, can I run a marketing idea by you, now that you've read our business plan?" I asked.

"Shoot." He sipped his grande latte and licked his lips, which was mildly distracting, but I soldiered on with my question.

"I'm thinking that we should combine our online matchmaking with live events, by city. Like the launch party. We partner with local establishments, and do traditional and online promotion, but get people into the same room to meet people whose profiles they've seen online. What do you think?"

"I like it. But the VCs won't see it as being as scalable as the online piece."

"I know that, but I'm concerned about quality of experience versus quantity. And long-term—"

"Yes, but you guys are going to be under huge pressure in the short term. You can't let yourself get distracted."

"Yes, but—"

"Save your energy," Paul replied. "Once you get this bridge done, you're going to have to please the venture guys. And all they care about are numbers going up fast. Trust me, I've just been through it. Live, place-based stuff will slow you down." He paused to sip and lip-lick again. "Annie, do you ever not think about work? I think you work too hard."

"What, I don't work any more than you, or Stephen."

"That's different. We own most of the equity in our companies. Stephen could someday make millions—tens of millions—out of GoodMatch."

"I have stock options," I said weakly, immediately regretting opening the topic, especially when Paul responded with raised eyebrows and a *you're kidding, right?* kind of look.

"I've seen your equity stake, Annie. If GoodMatch does well I'll fare much better than you for putting in 100K than you're going to get for all your time and sweat."

"Well, that's the difference between us, Paul. You have 100K, and all I have is me. And my time and sweat." Was that more edginess in my voice? How odd, and un-me. Especially considering I was talking to Paul. It was one thing for me to get a little testy with, for example, my mother, but another thing entirely for it to happen with a guy that I liked.

I could barely speak for the rest of our coffee date. (Okay, okay, it was *not* a date, but surely it was something more than simply beverage co-consumption?) It wasn't that I disagreed with what Paul was saying that made it so hard to hear; it was that he was right. One hundred percent right, and I had no idea what I was going to do about it.

Later, when I thought about it some more, I knew that it was not the first time I'd found myself in a discussion about money that left me feeling foolish and exposed, but it wasn't something I let happen often. Money was such a tricky topic that I rarely discussed it with anyone, least of all a guy like Paul, who seemed to have not a care in the world of the economic variety. For me, it was a truly dichotomous thing. Cold, hard cash, sure. But soft, hot, emotional, too. With the power to throw me into a paralyzed, insecure place. I didn't know what it was like to have money, because I had never had any. Even when I made a good salary before business school I spent it as fast as it came—on obscenely high Manhattan rent, too many clothes that all looked the same, and more than my share of drinks, dinners, and miscellany. My paycheck was a financial hot potato, burning a hole in my pocket. So now, having taken out eighty thousand dollars in student loans to finance grad school, and then accepting a job that paid almost nothing, I was a fiscal disaster. What made me do this? I could have had an excellent job in marketing for a big company, and I would've had plenty of money to pay my rent. But I chose the impoverished path, and contentedly, happily. Not just because I liked the excitement of a start-up. It was also because there was something comfortable and familiar and *easy* about having no money. It eliminated the pesky issue of choice and decision-making. And my self-serving logic held that my MBA degree bought me a safety net—if I absolutely had to, I could get a real job. I might not like it, but it would always be an option.

For now, I liked being part of something new and exciting and feeling like I was on the edge. But I was starting to feel unsettled about not owning a real piece of the action, about pouring my best, most creative self into the role with little hope of being rewarded for it. Yes, it was fun and safe to be part of a team, to let Stephen do all the major worrying and deal with the financial stuff. And I did have a stake in the company's success, but I couldn't imagine doing it this way forever. I would either have to renegotiate my deal with Stephen, or soon enough I would want to strike out on my own. For now, though, I would concentrate on learning and doing a great job and getting ready.

In the meantime, the GoodMatch.com numbers were growing by the day. Post-launch we set up a ticker in the main room of our office to keep track of new registrations and new subscribers. I'd pushed each member of our staff who was single to set up a profile, including Stephen and including me. It was the last thing I wanted to do, truth be told, but I didn't see how I could be an effective head of marketing if I didn't experience the service first-hand. And as well as things were going, there were many improvements we wanted to make and I needed to get a sense of them early, before frustrated customers started complaining. One of the biggest concerns was that the technology—cutting edge as it was—couldn't yet keep up with our ideas. The site could be clunky at times and a solution wasn't obvious—especially since so many people used dial-up connections from home instead of broadband.

But I was proud of my work. Our partnership efforts were driving people to the site, and my promotion ideas were starting to pay off in skyrocketing subscriber numbers. Among many other things, I'd given Elke a prominent place on our home page, which was working out well for everyone.

CHAPTER 30

Over our months of roommating, I had discovered a telltale sign that Elke was upset. She would get completely absorbed in cleaning or straightening of some kind. Difficult phone calls with her German lover, Holger, or the beau, Michael, she'd left behind in Providence could be followed by hours of closet rearranging, floor sweeping, tub scrubbing or all of the above. As I dropped my things at the dining room table and walked into the kitchen, Elke was drinking a Sam Adams and vigorously reorganizing the pantry. It had taken a few months, but something big enough must have happened for her to decide to tackle the "scheisse in the Speisekammer," which meant roughly the shit in the pantry. My greeting was tentative, and met with a "Hmmph" as Elke grunted a little, persistent in her project.

"Something wrong?" I asked. Elke didn't answer and I knew to leave her alone. I retreated to the living room to put the details together for a promotional idea I was newly excited about. When Elke resurfaced a half hour later she took a seat in the big round chair in the living room, long arms folded in front of her, staring straight ahead. I rearranged myself on the sofa in silence. Elke turned her head and looked at me.

"I have something to tell."

"Okay . . ." I was intensely curious. The behavior was so unlike Elke, who was always so poised and discreet.

"I have, what you call, a crush."

185

"A crush? On who?" As far as I knew there wasn't anyone new in her life, other than Terry, and he was clearly a Naked Friend only. Oh no. What if it was Paul? Please don't let it be Paul. Had Elke even met Paul?

Elke wordlessly pointed one long thin finger at the wall. I looked at her, completely not understanding. Then I realized that on the other side of said wall was Stephen's bedroom.

It took me a few seconds to register my genuine surprise.

"Stephen? *Stephen?* Noooooooo!" Could she really mean Stephen-our-roommate Stephen, who-we-share-a-house-with Stephen?!

"Yes. We did as you say, hook up."

EXCUSE ME? What did she say? I tried to contain my alarm.

"Did you say you *hooked up*? You hooked up with Stephen?" Maybe Elke didn't know what the phrase meant. I doubted her Merriam-Webster German-English dictionary would offer an accurate definition.

"Yes."

This affirmation was delivered with such conviction, too. This had me even more alarmed.

"Elke, hook up means different things to different people. What exactly do you mean, *hooked up*?"

"I think you would say we hooked all the way up."

"*All* the way up? You hooked all the way up with our roommate." I involuntarily began to stand and as I did, I reached over and grabbed Elke's arm.

"Come on. This calls for tequila."

CHAPTER 31

The Border Cafe had many distinctive qualities, not least of which was its tendency to impart its aroma on anyone who entered the premises. Simply stepping through the front doors was tacitly agreeing that you'd soon smell like a refried bean. But while you were inside all you knew was the food was scrumptious and the margaritas would knock you off your bar stool. Elke and I claimed a table by the window, and moments later a waitress appeared.

"Two frozen margaritas, please," I said.

"Salt?" asked the waitress. Elke nodded yes.

"One with, one without, thanks," I said. When the waitress disappeared I turned to my roommate, who was still looking crestfallen and staring out the window.

"Okay, spill the beans," I said.

"Spill the beans?" This came out like *spill zee beans*.

"Fess up, give me the scoop," I continued.

"Tell about Stephen, you mean," Elke responded.

"Yes, that's exactly what I mean!" I smiled anxiously. We'd agreed that I'd talk in everyday English to help Elke pick up colloquialisms and slang and we usually laughed a lot when phrases made no sense to Elke.

"It was just that one night. When we first met at the apartment. He struck me right away as handsome and sexy and, at first, I thought, it was just for fun, mutual pleasure, this kind of thing. But then something happened, and I felt my emotional self engaged. And I cannot stop thinking about him."

"Oh no. That's a disaster." I'd seen this a dozen times if I'd seen it once. "With him, I mean. He's in no place. He's not. Oh. I can't believe I didn't realize. I'm clueless. I really can't believe it, but it just never occurred to me."

"It just happened. It wasn't planned," Elke said.

"Well I should hope not! Doesn't anyone but me know you can destroy perfectly good relationships with sex?" I was only half kidding.

"Well . . ."

"Rhetorical question," I said.

The waitress arrived with our margaritas. Elke licked some salt off the rim of her glass while I gasped at the sharp tang of the fresh-squeezed lime juice and the shockingly large amount of tequila I could taste in every sip.

"I guess I'm just stunned that you guys would risk it, since you knew you had to live together afterward," I said, genuinely puzzled. Didn't they see how easily this would mess up the household equilibrium? "Maybe this explains why Stephen hasn't been around much at home."

"Maybe." Elke took a long drink of her margarita and put a graceful hand on her chest. "I feel this pain."

"I'm sorry. That sucks." I *was* sorry. It did suck. But I could've predicted this and saved Elke the heartache—if only I'd been consulted. My curiosity was piqued. I'd been a bystander for years watching a parade of women get their egos battered and fantasies dashed by Stephen's excessive charm and exceedingly casual approach to the opposite sex. He tended to be everything they wanted—he was handsome, playful, smart and someone everyone wanted to be around. But I never would have pictured Elke falling prey. What was it about Stephen that could turn even the strongest women to mush?

"Yes, it does suck," Elke continued. "And it leaves my bed empty more than I'd like." What?! I thought that seemed like a stretch. Elke had made lots of Naked Friends since the launch party when she announced her plans for maxing out on love affairs while she was here in the States. I'd met them, usually in the morning in the hallway on the way to the bathroom or late at night in the kitchen.

"Come on Elke, you've had more action in the last two weeks than I've had in two years." I smiled.

"Really? How long has it been?" Elke tilted her head and looked curious.

"Hmmm, oh, well, yes, about a year."

"Oh my, Anna. Batteries must be wearing out."

Batteries? What was she talking about? Oh! It took me a moment but once I got her point I could feel the embarrassment rise in my throat.

"No! No, I don't, no. Not me." I wondered if my face was turning red.

"No? Why not? You should," Elke replied.

"No. No way. It feels . . . desperate."

"No, actually it feels pretty good." Elke said it with such unembarrassed conviction, I noted her confidence and laughed.

As I sipped my drink I realized I felt genuinely sorry for Elke, which was a new emotion for me, at least as related to her. For the first time I realized she had a soft center and could be vulnerable, which was surprising because everything about her suggested strength. Competence. Intelligence. Organization. Control. She seemed bullet-proof and more like a guy than most guys I knew—at least when it came to matters of the heart, and body. Most important, I'd always thought of her as wildly different from me. Yet here she was telling me a story about a broken heart and dashed hopes that I could've told a dozen times over. I knew the sequence well—the immediate aftermath of the flash of possibility with a guy you thought you really liked, the fork in the road where you figured out if the initial connection was a fleeting spark or something that would have some staying power. And when you discovered it was the former the disappointment would replace hope, the early flash would be followed by disbelief, leaving you feeling heavy and sad. I was thankful I wasn't feeling like Elke was. I'd been there. I hated it.

"Back to your broken heart," I continued. "Now sorry if I misunderstand, but—haven't you been out with many guys in the past few weeks?"

"Ah, yes. For distraction. My love affairs are mostly for that these weeks."

"Well, they do say, get back on the horse . . ."

"I would like to get back on a Stephen-shaped horse, but I fear this is not in the cards. I fear I must accept it."

"So he's not giving you any indication he's interested in more?"

"None at all. At least it is unambiguous."

"Yeah, but what a bastard. He shouldn't have gone there in the first place."

"To be fair, I like to think I made it hard for him to make a different choice. *Very hard.*" Elke and I dissolved into margarita-fueled laughter. Our glasses were empty and Elke was looking around for the waitress. Her eyes lit up as she noticed someone at the bar.

"There are two horses, if you will." I turned to look. Over by the center bar, Paul Dennison and Eddie DiPietro were leaning in to look at a menu. *Oh, no.* Could it be that after months of successfully skirting the issue, I would finally be forced to introduce Elke to Paul?! I should've thought about this. I could've guessed that Paul might be at the Border Cafe on any given night, since he worked around the corner and loved Mexican. But why tonight? I'd been unconsciously (okay, deliberately) trying to avoid having him meet Elke. I just couldn't take it if he fell for her like so many of them did. And with her broken heart, surely she'd be looking for more "distraction."

"You know them?" Elke asked. "Should we invite them to join us?"

"Yes, and they were at the launch party." Consistent with my intention to delay the inevitable as long as possible, I strongly preferred that they not join us. Who knew what could happen? "We could invite them, but, well, don't you want to keep talking about Stephen?"

"Not really. I can't see how it will help beyond what I've already said. It does feel good to have it off my chest. I think it would be nice, you know, for your friends to join us. If you want them to."

"Ah, well, they're probably in a rush, I doubt they'll have time . . ."

It was too late. Elke had caught Eddie's eye and waved and pointed to me. She was truly shameless. Not more than thirty seconds later, Eddie and Paul had downed the last of their drinks and came over to join us. The waitress was a step behind them, and Paul ordered another round of margaritas while I made introductions.

"Eddie DiPietro, Paul Dennison, meet Elke Hermann, my roommate."

"El-kah. You must be . . . Russian?" Paul asked and Elke shook her head no.

"Deutsche."

While Paul attempted to converse with Elke in half-remembered high-school German, I tried to carry on a conversation with Eddie and still pay attention to what Paul and Elke were saying.

"I guess you don't speak German?" Eddie asked me.

"Nope," I replied. "It's one of my great mortifications, to be monolingual. What about you?"

"Same. But I try not to be mortified about things I can change," Eddie said.

Elke was coming on to Paul, who seemed to be enjoying the attention. I was watching them, and Eddie was watching me, and I felt a sick sensation in my stomach, which was now churning with tequila and anxiety.

"Huh?" I asked.

"Well, if it's really a problem, you can learn a language," Eddie continued. "No need to be mortified about it, either do something or accept that it isn't really that important."

"Huh. So you don't worry about things you can change— what about things you can't?"

"I try not to, but sometimes, I'm just human."

"What is the one thing you'd change if you could?" I asked. Eddie looked at me for a thoughtful moment while I tried to look interested and was really just straining to hear what Elke was saying. Something about medical school.

"I'll never tell," Eddie said.

The waitress came back to check on us. She was gorgeous but her accent took some of the sheen away. "You guys wannanotha rounda mahgaritis?"

"Yes, please, my friends are not nearly inebriated enough," Paul said. After taking our order, the waitress turned and disappeared.

"I must say the Massachusetts accent on a woman is like birth control," Paul said, and Eddie laughed with him.

"But is okay on a man?" Elke asked.

ANNIE BEGINS

"Well, I'm not interested in sleeping with them so it's less of an issue, yes. See, I can tolerate Eddie here."

"Eddie doesn't have a bad accent," I defended. He did have traces of one, but it could've been much worse.

"Yeah, I'm wicked suhfisticadid," Eddie said.

"Well, me too," I said. "I'm wicked smaht. And, I can pahty like a rock stah."

Paul found this hilarious, but Elke didn't quite get it.

"Hey, that's pretty good," Paul said to me.

"You don't know the half of it." I was thinking of how strong my accent really was, under my practiced new manner of speaking, the one I picked up in college, practiced in New York City just a few years ago, and perfected in business school.

Eddie turned to me. "See, you are bilingual." I giggled. We were all a bit tipsy then.

Normally when I was out with Paul our conversations wandered around the same sets of topics—men, women, relationships, work, and occasionally our friends. Tonight, Paul was contemplating aloud his reentry into the dating scene, and it was not lost on me that Elke's presence was fueling the choice of subject. I tried to stay cool, but I had a lump in my throat and a matching one in my stomach. If Paul was interested in Elke, well, this might be my worst fear realized.

"I haven't been on a date in over ten years. I don't know what's in vogue on the dating scene anymore," Paul said.

Of course I didn't know much either, but I was a girl, and girls talk, so I had the collateral benefit of having all of my friends' stories and statistics.

"Same old stuff, except people sleep together sooner now," I offered.

Elke shrugged in tacit agreement and Eddie sipped his margarita. Why I was encouraging this line of discussion was beyond me, but I couldn't seem to stop myself.

"Really. How soon?" Paul asked, now disturbingly attentive. Eddie was still sipping his drink.

"Well, I don't know for sure, but I'm hearing like the third date."

Elke shrugged again, but this time in clear disagreement. I was pretty sure it was Elke's habit to sleep with someone whenever the mood struck.

"Huh. Interesting. Now that is going to be weird," Paul said.

"What?" Elke asked.

"The first time I sleep with someone other than my soon-to-be ex-wife."

Oh, puhleeze. What a cheesefest we were having. And Elke was playing right into it.

"When do you expect that will be?" she asked. I wanted to crawl under the table. This was the worst. And a mere hour-and-a-half ago I'd been feeling sorry for Elke's wounded heart. *Ja, right.*

"Ah, as soon as possible? I think."

"You think?" Elke asked.

"You're a guy," I noted, stating the obvious. "You must be looking forward to it." I had no idea, none whatsoever, why I was assisting in this conversation. Blame it on the tequila. Then I made the mistake of glancing over at Eddie.

"What does being a guy have to do with it?" Eddie asked. "Don't women look forward to it, too? Don't you?" This caught me off guard, especially coming from him. And I didn't want him to start another conversation with me that left Elke and Paul alone! Gawd, didn't he get it at all?

"The truth is," I responded, looking around to include everyone in the conversation, "I'm Catholic. So casual sex has never worked. Too much guilt." I tried to smile and keep it light.

"Ah, I see now." Paul laughed. "In my experience, Catholic girls are the most fun in bed, once you get them there."

Well isn't that a fun fact.

"Really. Is the ex-wife Catholic?" Elke asked.

"Oh, yeah. All the same hang-ups. But also this incredible desire to please."

"I think I have that too," I said, jumping in before Elke could say anything. It was pathetic. *I* was pathetic.

"A good quality in a lover," Paul said and winked at me. Yes, he winked. *He just winked!* And in the direct presence of Elke. I felt much better. The waitress came by again, and we ordered yet more margaritas and individual tequila shots while I mentally counted the hours before I'd have to be at work. I was too drunk to do the math, and mercifully we got off of the topic of sex and soon everything that everyone said was hysterically funny and Elke wasn't dominating Paul's attention so much and I couldn't have cared less about the time, especially when Eddie and Elke started talking and I finally had the chance to connect a little with just Paul. The four of us then bounced around from topic to topic, and somehow the three of us Americans had decided that teaching Elke the lyrics of "Schoolhouse Rock" was an essential exercise for her mastery of English and America. The waitress finally gave last call, then brought the check and I vaguely recalled that Eddie retrieved it, and my panic from earlier in the evening resettled in my throat, as I realized that the end of the night was approaching and I had no idea how it was going to play out, and I was drunk off my ass.

Elke excused herself to go to the restroom and I stumbled after her. It was late, and a work night, so it was quiet in the ladies' room.

"Anna, these boys are so much fun, why have you been hiding them from me?" she asked, seeming far less drunk than I felt.

"Oh, not hiding them, I just, well, I ummm, I maybe, yes, well, ah . . ." Elke was looking at me strangely, then disappeared into a stall, allowing me to catch my breath. "Well, iss juss that you're the supervixen." I spoke under my breath and Elke couldn't possibly have heard me.

"Excuse me?" Elke reemerged and washed her hands, looking puzzled.

"Sorry, I don't mean this to sound bad, but, well, you may have noticed . . . Well, lemme put it this way. You know how you've been feeling about Stephen? How you said you have this, thiss pain, the heart hurt?" I put my hand to my chest, which created just enough imbalance that I needed to steady myself against the sink. How had Elke managed to stay sober? Jeez, she was even better at drinking than I was.

Elke nodded yes.

"That is, well, um, that's how I feel about Paul." The words came out in an embarrassed jumble. I was afraid, in saying it out loud, that the outside world would critique me and Paul as a terrible mismatch, especially if they didn't know about our friendship, our more-than-skin-deep connection. Sure, Paul was A-list and I was B at best, but if you squinted I really thought you could see us together. We made sense on a level beyond the superficial. I desperately wanted Elke to know how I felt, so she wouldn't accidentally ruin everything with a casual romp that didn't mean anything.

I couldn't exactly tell Elke that sometimes when I laid in bed, just before falling asleep, I would fast forward through his divorce and our courtship, and imagine what would happen if things worked out, if we became a couple, and got married some day. This was not how a supervixen thinks. A supervixen wouldn't get so far ahead of herself. She wouldn't need to. I was sure she wouldn't understand.

"Really, you like Paul," Elke said, less a question and more musing aloud. "I would never have guessed based on your actions. You behave like a sister or friend. No flirting?"

"Well, I washz juss waiting for the right time . . ."

"Plus it appears to me that is how Eddie feels about you."

"You think so? Yeah, I guessh that could be true."

"And you are not interested?"

"No, not at all. I mean, I like him, very vrrry much, but I just don't feel *that* way about him."

"So what we have here is—what do you call this thing where the horses go around, but stay still, on posts?" Elke was searching for the words.

"A merry-go-round?"

"Yes, we have a merry-go-round of unrequited passions."

"Yes, we do. I guess I wanted you to know how I felt about Paul, so, you *know*."

Elke let my shy request hang out there in the air. My head was squeezing itself. "Paul seems to adore you, but I had the impression it is in a sister-type way."

"Well, yessssh, you're right," I agreed. "We've always been jusss friends. He was married . . . But I have a crush. Such a crush. I was hoping, hoping, I mean, once he gets past the divorce, that maybe . . ." *And he winked at me. Didn't you see that wink?*

Elke seemed to understand. "I see. So you would like me to not interfere."

When she said it out loud, I realized that I sounded terrible if not pathetic. I couldn't put a red dot on Paul's forehead to claim him for myself and keep other women from him. But if there'd been a red Sharpie in grasping distance, I probably would've tried.

"Gosh, I feel so weird," I continued. "But yes, I guess that is what I'm saying." My desire for Paul outweighed the loss of pride at admitting this all to my roommate. *Please stay away from Paul. For me. Just until I see where this goes.* I almost died. I wished I were the kind of woman who didn't need to plot and plan. For whom good things just happened, like they seemed to for Elke. But I wasn't. I just wasn't that woman. I had to work harder than most.

At closing time the hot waitress ushered the four of us out the door and locked up behind us. We stumbled across the sidewalk and toward home.

CHAPTER 32

That was the last I remembered until the next morning, when I woke up to bright sunlight. My head ached, my teeth were hot, and I knew I was thirsty before I even opened my mouth, remembering, or at least trying to, the end of last night. I dragged myself out of bed and toward the kitchen, the obvious source of fluids. Passing Elke's room, I looked around for evidence of overnight guests, but there was none. Elke's door was ajar and she appeared to be alone. Whew.

Pulling a Diet Coke from the door of the fridge, I popped it open and took a sip, leaning against the counter as the cold liquid cleared my throat and arrived in my stomach, the carbonation mixing with its emptiness and reminding me I should eat something, or maybe not. I might puke. I opened the cabinets and pulled out Alka-Seltzer.

"You are sick?" Elke asked. I jumped slightly. My roommate looked surprisingly rested and pretty given the previous night's excesses. So unfair. I was sure I looked like death warmed over.

"Oh, hey. Not sick-sick. Just hangover-sick."

"Ah, yes. In Germany we call it like Katzenjammer, which means, roughly, wailing of cats."

"Exactly, that's it," I replied. "This is Stephen's secret remedy. It really works. Someday they'll market it as a hangover cure, just you wait. Want some?"

"Definitely."

I prepared two glasses of Alka-Seltzer. "That was fun last night. What I can remember."

"Yes, for me, too," Elke said. "I have some uncertainty surrounding the final moments."

"Did we come home alone?" I honestly couldn't remember. Well, I was pretty sure I came home alone, but less certain about Elke. Dying to know, afraid to find out. The memory of the evening's end was showing up in fuzzy spurts in my mind. Did we all walk home? Past Eddie's? Did someone have the good sense to suggest we all go to bed rather than continue our drunk night? If anyone had made such a sensible suggestion, it was probably Eddie.

"Yes. I insisted that we come home," Elke continued. "We had fun, but in the end it seemed best to leave them and make our way here."

"Ohthankgod."

"Yes, you made it clear that you didn't want me to interfere with your Paul," Elke said.

The night was coming back to me, when I embarrassingly asked Elke to stay away from Paul. I was pretty sure I'd called her a supervixen. I wanted to crawl back into my bed.

"I'm sorry, Elke. I know it sounds pathetic."

"No, no. It is just a bit new to me. Where I am from we have more the pattern of letting things happen."

Well, where I'm from, I have a pattern of doing whatever I can to avoid awkward situations like my roommates sleeping together, or casually hooking up with my crush. Was that so wrong?!

"Well, I was just waiting until the time was right to let him know how I feel." What I was really thinking was: *He's mine! Please, Elke, don't screw things up with your leggy sophisticated sex appeal.*

"Perhaps you can show him," Elke offered, and I was taken

by her ability to move instantly from rival to supporter. "Showing is so much better than talking sometimes." Elke finished her Alka-Seltzer and retreated to her bedroom to sleep off her hangover, allowing me to contemplate what "showing" Paul might look like. Then, despite my raging hangover, indeed the wailing of cats, I dragged myself to work.

CHAPTER 33

A college roommate of mine once called me controlling. I was aghast, feeling misjudged and hurt. For a split second I had wanted to argue with her, until I realized with more than a small dose of shame that it was technically probably true, because I did go to exceptional lengths to make things in my life work out the way I wanted. The way I hoped and dreamed. But I preferred to think of myself as hard-working. Planful. The think-ahead, organized type. I didn't purposely cause anyone pain, I just did it in an attempt to get my life to work out, because I sure as hell didn't think it was going to happen on its own. Didn't that make it okay? Since my compulsion to orchestrate came from such an inferior place, from deep and hidden insecurities unknown even to me most of the time, I never thought of my behavior as problematic, or unfair, but really just a leveling of the playing field. People like Paul, or Stephen, or Elke, they had the world wrapped around their fingers. I was just trying to keep up.

This controlling propensity was what guided me to put Elke and Paul at opposite sides of the launch party, for example. Not to *prevent* them from meeting and falling in lust as I certainly feared and half-expected, but to make it slightly less likely. Or postpone it. Was that pathetic? Well, so be it. It was the same instinct that made me ask Elke again, over hangovers and Alka-Seltzer, not to go after Paul. And it was the same propensity that caused me to notice Stephen's new habit of spending every night at the office, and why I hatched a plan to get my roommate situation normal again.

The following Thursday, I raced into the kitchen after work hauling three Bread and Circus bags, and called to my roommate. "Elke! I need your help!"

Elke emerged. "What for?"

"We're having our roommate dinner tonight. You promised to come. So did Stephen. Goddammit. You better both be here. We are getting this household back to normal once and for all." I was joking, but in a serious kind of way.

Elke didn't move from her spot. Instead she leaned against the doorjamb, inspecting her fingernails. "Are you sure you know what normal is? And that you really want that?"

Unloading chicken breasts, haricot verts and the makings of mashed potatoes, I stopped to address my roommate, plunking a hand on my hip like my mother might do if she wanted to make a point.

"Elke, sweetie, I don't have time for philosophy. I just want everyone to be willing to be in this apartment at the same time and talk to each other once in a while." I was undeterred by Elke's misgivings, having flip-flopped between sympathy for my friend's hurting heart and annoyance that both of my roommates left me in the dark for so long about their disruptive fling.

"Okay, how do you plan to accomplish that?" Elke was curious.

"How else?" I pulled out three bottles of wine and a liter of Jaegermeister from one of my bags.

Elke picked up the bottle of Jaeger.

"His favorite," I said.

"In Germany only old men and alcoholics drink this."

"Don't tell Stephen, he thinks he's cool."

Half an hour later, with chicken sautéing in a Marsala sauce, beans steaming and potatoes boiling, I was uncorking wine while Elke got changed, probably into something understated but fabulous. Then the front door slammed and sent reverberations through the house. Stephen bounded up the stairs and into the apartment, bursting into the living room, huffing and puffing and sort of laughing, hunched over to catch his breath, unable to speak. Seconds later, the doorbell rang. Whoever it was, he or she was leaning on it insistently. Stephen glanced at the general direction of the sound, and then at me.

"Someone has to get the door. Tell her I'm not here."

"Who?" I asked, stepping toward Stephen, who was in the living room.

"Blake. From the *Herald*. She won't leave me alone." I knew that Stephen had tried to end his short-lived fling with Blake weeks ago. Apparently it wasn't going as planned.

"What, is she stalking you?" I was now in the living room, too. Stephen laughed but he was serious.

"I can't get away from her. Will you answer the door, tell her I'm not here?"

Was he crazy? I knew Blake, too. We'd met multiple times through work, and, as it turned out, she was friends with many of our friends in our small-world social circle. He seemed to be forgetting that we lived in a town where everyone knew everyone. "I'm not going to lie to her face," I said.

Then, from behind us, Elke stepped out of her bedroom and headed for the front door without glancing back. "I will tell her goodbye."

Lucky bastard. There was always someone willing to step in and help Stephen out of sticky situations. Stalking crisis apparently averted, I put Stephen in charge of drinks. "Dinner's almost ready. Can you fix this?" I handed him a bottle of Trader

Joe's Charles Shaw merlot with a broken corkscrew sticking out of the top, victimized by my excessive poking with the cheap contraption I found in the junk drawer. I pointed to the Jaegermeister on the counter. "For you."

"Are you trying to get me drunk, Miss Annie? It's a school night, you know." Stephen raised his eyebrows in my general direction.

"I just want you to be happy and comfortable in your own home." I really meant it. I hated the idea of losing Stephen's companionship because of some unthinking slip-up made on a whim—a short-sighted pleasure grab that, by the way, put our household peace in jeopardy. Okay, maybe I was being a little dramatic here. But I did want the two of them to air things out, return to the way things were, more like when Mallory Weiss was there and we often ate take-out or had beers together or brunch on the weekends.

The truth was I missed him. And I had handled it better when I thought it was all because of work. It was one thing to be MIA because of the demands of your start-up company, another thing entirely if you were not coming home for personal reasons like avoiding your hookup. Now that I knew it was this secret awkward unrequited lust thing with Elke, I thought the least I could do was get it out in the open and make it "discussable," as we said in the corporate world. It was momentarily lost on me that our household was anything but the corporate world. All I knew was that I wanted everyone to get over it and get back to normal.

When Elke surfaced from shooing away Stephen's stalker girl, she set the table while I mashed the potatoes and started plating them along with the chicken and veggies. Our table was another hand-me-down, but Elke had dressed it up with a trio of placemats the color of moss and pulled out a few votives and two chunky pillar candles that smelled of freesia and provided a gorgeous, flickering glow instead of the harsh overhead light normally shining in from the kitchen. She managed to find three sets of matching knives, forks and spoons, too. Well, each set matched itself, if not the other two.

Stephen was able to extract the cork and poured the wine into the goblets at each place setting, jostling for position and bumping into Elke as she finished laying the flatware out. I wondered if he was flirting. Please don't give her any false hope! I thought Elke was finally moving on, and this dinner needed to reinforce that nothing was going to happen with Stephen, not reopen her longing! Maybe Stephen misunderstood the purpose, or selfishly enjoyed the attention.

This was the first time the three of us had actually sat down for a meal together since the second roommate dinner. Our best intentions went unrealized due to schedules and such. But we'd been living under one roof for months now, and with the aid of wine and Jaeger, it seemed easy for us to relax and laugh and tease each other. We did the normal catch-up conversation on work and people we have in common, then when we were good and tipsy the talk turned to relationships.

"So what is this story with this Blake?" asked Elke. Good question, and I thought Elke had earned the right to ask since she did the dirty work of getting rid of her. Stephen was grinning but not saying much.

"There's nothing to tell, really. We saw each other for a while, hooked up here and there, and then she wanted it to get all serious and I didn't, so I stopped calling and she freaked out and now she's pretty much stalking me. Hopefully she'll lose interest soon. She's a little crazy." Hmmm, interesting. It was probably true that Blake was a little crazy—but Stephen seemed to inspire more than his share of this reaction in women.

"Your stalker girl confirms my theory," I said. "In this life you're either a pursuer or you're pursued. You are both the pursued."

"I think we are all both," said Elke. "Usually pursuing people who are not responsive and being pursued by people we are not interested in. If approximately half of us would turn around, wouldn't that solve it?" She was right on some level. Nearly everyone I knew was trying to hook up with someone who wanted someone else. Was it all just coincidence, or the tide and moon cycle, or something else entirely?

By dessert, which consisted of a shared pint of Ben & Jerry's Phish Food ice cream, the three of us had put away two bottles of the wine and succumbed to Stephen's insistence that we all do multiple ceremonial shots of Jaegermeister. The *Best of Barry White* CD was replaying itself for a third time, and the candles had dripped an elegant pool of wax onto the table. Stephen leaned back in his chair and rested his hands on his protruding stomach.

"Well, Annie, have we diffused the sexual tension enough for you?" he asked with a wink.

"I don't have so much trouble with sexual tension," responded Elke, before I had time to react. "I could have handled this."

"Oh, me too," Stephen replied, grinning to Elke. "But Annie couldn't have." Now the two of them were looking at me, waiting for an answer.

"Pardon? How did I become in the wrong here?"

"Not in the wrong, just a little . . ." Stephen hesitated.

"A little what?" I braced myself for whatever was coming next.

"A little closed off. A little uncomfortable with sexual tension. In general." Stephen was smiling and Elke was too. I was stunned.

"How did this become about me? And you're not right anyway."

"But you could be a little more open. Perhaps even aggressive," continued Stephen.

Elke jumped in. "Yes, I, since I have known you, you are not exactly attuned to your sex life."

"Some might say prudish. I'm not saying I would, but some might," agreed Stephen. I swallowed my disbelief, surprised that either of them would have the gall to mention this all in a group setting. A small group, but a group nonetheless.

"Are you drunk?" I asked. I felt defensive and the accusation hurt. "I can't believe you're saying that to me."

"Annie, why is this such a surprise?" asked Elke. "In the months I have been here, there has been not one man in your bed. Except Stephen, who usually has his shoes on and is snoring."

It took several seconds for this all to sink in. I would never have expected these two to start commenting on my sex life, or lack of one, certainly not together, over a dinner that was meant to be about the two of *them* and *their* sex lives. Sure, it was probably true that I was a little gun-shy these days, a bit reserved, hesitant to put myself out there. But I had good reason. I'd been burned a dozen times by guys and I wasn't in favor of having it happen again. So I was accustomed to taking it all a little slow. But couldn't they see? I was totally into Paul, just waiting for the right moment. And I resented the implication that I was frigid. That wasn't fair. It might even be funny if it weren't so unfair. Although if I were honestly assessing the state of my sex life I'd have to do serious math to calculate the last time I'd seen any action.

"You two don't even know what you're talking about. I am *not* a prude." They didn't look convinced. In fact, I was willing to bet they were humoring me, independently if not conspiratorially, which might be worse, trying to keep their comments in check so as not to offend me. I found it hard to process in the moment, accustomed as I was to processing deliberately and over time, running things through my analytical mind over and over again. But there was no time for analytics here. I was coaxed by my buzz to go with my gut, and while I in theory could have just kept to myself and said nothing, since my otherwise-controlled demeanor was mixed with generous amounts of wine and spirits, everything pretty much came out from thought to mouth in one stream.

"I've done what you two do. I've done *worse*." Suddenly, my solution to defending myself against prude status was to pull from my store of Most Embarrassing Dating Secrets.

"Once I dated three guys at the same time. Two of them stepbrothers." I did, and that sibling thing was definitely a bit of a disaster. I was a lot younger then, but I could still remember the sting of embarrassment when it came out in the open. "I can remember one summer on the Cape when I dated a different guy every week. So what are you two saying? This is fucking ridiculous."

I knew it was on some level comical that this conversation was even happening, but it was, and instead of being funny to me it was unbelievably painful, to have to admit that I was so messed up in relationships, and to have it publicly acknowledged in this way.

"Hey, okay, okay. We were just kidding," Stephen said.

"I know. But you hit a sore spot," I said.

"Apparently so," replied Stephen, and we all laughed a little.

"I just think maybe you should go back to that time of multiple men. I see nothing wrong," Elke offered. And she was serious.

"Okay, Annie, don't be so hard on yourself," Stephen added. "There's nothing wrong with you."

"But there is," I squeaked, and then the tears were coming. Damn Stephen and the Jaeger shots! And after the tears, the confessions started. And the acknowledgment of things I'd known deep down but had never put words to. "I'm either too nice or too much. I can never seem to get it quite right. And I'm tired of it. I just don't like me when I'm with guys. I don't like the way I am with them." I paused to take a breath and let out a long, complicated sigh, the kind that ends with your lips sputtering. "Do you think it's coincidental that I have my sights set on a man who is only months into a divorce he didn't want? Could I pinpoint a less available man?" *Where'd that insight come from?* It had surely been hovering around the edges of my mind while I indulged in my crush, yet I hadn't let myself really acknowledge the reality. But it was true.

Elke seemed to agree. "Yes, you seem to be in pretty safe territory there, with little risk of much happening beyond a fling. But then again, you've got an important friendship, if anything happens romantically it could be different from what you fear."

"Maybe," I said.

Stephen spoke up. "I don't know. I don't know about Paul. I'm not sure he's good enough for you."

I thought surely this was a joke. How in the world could Paul Dennison not be good enough for *me*? I let out a disbelieving "hah," and Stephen countered.

"I'm serious. He's a decent guy, but I just might have different criteria about what's good for you." Stephen stood up and pulled me to him, hugging me and kissing my temple. "You deserve good things, Annie." Then he let me go and reached for a dirty dish. "Okay, we'll clean this up, Annie. You can go to bed." Elke stood, too, and began stacking plates and waving me away.

I liked the idea of letting them take care of the mess. I'd been going nonstop for days, so I shuffled down the hallway and flopped on my bed and laid there for a long time. I must have dozed off for a bit, and woke up sometime later, still alone in my bedroom with the lights on. I rolled over onto my side and noticed the clock. More than two hours had passed. I started mentally reviewing my to-do list for the next day, then sat up and reached for my backpack, sifting through it to retrieve my datebook and cell phone. The latter had a blinking light indicating a voice message. Scrolling through the caller ID list, I saw MOM AND DAD listed twice and dialed into my voicemail system. It was my mother's voice sounding concerned. Something about April. At Mass General. It was serious, and if I could come soon, that would be good. The last message was left at eight thirty-five that evening. I checked my watch; it was after eleven p.m. I made sure I had sobered up enough to drive, found my keys, slipped into my boots, and careened down the stairs, yelling to Elke and Stephen as I left that I'd be back later.

CHAPTER 34

By the time I arrived at the oncology ward it was close to eleven thirty and only Liz was with April in her hospital room. Liz looked up as I tiptoed in, and whispered hello to me.

"Hi," I said tentatively. I hadn't been able to reach my parents to get any details about what was going on.

My cousin looked pale and stricken, like you'd expect from a mother with a gravely ill child. April was half-asleep, attached to an IV and covered in a rose-colored cotton blanket, her small left hand resting on a stuffed lamb named Fleece, her favorite Beanie Baby. She waved limply then closed her eyes again. I looked at my cousin.

"Liz, I just heard. I guess everyone's gone?"

"Yeah, they all had to get home."

I approached April's bed and kissed her on the forehead. She opened her eyes.

"You smell like beer," she whispered. I made a *Shhh* sign, smiled and turned back to my cousin, speaking softly.

"I only got a message. I don't really know what's happening."

Liz looked exhausted, with the day's mascara smudged across the skin around her red-rimmed eyes and faded lipstick feathered at the edges of her lips. She walked with me toward the door, so we could talk without disturbing April. Liz looked at me for a long time and sighed before speaking.

"Her tumor is back. It's worse than before, growing not shrinking. Her doctors seemed surprised and they wanted to try a new experimental thing. With something called stem cells. It's pretty dramatic. She'll come back here in about a month. She stays five weeks. Then we'll see."

"Oh, God. I'm so sorry. I'm so sorry I didn't come sooner."

"That's okay. It was a madhouse a couple of hours ago. Everyone was here. My mother took Melody to her house."

"Are they hopeful about the treatment?" I didn't want to pry, but I desperately wanted to know what we were dealing with.

"They haven't given me any percentages. They're going to tell me more tomorrow." She and I wandered back toward April's bed, as Liz continued, "She's afraid she'll miss her birthday. So we're going to have it early. In two weeks, before she starts her treatment. It'll be good for her to see everyone because no one can visit during the treatment period."

"No one can visit?"

"The treatment's gonna weaken her immune system in a big way, so they have to limit her exposure to people. You know, germs and stuff. I'll be able to see her, but that's it."

It all sounded so terrifying and grim. Liz yawned, gasping for oxygen and tipping over a little.

"You're exhausted," I said.

"I haven't slept in three days," Liz said flatly.

"Liz!"

"April wakes up at odd hours. It's the medicine. I don't want her to be awake and alone."

"I'll stay," I offered. "I pull all-nighters all the time. You sleep." Screw the to-do list—I couldn't imagine leaving my cousin alone right now.

Liz was practically in tears, probably from the sleep deprivation. "Really? Thank you. Thank you." There was a sitting room adjacent to April's and we borrowed a blanket and pillow from the nurse's station to make a bed for Liz. As soon as her head hit the pillow, she was passed out cold.

I went back to April's room and took Liz's spot next to the bed while April dozed. I couldn't use my cell phone in the hospital, so Stephen would just have to wait until tomorrow for me to explain my absence. I sipped water and thought about the enormity of the situation. We'd never faced anything like this in our family. No one had ever been seriously ill. Even all of our grandparents were still alive. I could feel that I was bracing myself, not feeling the expected emotions. I was aware in my head that it was a frightening situation, but I was numb about it otherwise. I let my mind wander. An early birthday party. The idea made me smile. April's spirit was remarkable. Barely ten years old but she'd figured out what really mattered to her—presents. A short while later, April stirred and looked around.

"Where's my mom?" she croaked, her throat sounding parched. I poured some water from a plastic pitcher into a cup and handed it to her with a straw.

"She's sleeping, right next door. She's just around the corner."

"Oh good. She needs her sleep," April said sternly.

April was a nurturer, but she had an edge, too. An edge that I admired for its blunt realness. I reached out and touched her hand, lacing our fingers together.

"I'm so sorry you're sick again." It came out as a whisper. I moved to position myself on the edge of the bed and sat close, like Melody would.

"Me, too, for crying out loud," said April. "Annie, do you have a boyfriend yet? Did the Relationship Box work?"

"Oh, sweetie, not yet. You know, it isn't the box's fault. I've been working a lot."

"Working? What does that have to do with anything?"

"I've just been busy . . ."

"Annie, come on. What is more important than having a boyfriend? For crying out loud."

"Well, some people would say . . ."

"But really, Annie, there's *nothing* more important." April looked pained.

"Well, I have a very good friend that's a boy. Does that count? And maybe it will turn into something more."

"Well, that's better than nothing, I suppose." April suddenly looked surprisingly awake for one a.m.

"Do you want to play a game?" I asked, and her face lit up.

"How about Pretty Pretty Princess?"

CHAPTER 35

The next two weeks passed quickly. There was so much mindless work to be done after the launch party at GoodMatch—copyediting Web pages, debugging software, securing additional partnerships—that I managed to maintain my productivity even while thoroughly distracted by the anxiety of April's situation. I visited April each night of the week she spent in the hospital, often bumping into Eddie, whose quiet friendship had become one of the mainstays I relied on. He would come with Barbara and Jimmy sometimes, and sometimes by himself. Sometimes staying for hours, other times just popping in for a few minutes to drop off some Rolos or Good & Plenty. It became clear to me quickly that April had become increasingly attentive to my friendship with Eddie, and would keep a close eye on our interaction, probably hoping to see some sign of romance. It was only a little embarrassing for us, and we both let it roll off our backs, though I was aware on some level that Eddie might've liked it to be true. How could it be, though, given my feelings for Paul? Was Eddie unaware of them? Could he not tell there was something there? Or did he have other information from Paul's perspective about the prospect of our relationship growing into something more?

Eddie was always on the quiet side, hanging out on the fringes of the conversations, yet I always got the sense that he was really listening. If he and I drove home together, we would more naturally spend time chatting, since too much silence on a car ride didn't sit well with either of us. Plus I liked to park in front of his apartment with him, imagining that Paul might come by at any moment, although so far he never had.

One night we left the hospital on the late side, since Liz had been napping and April wide awake. We passed the security guard and exchanged goodbyes, and headed to the garage. Eddie always insisted on paying for parking when I drove, which was all the time. Come to think of it, Eddie never drove.

"Eddie, it has occurred to me that you sell cars for a living and yet you never drive. What's up with that?"

"Truth be told, I prefer to walk or ride my bike when I can," he answered, settling into the passenger seat, playing with the radio.

"Where is your dealership?" I asked. I'd always pictured him in one of those corner lots full of used cars, with ubiquitous blue and white triangle banners and "0% APR" signs in neon. I also wondered if his fellow sales guys also had mullets. It seemed fitting for the industry, if I wanted to stereotype. I'd always been hesitant to talk to Eddie about his job, and I couldn't exactly pinpoint why it made me so uncomfortable. It had something to do with not putting him on the spot, especially since his comments about used-car salesmen being so disrespected. I wasn't going to be able to feign interest easily in used-car sales, and I didn't want to be patronizing, but now I was curious.

"My offices are all over eastern New England. I work for TrekStar," Eddie replied.

"The car rental company? 'We pick you up,' that TrekStar?" I asked.

"Yup, that's us."

"I didn't know TrekStar sold cars. I thought it was just a rental company." I knew TrekStar was one of the leading private companies in the U.S., based on a case study I'd done in business school. I knew they hired the best talent, based on a combination of smarts and personality, from good colleges, and gave them significant opportunities for advancement if they performed well. It was an interesting model, based on valuing certain people-skills as highly as intellect, and seemed to be working.

"We started selling the cars we've retired from our rental fleet in 1962. We were the pioneers of no-haggle pricing for cars. Trying to remake the industry by becoming the most trustworthy used-car sales company in the country, no haggling, no hidden fees, everything systematic and aboveboard."

"That *would* be transformative, if people felt they could trust a used-car dealer," I said. "No offense. But you said yourself that people don't trust you."

Eddie nodded, and smiled.

"So do you actually sell the cars?" I asked.

"Not directly, not anymore. But I used to. Now I manage ten of our offices."

"Really?!" I was intrigued.

"Yup, so I spend a lot of time driving between them."

It sounded like fun—to manage something so tangible and substantial as the process of selling huge contraptions of glass and steel. A car was something so real, whereas so much of what my B-school classmates and I did was intangible. Most people took six-figure jobs with professional services like consulting or investment banking in cities like New York and San Francisco and London. Now with the Internet, a small but growing percentage was, like Stephen, taking the leap into technology ventures. But still, most of what we did was remote and service-based and intangible. Even our Internet matchmaking service felt a bit abstract and fleeting. Disconnected from the real people. I loved the idea of GoodMatch, helping people meet people and fall in love. It was just that I preferred real-life interactions, like watching the chemistry happen between people at the launch party, or feeling as I did for the very real, very unattainable Paul Dennison, who, as I pulled up to his and Eddie's apartment, appeared to be nowhere in sight.

I said good night to Eddie and made the few-block trip home, feeling lucky to find a parking spot on the street near our apartment. Once inside, I passed through the narrow hallway to the living room and spied Elke sitting cross-legged on the sofa, drinking chamomile tea. She looked so content and organized, sitting there, having somehow found the time and energy to yet again *make tea*. I was in awe of her European sensibilities; everything about her seemed so effortless. And stylish. I felt lumpy and awkward by comparison. Over the months that we'd been together, I found myself mimicking certain things about Elke's manner. She had a less-is-more approach, dictated at least in part by the fact that she had almost no stuff. But it prompted me to start hauling old brown clothes out of my closet and dropping them by Goodwill or giving them away to cousins.

"Hey, Annika."

"Hi, Elkster," I replied, dropping my bag and joining my roommate on the couch, exchanging small talk and catching up on the day.

"How are you? How is April?" Elke asked. I provided her with the latest news.

Elke had been a source of real comfort, gently inquiring after April's health, but also helping me deal with practical issues exacerbated by the nights and weekends spent at the hospital. Elke had taken more and more responsibility for paying the bills, organizing our rent checks, cleaning up, the occasional roommate dinner, toilet-paper shopping and generally keeping our household going, and I felt deeply appreciative. I could accept this generosity from Elke in a way I normally found difficult. Normally I would just soldier on and find a way to keep doing it all myself. Somehow with Elke it was different. I could accept her help, and I had no idea why. She was becoming a good friend, and I trusted her.

On Saturday morning, the day of April's early birthday party, Eddie arrived at my apartment holding an overstuffed bear with a bow around its neck.

"Ooooh. She's going to love that! But you have to wrap it," I said.

"It's got a bow." Eddie pointed to the red ribbon around the bear's neck.

"Oh, no. April loves *opening* presents." I guided him upstairs to the dining room table where I'd been wrapping a new collection of Ty Beanie Babies in sheets of pink and purple.

"Here." I tossed Eddie some birthday wrapping paper featuring balloons and monkeys, and tape.

He looked at the raw materials as though he'd never gift-wrapped a thing in his life, and proceeded to use the entire roll of tape, having decided to wrap the head, torso and each limb individually, so that the finished present was still clearly a bear, or possibly an aardvark, based on the way that Eddie had wrapped the head, which made me laugh. Many minutes later, Eddie and I descended the stairs and headed out to the sidewalk, arms laden with April's gifts, bottles of wine and a bag of Rolos, her absolute favorite.

"I can drive." Eddie pulled his keys from his pants pocket.

"Shotgun," I replied. We had some distance to cover to get to the Cape, and it went without saying that Eddie's company car offered a more enjoyable ride than my Corolla.

"Where'd you get this car?" I asked as Eddie opened the door of a brand new Nissan Pathfinder, black with gray leather seats.

Eddie shrugged. "It's what I had on the lot. I just take what's available from my inventory when I leave at night."

"Oh." That sounded appealing to me. I loved variety. It would be an excellent way to keep from filling your car up with junk, too, if you had to switch every day. I settled in for the drive, noticing that Eddie took the same back streets to get to the highway as I did. When we were on Route 3 and passing Chester I called Liz from my cell phone to check in. To me, my cousin sounded preoccupied, as one might expect given she was hosting a months-early birthday party for her cancer-stricken not-yet ten-year-old.

"I'm just checking to see if you need anything," I asked into the mouthpiece. I listened for a few minutes, responding with things like "Okay, uh-huh, that's too bad, yup" then hung up and stared out the window for a minute before turning to Eddie.

"Liz said April's having a pretty bad day. She's so tired. She has to stay in bed for the party."

Eddie let out a quiet sigh and tapped his finger against the steering wheel.

"But she's still having the party?"

"Oh yeah, April wouldn't hear of anything else. This is really important to her."

Eddie laughed. April was amusing in her single-minded focus on presents and celebration. It took us another hour to get there, and we passed the time mostly in silence, listening to the radio. When we arrived at Liz's compact ranch it was packed with people, only half of whom I knew. Who were they all? I spotted members of my family scattered around the house, but didn't see Liz, guessing she was with April in her bedroom. I hadn't been to their house in quite a while, but it looked the same, except every available sitting spot was occupied and most of the floor space, too.

There was a line, actually, waiting to see the birthday girl. Fifteen minutes later, when Eddie and I took our turn, we saw April in the middle of a big bed wearing silky navy blue pajamas with little flowers all over. She'd never worn a wig and had even given up on wearing hats, so her bald head peeked out from the covers. Her skin was so pale she faded into the off-white of her sheets. In a word, she looked terrible. Awful. Unbelievably sick and fragile. It was terrifying.

There were piles of presents gathering at the foot of April's bed and covering her dresser. Only two or three people could fit in her room at a time, so the presents seemed like stand-ins for the guests hovering outside the door. Piles and piles of presents.

When Liz saw Eddie and me she got up to hug us. "Hi, you two," Liz whispered. "April, look, it's Eddie and Annie."

April opened her eyes and waved from her bed, trying to smile. We moved close enough to touch her hand, but she was dozing again.

I looked around at the light-wood furniture set. It was the first fully matching set of furniture I'd seen in our entire family, which was more of a mismatched furniture kind of crowd. But April's room had a beautiful bed with tall posts and a headboard stenciled with flowers, with a matching L-shaped desk and chair, and a dresser combination that had a tall mirror with tiny white lights draped along the edges. I touched it.

"This is beautiful."

"It's her Make-A-Wish present." Liz reached out and ran her hand along the bedpost.

Her Make-A-Wish present? For the dying kids? I felt a chill. Why would April have a Make-A-Wish present?

"I thought—"

"No, they give presents to kids who are just very sick, too."

Liz then ran her hand along the frame of the mirror. "You know," she continued, "the first thing she asked for was 'a reliable car for her mother.' But they said no, the presents had to be for the kids, and she picked this." And after a pause, she added, "I'm glad."

April opened her eyes and Eddie and I were able to visit for a few minutes. She wanted to hold our hands at the same time, each of hers holding one of ours.

"Don't forget, Annie, that friends can become boyfriends," April whispered. Then there was another party guest at the door, and we made room so he could visit. It was all quietly awkward and sad, with April too sick to even sit up.

Back in the kitchen, my eyes took in the countertops laden with food and drink—Delmonico potatoes, a pink boiled ham, a casserole involving cream-of-something soup. Desserts covered every inch of the kitchen island, hiding its chipped linoleum. Plates of cream cheese brownies, angel food cake with a bowl of frozen strawberries for topping and Toll House cookies bumping up against store-bought cupcakes and a sheet cake that said *Happy Birthday April—We Love You*. Offerings meant to attest love and caring and to soothe Liz's and April's and Melody's pain, and our own. Then there was the soda. Two liter bottles of every kind, dominated by Sprite and Pepsi. They could open a 7-Eleven with this supply. I felt no particular thirst, but poured myself a tall cup of Diet Coke and drank it in a long series of gulps.

Eddie had followed me out of April's room, and now across the room I saw him scoop up Melody, wrapping his arms around her, squeezing her into a hug and kissing her cheek. Melody seemed lost, her huge blue eyes dulled and vacant. Liz said she didn't really understand what was happening, and felt just as disconcerted by all the attention flowing away from her as she did with her sister's condition. No one expected a six-year-old to understand. To look at Eddie with her, you'd think Melody was the sole reason he'd trekked down from Cambridge. She brightened under the warmth of his attention, giggling as he tickled her neck. I set down my empty cup and maneuvered among the guests to join them, offering silent hellos to the people I didn't know and hugs to the people I did as I passed through.

"Hi, sweetheart." I touched the back of my hand to the soft skin of Melody's cheek then kissed the same spot. She smelled like Johnson's Baby Shampoo.

"Hi, Annie. Eddie is going to take me to the Children's Museum."

"He is?!" I looked at Eddie, who confirmed with a nod.

"Next week or the next week or the next week. While April's away," Melody continued.

"Well that sounds like a nice time," I said.

"Yeah but you can't come. It's just for me." Melody smiled as she said it, but with a certain firmness. I turned to Eddie, who shrugged as if to say, "You heard the girl, you aren't coming."

"Do you want a drink?" I asked in the direction of Eddie and Melody. They both nodded yes and the three of us moved toward the 7-Eleven section, settling in against the counter, occasionally chatting in quiet tones with relatives and friends who'd also come to the kitchen in search of chocolate-covered distraction or a cream-of-mushroom diversion.

Later, when it was time to leave, I remembered that I had a special gift for April and headed back to her room to give it to her and to say goodbye for now. Liz was alone in the room, sitting on the desk chair; the sun had set and the glow of the white lights gave the room a peaceful sheen.

"Hi, can I come in?" I asked. Liz and April waved me back in.

"I have a special present for you, sweetie." I eased myself onto the bed and handed April a gift in the Tiffany box. "It's just a little something."

April untied the bow and opened the box. It was a necklace, an angel suspended from a delicate gold chain.

April smiled. "I love it."

"I love you. I was hoping you could wear your angel to the hospital and she'll watch over you during your treatment. I'm going to miss seeing you but I will think about you every day."

"You better," April said. "When this works, I'll be in the medical books, you know."

Liz mentioned that they'd be admitted the next week.

"And everyone's hopeful?"

"Yeah, as far as I can tell, they think she has an excellent chance of responding to the treatment."

There was a noise outside the window, which was open, just a crack. April's eyes moved in that direction but she herself stayed still. A smile tugged at the corners of her chapped lips as she heard the kids singing. Liz and I peeked out the window and saw about a dozen neighborhood children and a few parents gathering outside holding candles. When the singing started—the first song was "Happy Birthday"—April's eyes closed and her smile broadened.

I wasn't used to this much direct expression of love and compassion and sadness and encouragement. I found it almost overwhelming, the sweetness of the gesture and the way tragic circumstances brought out such goodness in people—the same people whose kids trample your lawn and accidentally hit your house with errant Frisbees now organizing themselves to sing "Happy Birthday" and "Angels Among Us," a favorite song of April's. The sincerity, the kindness, the thoughtfulness. I had to get the hell out of there.

The next time I saw April and Liz was the following week,

when a few relatives gathered at the hospital to wish April well, to give hugs, kisses, temporary goodbyes.

"We'll see you in five weeks, sweetie. And hopefully you'll be all better!" I whispered into her ear when it was my turn to say bye.

April smiled and squeezed my hand. "And I'll be officially ten by then!"

CHAPTER 36

Sitting at opposite sides of his desk, Stephen and I were painstakingly reviewing details of a partnership agreement with Yahoo! that would make GoodMatch.com their preferred online dating provider. I enjoyed this like a hole in the head. I appreciated that it was a necessary evil, but the evil part was what really stuck for me. It was late. I'd rather be sleeping. Or scrubbing the toilet. Anything but legalese.

"Long day, Anna-belle. Want a beer?" Stephen reached toward the mini-fridge. A beer seemed like just what I needed.

"Absolutely."

Stephen removed a Guinness and a Sam Adams from the cube and handed the latter to me, then kicked back and propped his legs up on the desk.

"Any news about April?" Stephen asked, passing the bottle opener across the desk.

"We won't know anything for a while. So it's all prayers and finger-crossing for now." I was grateful for the five-week reprieve, where there was a real reason to hope, and even more grateful that it coincided with a particularly busy time at the office, which kept me distracted. We'd have to wait and see, and in the meantime, I hoped to make major progress on the marketing of GoodMatch.com.

"So what is happening with Paul?" asked Stephen.

"Not very much. We seem to be securely planted in the 'just

friends' bucket. What the hell." I kept working. Stephen looked thoughtful. In general I appreciated when my friends stopped to give me dating advice, to reflect and commiserate about the complications of finding a partner now that we were out of the social milieu of a university, with arguably fewer single people to choose from. To offer a perspective on whatever or whomever I was interested in. It was not lost on me that Stephen, as founder and president and CEO of GoodMatch.com, needed to have a better-than-average understanding of the dating scene, and that sooner or later I was going to be forced onto GoodMatch.com.

"I think the problem is that Paul wants to date a different kind of woman right now," continued Stephen.

"What do you mean Paul wants to date a different kind of woman? What the hell are you talking about?" *Why the hell was I getting all feisty?* And how did Stephen know this? Did he and Paul discuss it? Did Paul confess to Stephen over beers what kind of woman he wanted, and it was clearly not the "me" kind?

"I mean that he's single for the first time in ten years and he wants to get laid by the hottest and most uncomplicated babes that he can."

I tried to hide my disappointment that apparently I wasn't hot. Phooey, I knew this, of course, but I didn't particularly like it said out loud. And the uncomplicated part. Hmmmm. I'd rather be complicated than uncomplicated if I were forced to choose.

"Just because that is what you'd do doesn't mean Paul would." I sounded like a fifth grader with the "just because" argument. Oh shit. Stephen was right. That was probably exactly what was happening. "This is so wrong, you know," I continued. "He should feel an obligation to date smart women. No bimbos. Smart."

Stephen looked at me in genuine confusion. Apparently he'd never considered the smart-hot continuum before.

"An obligation?" Stephen asked between sips of his stout.

"I mean it goes back to the normal distribution curve of most desirable attributes in the opposite sex."

Stephen looked at me quizzically and continued to drink his beer, smiling into the can, while I picked up a dry-erase marker and drew on the whiteboard. I drew a generic bell curve and continued to verbalize my theory. "This is something we have to figure out for GoodMatch, too. If most smart, successful—or at least high-potential—guys are generally going to want to date someone who is possibly as smart, but not smarter than they are . . ." I indicated on the graph that a smart guy had almost the entire population of women to choose from. "Or you could substitute 'successful' here."

I indicated that smart and successful correlated on my graph.

"Go on," said Stephen.

"But a smart, successful woman, who generally wants to date someone who is at least as smart as or more successful than she is, has only this little tail." I pointed to the small rightmost end of the graph. "So, while Paul, and you for that matter, get to choose from almost all of the women in the world, smart and successful women have this little tiny splotch into which must go not just smart but kind and fun and honest and, ideally, a decent ability to kiss. This is not easy."

"Annie, it's simple. You just need to lower your standards."

"*What?*" I'd been fighting my entire life to raise my standards. I was finally past the point of being attracted to lughead football players and Stephen was telling me to go back? It couldn't be.

He was studying the curve. "On the other hand, you could draw the same graph for looks," he continued. "Guys care a lot, women not as much."

"And this is supposed to make me feel better?" I fell to my chair in defeat.

"Okay. By this analysis, you're kinda screwed. But as far as Paul is concerned, the guy's wife left him for their landscaper. He's gotta want to let out some steam. I have to believe he is putting T and A ahead of IQ right now." Stephen paused and appeared to be thinking. "Give Paul some time. He may come around."

CHAPTER 37

Elke offered me some Orange Mint Fusion tea, which at first sounded awful, since I could think only of the taste of orange juice drunk too soon after brushing my teeth. But it turned out to be quite soothing and delicious. It was a gorgeous and unexpectedly sunny day and I was playing hooky. I couldn't bring myself to head immediately to the office for the umpteenth Saturday in a row. I needed a tiny break, to properly obsess about my crush on Paul over tea with Elke.

"I can't stand not knowing how Paul feels. He sends confusing signals. I mean, he confides in me all the time about everything. About everything but me. Maybe I should just come out and tell him how I feel and see what he says."

Elke looked thoughtful and skeptical. I sensed a head tilt coming on.

"Everything that is true does not have to be said," she offered. "If you tell him exactly how you feel, you will force him to deal with his own ambiguity about your relationship. And when men are forced to confront their ambiguity about a woman they haven't already decided to pursue, well, it doesn't usually go well."

"Huh."

"Yes."

"Maybe I could just *casually* ask him how he feels about me?" I didn't want to give up in my quest for information. To fill the knowledge gap. To feed my need to know, definitively, what was going on inside Paul's attractive head. Now Elke was doing a lip-purse *and* a head tilt.

"If you want my advice, I would say that you already know how Paul feels about you and asking him will get you nothing except embarrassed. He likes you very much. As a friend."

I loved and hated how Elke told me the truth. She was so different from my American girlfriends, more likely to be caught in their own obsessive webs, where it was soothing and enjoyable to take turns yakking about every little detail, each word, each gesture made by the object of one's obsession, regardless of whether the obsession was returned.

"So you think there's no chance of anything happening between us?"

"Oh, Anna, I don't know. It seems nice that Paul is pursuing such an intimate . . ." Oh, intimate, yes intimate. Such a good word.

". . . though *platonic . . .*" Ooh. Platonic, not such a good word. Perhaps more accurate, but not so good.

". . . relationship with you after this divorce. It says good things about a man who wants that connection. But it seems he hasn't given you any indication of wanting more, and until you have such a thing, I wouldn't spend too much time in the imagination."

"Well, what else can I do?"

Elke looked hesitant, like she wasn't sure she wanted to encourage me on this one.

"It does seem you are terribly convenient to Paul. You have a crazy life, yet you are always available should he indicate the tiniest inkling of need."

"Is that your way of telling me I should play hard to get?" I asked.

"No, I am more saying you should *be* hard to get."

Be hard to get? The words sound as foreign to me as an obscure dialect of Mandarin Chinese. I had never been hard to get in my life unless I was truly uninterested. I never wanted to tempt fate that way. Always wanted to be honest and clear. A good girl, not a player girl. We paused, sipping tea and looking past each other.

"Why am I obsessing about this?" I wondered into the air.

"Maybe it keeps you from facing up to other things." This was Elke's way. She'd drop her observations and insights innocuously into conversation, and give me something to ponder at night before bed, or in the shower, or on the car ride to work.

"Really?" I asked.

"Really."

For half a second, I contemplated thinking about what this all meant, letting go of my ruminating about Paul and trying to get underneath it. But I couldn't. All of the parts of me wanted to stay focused on Paul and avoid whatever it was I was trying to avoid that I couldn't name and I didn't understand and I didn't want to.

"I don't know, though. I think I really like him. He's so—so likable! He's just amazing. Maybe I could figure out a way for him to see me in another light. To reframe his view of me. Like positioning an old product in a new way."

"Anna, you are not washing detergent."

"I know. I just mean to say that sometimes you need to make a little extra effort to influence the things you want to happen." This was understatement at its best. I was generally willing to go to great and remarkable lengths for something I considered a good cause, like reigniting my love life.

"Little Annie, you are not, as we say, the General Manager of the Universe," Elke admonished.

"I know, I know. But that would be a killer job, huh?"

CHAPTER 38

"Stephen, does it concern you that 80 percent of your time these days is spent on raising money? The business suffers when you're not around, boss."

I was seeing Stephen for the first time that week, and it was already Wednesday. He'd been in VC meeting after VC meeting, trying to put together a group of investors for our first major round of institutional financing. The Denny money was almost gone; we really needed something to happen soon or we'd be out of luck and out of time.

"I know, but what can I do?" he answered. "We need money to grow. It's a rock and a hard place."

"It seems like everyone goes through this. The constant battle to have access to capital, when what you really want to be doing is making a good product."

Stephen looked like his mind was on other things.

"Annie, I have to tell you what I'm hearing from the VCs. If we raise this money, the chances are very good that they'll want to bring in a seasoned CEO."

"Excuse me? But what does that mean for you?" I felt a wave of panic. I'd never imagined anyone but Stephen in charge, and certainly wasn't sure I wanted to work with anyone else as my boss.

"That I'd be president or some other role, but that there'd be someone with actual experience running the show."

"Huh. I can understand that, it happens all the time to technology entrepreneurs, but I guess I thought it might be different for you." It registered for both me and Stephen that the money guys often replaced company founders with experienced management, but I thought that was because the entrepreneurs were typically narrowly skilled, like deep technologists or scientists without general management talent to run a whole growing company. Not that I thought inexperienced MBAs should be left unchecked inside funded start-ups, but Stephen had all the basic skills of a general manager, if less real-world practice than some.

"Well, it isn't." Stephen was looking toward the floor, then back up toward but not directly at me. "And . . . they also consider the VP of Marketing a critical role."

"Oh, so I'd be out of my job, too?" I sounded flippant, but inside I was shocked.

"Not out of your job, just with someone else in charge of your area."

"Hmmmph." I felt a familiar sinking sensation in my midsection, the kind of anxious emptiness that comes from feeling deeply uncertain about a matter absolutely crucial to your well-being. I was interrupted, though, by my cell phone ringing. It was Elke, looking to rally a roommate dinner for that night. I wasn't convinced that she was entirely over Stephen, but for the most part things were fairly normal in our apartment. Unfortunately, Stephen had to work and I had plans to see Paul, so Elke was out of luck.

Hours later, I raced in the front door and bounded up the stairs to our apartment two at a time. I had maybe thirty minutes to get ready for dinner and drinks with Paul. Argh! Always rushing. Never enough time to feel really ready. As I opened drawers and my closet and pulled out option after option, Elke poked her head in the door and we exchanged hellos and she asked me where I was rushing to.

"I have dinner with Paul tonight, remember?" I smiled conspiratorially to my roommate, who came into the room and arranged herself on the bed, eating something familiar, yellow and cake-like. I couldn't let this go without comment, despite my panic over diminishing getting-ready time.

"Elkeee, what are you eating?" It was highly unusual to see Elke eating processed snacks at all, but lately she'd become enamored of trying out the American staples.

"What? It's a Twinkie. I bought a box. I just wanted to try one. The rest will sit in the Speisekammer for a year. Fortunately the shelf life will allow that, I checked." Elke smiled and I laughed, then emerged from my closet in a putty-colored Gap sweater and my best jeans.

"Anna, have you not been listening to me?"

"Pardon?" I said.

Elke popped the last of her Twinkie into her mouth, stood and approached me and my closet.

"This outfit will not do. You are trying to attract Paul's attention and yet you continue to dress so that you're practically invisible. And asexual." Elke reached into the closet.

"Here, try this." Elke handed me the infamous sexy Prada top. I looked at my roommate with uncertainty as she reached out and ran her fingers through my hair. "And I can help with this style if you like. I have done my share of haircutting and styling in the past."

"Elke, this is not *Grease*." She didn't fully understand the reference, never having seen the John Travolta–Olivia Newton-John classic. "You can't just dress me in a low-cut top and curl my hair and expect it to be that simple," I explained.

Elke just looked at me, unmoved and unconvinced.

And it dawned on me. "Oh shit, it can be that simple, can't it."

CHAPTER 39

Some days you wake up and despite best efforts, good intentions and all that, you just look like shit. Whether from lack of sleep, sun, vitamins, vegetables or of genetic material of the beautiful type, it's just not working. Then there's the altogether rare, exceptional day when the stars align, the benevolent forces in the universe are smiling and the temperature and relative humidity mix with your hair products and styling choices—especially when aided by a more talented roommate—in such a way that you end up with—what to call it? A good hair day?—and then your skin coincidentally is blemish-free and your makeup actually works and, holy shit, you look hot. Certifiably hot. And so now you have to do something with this. You cannot stay home, or in your office, or whatnot. You must be seen. So you call your best girlfriend and you drag her out, hoping to be seen by someone see-worthy. Unless you have a date, or a pseudo-date, which luckily I did that night. Then you go into that date-like situation with an unprecedented amount of confidence and verve.

I met Paul at Grafton Street on Mass Ave, an Irish pub packed with graduate students and young professionals that offered simple, scrumptious food and a well-stocked bar. From the instant we spoke I sensed that something was different, and I could not tell if it was me, him, or us that was responsible for it. I was trying not to seem self-conscious in my sexy Prada top, knowing that the slightest hint of discomfort could ruin the look entirely, that the sexiest thing was looking comfortable in my own skin. And since quite a lot of my skin was showing, it was a good time to get cozy in it. Elke had applied my makeup, giving me smoky eyes and pouty lips. I caught my reflection in the gigantic mirror that ran the length of the bar and noticed my hair looking super sleek, thanks to Elke's efforts with scissors and a flat iron. Next to me, Paul was drinking and picking at his hamburger like a finicky five-year-old.

"Aren't you hungry?" I asked.

"Not really. My stomach's not quite right." He signaled to the waiter, who came over immediately. "Hey man, can I have a Grey Goose martini, up?"

"Yeah, that'll help," I smiled.

Paul put away at least four "geese" martinis—I had lost count. It was hard to hear in the crowded restaurant. He was laughing a lot, though with even more sarcasm than usual. After an hour's worth of chatter and catching up during which there had been an unparalleled lack of Susie talk, I wondered if he was starting to get past the whole troubling situation. It had been months. It was possible, right?

Paul stood up and pulled me to my feet.

"Let's dance."

"Paul, there's no dance floor."

"C'mon."

Paul pulled me to a corner of the bar in front of the jukebox. He picked U2's "With or Without You" and danced close to me, holding me at the waist, marking the first time he'd ever touched me beyond a friendly hug. Feeling a little stunned by this sudden change in demeanor, I tried to go with the flow. Paul picked up a wayward ribbon connected to my top that didn't seem to perform any particular function and rolled it between two fingers. With his other hand around my neck he pulled me toward him, kissing my forehead—or at least resting his lips there—and playing with my hair. I was about to fall over. I couldn't believe he was actually finally really touching me. I sucked in my gut.

"I have an idea." Paul grabbed me by the hand. After paying the bill he pulled me outside and down along Mass Ave, headed toward Central Square without telling me where we were going. It didn't appear we were going home, which I would've liked very much. It did appear that Paul's Grey Goose had taken over and decided a pub crawl was in order.

"We're here," announced Paul. I looked up at the sign for the Cantab Lounge, a Cambridge institution, known for its mix of locals and students who came to drink and dance in one of the darkest dive bars in town. Little Joe Cook was playing. He stood about four feet tall atop a milk crate so he could reach the microphone. We heard the first strains of "Beauty Shop" from the sidewalk . . . *Sexy lady, from the beauty shop. You make my heart go bibbity bop* . . . We knew the songs by heart, all with a predictable beat that anyone could dance to, so long as they had a few drinks in them.

Paul stopped only to get a round of drinks at the bar, then pulled me to the middle of the dimly lit space used as a dance floor, where he turned every song into a slow song, and seemed to use the crowdedness as his excuse to hold me close to him, to rub the small of my back underneath the silky fabric, touching my actual skin. To play with my hair, and to kiss my cheek, my ear, my neck. I was deeply puzzled—how did this happen? Why now?—and deeply excited. If only he would kiss my mouth, then I would know he was serious and I could kiss him back.

Later, Paul pulled me into Eddie's apartment and left the

lights off. I wondered for a second about Eddie, but it seemed he wasn't home.

Paul was swaying a little. He pulled me toward him, talking into my hair, wrapping his arms around me then letting his hands drop to my hips.

"You're so beautiful, Annie." Did he just say that out loud? I couldn't respond to such a direct compliment, so I was particularly grateful when he occupied my mouth by leaning over and kissing me lightly while tucking two of his fingers into the waistband of my jeans, running around the front edges, brushing my stomach, stopping at my navel, teasing. God it felt good. I wanted to touch him back but felt frozen in my place. Instead I rested my hands, rather gracefully I thought, on his forearms and deepened our kiss, hoping he could tell how much I wanted this to happen. Paul's free hand moved from my hip to my shoulder, making circles, or tracing the alphabet perhaps, into the bare skin above my perfect and by then worth-every-penny Prada top. My arms fell to my side as his hand drifted down and he cupped my breast through the thin fabric, sensing my nipple harden and teasing it further with his thumb. Everything seemed to be moving in slow motion and I couldn't tell if it was on purpose or because Paul was drunk. He pulled his hand away from my belly and touched my other breast while kissing my neck. I struggled to stay acquainted with gravity; I wanted to fall into his arms and kiss him all night long.

"You have fucking incredible tits," he groaned into my hair, jolting me a little. But then he caressed and teased and kissed me again and it was all soft and warm and mesmerizing. He pressed his body against mine and I could feel his hardness and wondered if he could tell how excited I was.

When Paul grabbed for my waistband and started to fiddle with my zipper, I snapped to attention. I wasn't ready for this! So not ready!!! With an apologetic look that hopefully said, *Hold on for just one second, big guy,* I slinked off into the bathroom, waiting until the door was shut to turn on the light. I stood in front of the mirror and took a deep breath. With a quick unzipping of my exceptionally tight jeans my worst fears were realized. Shitshitshit. I reached down to feel my legs, which were in the perfect unshaven state of full stubble that hurt to the touch. Oh, fuckfuckfuck. After months of thwarted hopes I had given up on this happening, and now I wasn't prepared. But instead of taking my lack of readiness as a sign of my, well, lack of readiness I ignored it and searched for hasty solutions. I didn't want to lose this chance—what if it never came again? I was aware that every minute away from Paul was one minute closer to his passing out or sobering up or—goodness forbid—changing his mind. I heard a light knock. Paul met me at the bathroom door.

"Hey."

"Hey you," I said back.

Paul was slurring his words, slightly. "Are you going to stay? Please stay." He pulled me toward him and kissed me hard, with a little more saliva than I'd have preferred. He took my hand and led me across the living room toward Eddie's second bedroom, opening the door in the dark and kicking aside a balled-up sweatshirt and a pair of jeans to clear a path to the opened sofa bed. I remained overcome by disbelief, despite having imagined this scene a hundred times. Though, in my fantasies, the room was candlelit and the bed linens were crisp and white. In this reality the sofa bed appeared to be made with red flannel sheets and a Patriots sleeping bag.

Paul sat down on the edge and tugged my belt loops to guide me toward him, and when I was close enough he leaned in to rest his forehead between my breasts, exhaling hot breath that passed through the Prada silk and hit my skin in short bursts. His hands were wrapped around the backs of my thighs, his legs touching the outsides of my weak knees. I placed both hands on his chest and pushed him back until he was lying flat, feet still on the floor. I laid down beside him and let him roll over on top of me, his heaviness surprising me and pressing the backs of my thighs uncomfortably into the edge of the bed frame. We were awkwardly positioned but he seemed not to notice. Paul moaned again into my ear and my stomach flipped and my breath quickened and then I didn't care if it hurt a little. He moved against me. His mouth rested near my ear, and I picked up a few more moans and other indecipherables that I imagined to be— just maybe—declarations of love and prolonged wanting.

"Will you stay, Annie?"

He pulled me closer and buried his face in my neck and caught his fingers in my hair and all I could smell was booze. But it didn't matter, I still wanted to be there, with him. Suddenly he stopped and became obsessed with taking off my top, which he did rather indelicately, leaving me in just my pink lace bra distracted with concern for the condition of my fancy shirt. The room was drafty, I was cold, I was stubbly, I couldn't get past my desire for our first time to be perfect, and this definitely wasn't it. Seconds later I heard the kind of deep guttural burst of a snore that usually jolts the snorer awake, but in Paul's case it just seemed to precede his passing out fully and falling, deadweight, against me.

"Paul? Hey. Paul?" I shook him pretty hard with my free arm. Nothing, then another burst of snoring.

I still might've stayed there all night, just for the experience of sleeping next to him, but the combination of my arm starting to ache from the weight of his head now pinning my bicep to the bed and the alarming sound of Eddie's keys in the front door changed my mind. I inched my way out from under Paul, found my top and re-dressed as quickly as possible—no small task in the darkness of the room—and scrawled a note to Paul on a Post-it note I found on his dresser so that we might continue this evening, another time, hopefully very soon. I was having a hard time giving up on this night. (Okay, I admit, I wrote the Post-it over just a few times before settling on the simple *Let's pick up where we left off, tomorrow night? —A.)*

I exited the room as quietly as I could, hoping to slip past Eddie unnoticed.

"Annie?" Eddie's voice came from behind me. I jumped and turned to see him eating a bowl of cereal.

"Oh, hey, Eddie. I didn't see you. I was just getting Paul to his room. He's kinda drunk."

"Oh, sure. Hey, *that's* a cool shirt."

"Wha, oh, this?" I glanced down only to realize my fancy Prada top was on inside out, *and backwards.* "Ah, designers, you know, always deconstructing things."

"Are you headed home? Let me walk you," Eddie offered.

"You're sweet but I'm fine—it's just around the corner."

I departed quickly with a wave goodbye. Once outside the door, I found it hard to actually leave the hallway. Instead I paused at the door, letting the evening sink in. I tiptoed down the stairs and headed home, trying to contain my excitement about the next time I'd see Paul; hopefully he'd be much less drunk, and hopefully it would be as soon as possible, like tomorrow night.

CHAPTER 40

The next day I was having a panic attack. I'd wasted an hour and a half thinking about Paul when I should have been working up a proposal for a partnership agreement with Excite, the search engine. But focus was elusive and I let my hands rest still and silent on the keyboard and drifted back to thoughts of Paul, replaying the details of last night. Then I absently moved the mouse around to no place in particular on the page, running over in my mind what he said, how he looked, how he touched me, kissed me, asked me to stay. It gave me delicious chills when I thought of him crossing the line from friendship to more. I started over from the beginning, savoring the recollection of words, touches, kisses—and grinning inside.

Elke would call this repetition ruminating, to put a good pathological spin on the more innocuous "daydreaming" that I might name it. But I was not dreaming, this had really happened. It really, really happened. And I, who needed variety like most need oxygen, was now capable of fixating on one set of experiences, never tiring of the details, wafting away from them only to imagine what might happen tonight when we were together again. One thing was for certain, I'd be ready this time. In my conviction that this occasion warranted new underthings, I hatched a plan to sneak out to Victoria's Secret at lunch—after all, it was entirely possible that our continuation of last evening could happen as soon as tonight, if Paul agreed with my Post-it note. I would figure out some way to guarantee I had time tonight to shower and primp before seeing Paul. Feigning illness was not beyond me—I would simply not let another work emergency leave me incapable of consummating this new twist in my relationship with Paul. I typed a few more sentences into the Excite document, and then allowed myself to contemplate the evening ahead.

What would we do first? Go out to dinner? Or just stay in, to finish what we started last night? Hmmmmm. Either would be nice. I'd let Paul decide, and be flexible and fun either way. I forced myself to smile and sit up straight just thinking about how I'd behave in our next encounter. Flirty, confident, sexy. I stifled a yawn. And I'd be awake! Despite my inability to sleep last night, I'd have to psych myself into being energetic.

I glanced at the clock on the lower right corner of my computer screen. 11:37 a.m. I would've expected to hear from him on the early side of the day, just to make sure we were coordinated in our follow-up plans. But planful and coordinated was my style, not Paul's. He was more laid-back, and I'd just have to wait. Surely I'd hear from him by early afternoon.

By twelve thirty I'd managed to write about half the Excite agreement, knowing it should have taken an hour, tops, for the entire thing, but I considered halfway done sufficient progress for my distracted, lovesick brain and escaped my desk without a word to run over to the Galleria Mall.

An hour later, leaving the Victoria's Secret bag in the trunk of my car, I slinked back into the office, which was buzzing with its normal intensity—questions flew across the room, Jeet hopped from workstation to workstation, solving problems and giving direction. Stephen was looking particularly focused. I could see him through the opening to his office, hovering over a spread of papers that could be the financials. I nodded hello to everyone I passed and slid into my desk chair, mirroring their energy but focused on an entirely different set of questions. Had Paul called? Or emailed? I reflexively pressed "Send/Receive" to check my email. A dozen work messages, otherwise nothing new. The only messages in my voicemail box were from vendors. I rechecked my cell phone. Nothing. I returned to my document, managed a few more sentences and some math, calculating revenue-sharing options based on volume and click-through and registration of new GoodMatch.com visitors and members. A few minutes later I checked email again. Nothing. One more time. Nothing again!

The absence of any contact from Paul was starting to rattle me. I'd been in this situation before. And I hated the waiting game, possessed negligible capacity to be in the dark about what would happen next. I couldn't stand sitting there a moment longer. I wandered to the kitchenette and pulled a Diet Coke from the mini-fridge and tapped the side of the can. The soft tips of my fingers hit the aluminum in a series of dull, light thumps instead of the clicking of graceful, polished fingernails I wanted to hear. I'd bitten my just-starting-to-grow nails to the quick in nervous excitement after last night. I resolved to get serious about letting them grow again. Perhaps I'd squeeze in a subtle self-manicure before tonight, since even a quick coat of clear or light polish was wildly preferable to dry, stubby nails.

Through the door to his office, I could see Stephen concentrating on the printout of an immense spreadsheet, covering most of his desk and his small conference table. He looked busy, but I couldn't help myself. I normally wouldn't interrupt real work for gossip, but it was Sunday after all and this was really good stuff and I was dying to tell someone.

"Guess what happened last night." I shut the door behind me, and Stephen looked up and patiently listened to me recount in precise detail the events of last evening, though it seemed he was struggling to concentrate on my story. I was surprised at his distraction. I sped up my summary and waited for his reaction.

"Really," replied Stephen. "I hope you don't mind mixing business and pleasure."

"What do you mean by that?"

"Well, do you remember when Ben West told us the only way that companies fail is by running out of cash, and we all said 'duh'?" Ben West had been our first-year Finance professor.

"Yeeeess." What flashed through my mind was the sudden departure last week of our nominal chief financial officer, a well-meaning but underqualified fraternity brother of Stephen's who'd been doing the books for GoodMatch during the last several months. As we got closer to securing the next round of financing, Stephen had stepped in to take a closer look and tighter hold on the financials. Now Stephen turned the critical section of the financial statements toward me.

"Well, here's our 'duh' moment." I glanced at the figures, which clearly showed that our available cash wasn't going to cover us through the end of the next month. Something had to be done, quickly.

"Oh Stephen. This isn't good."

"Nope."

"But our subscriber numbers are so good. We're killing our projections, even!"

"I know, but it doesn't matter how fast we grow if we can't fund it. If we can't keep the lights on."

"I'm so sorry to babble on about my silly Paul news. No wonder you're working around the clock. What about the bridge financing?"

"It's actually looking okay. If Paul comes through I think we can put the round together." Herein was the business-and-pleasure issue.

"Why Paul?"

"Simple, he's talking about putting in the most money; others are willing to follow but not lead."

"How does Paul have so much money?"

"It's his family trust," Stephen explained. "Remember, he handles the investments."

"Right, I remember that. I just didn't realize he'd be the lead. Well, is there anything I can do?"

"Nah. Just don't piss him off. At least not until after he cuts us a check."

The precariousness of our business situation helped me snap back into work mode, and I was grateful in a way for the pressure because I didn't hear from Paul that day, or that night, or the next day or night, or the next day after that, Tuesday. I was sure there must be some explanation, and I would hear from Paul soon enough, and then we'd reconnect. After all, there hadn't been any *guarantee* that we'd pick up on Sunday where we'd left things on Saturday—that was just my Post-it suggestion and my deepest desire, felt so strongly I had to do special breathing to stay standing straight. I hadn't wanted something so much in so long, and the idea that it was so, so close to happening made me ecstatic and terrified all at once. I was aware that I was expecting something different from Paul than if the same situation had occurred with a regular guy, but Paul was my *friend*, and I trusted that he would not have kissed me or asked me to stay if he wasn't sure he wanted to take our relationship in this new direction. So my excitement overwhelmed any other concerns I might've had, because in my heart of hearts, Paul and I together, well, it just all made sense.

To keep my mind off of Paul I simply redoubled my efforts to help shore up GoodMatch.com's position with its prospective funders by working to secure more distribution deals and partnership arrangements. The more access we had to singles, the more faith the money guys would have in our ability to pull it off.

A full two days after I'd last seen Paul, with still no word from him about getting together the previous Sunday night or any night, I snuck into the one small office in the corner of our space and shut the door behind me. I looked around to make sure no one was watching and pulled out a piece of paper with a script I'd written and rewritten over lunch. I was past the point of waiting and had decided to take matters back into my own control. I knew that as soon as I'd placed the call I'd then be waiting again, and no longer in control, but I needed to act. I needed to know what was going on. I picked up the telephone receiver and dialed. It was his voicemail. *Hello. You've reached Paulson Dennison. Please leave a message.* After enduring the long, grating beep I read from my prepared notes.

"Hi Paul. It's Annie. It was great to see you Saturday night. It's Tuesday afternoon and I thought I'd touch base and see when we might get together again. I know we're both so busy, but call me on my cell phone and we can make plans. Talk to you soon. Bye." I winced at the flatness of my voice and the hint of anxiety I could hear in my speech. I pressed the pound key. The affected female voice of the automated voicemail system directed me. *If you are satisfied with your message, press one. To listen to your message, press two. To erase and re-record, press three.* Satisfied? No. I sputtered a shallow breath and pressed three. I needed to get this right. This time I'd speak a little more quickly in an attempt to be breezy yet casual, and in an effort to add authenticity to my voice I forced myself to hold a big fake smile accompanied by a hair flip.

"Hi Paul. It's Annie. Great to see you Saturday. It's Tuesday, uh, afternoon and I thought I'd see when we might touch again. I mean, touch base, and see each other again—" Now there's a Freudian slip, I sighed, and pressed three. I shook my head quickly to clear my mind. I took another breath, deep to my diaphragm this time. *C'mon, Annie. You can do this.* I tried the script again. Shit! So close but I stumbled on the last line. I pressed three yet again and tried again—stopping halfway through, realizing I'd said the wrong date. The next time I sounded too desperate. Then too whiny. Too cold. Three, three, *three.*

I leaned on the table, fatigued, then stood up to get more energy and tried one more time. The digital timer on the phone indicated I'd been at this for twenty-three minutes, and I was starting to feel ridiculous. My voice was hoarse and cracking. I pressed three once again while working my way over to the water cooler, stretching the phone cord so I could reach and get a drink to soothe my parched throat. Exasperated, I made one last attempt and my voice was flat and mildly cold and I didn't care.

"Paul, it's Annie. Call me back, would you?"

I couldn't concentrate and left work much earlier than usual and got home in time to help Elke prepare dinner. We were chopping ingredients for kale and vegetable soup, surrounded by carrots and onions and green leafy stuff. I'd never have done this on my own, but I liked doing it.

"Have you heard back from Paul?" she asked, reaching for a carrot. The question ignited a burning commotion in my chest. I'd heard nothing but shattering silence from Paul, silence which had left me disbelieving and stunned and now, with Elke putting the question out there right in the open, I felt more than a little humiliated at the truth. He hadn't returned my call. Hadn't emailed. Nothing. For a second I let myself imagine he hadn't gotten my message. But really, who was I kidding.

"No. He's probably swamped with work," I replied. I

couldn't bear to acknowledge out loud that I was being blown off. It was too much—how could I have been so hopeful and excited? I felt like a fool and I wanted to cry but instead I forced myself to feel nothing and chop.

"Still, I'd be a touch angry," said Elke.

I paused my chopping, resting my knife-holding hand in a fist on the counter, and stared out the window. "Huh. I don't get angry." I saw anger as such an undesirable trait that in the unusual event I experienced a wave of it I managed to control it, rarely letting it reach the surface. I thought it made me a nicer, better person. I learned that from my mother. She never got angry, either.

"Really?"

I felt surprised by Elke's surprise. "Really. Almost never. You do?"

"Oh ja," Elke answered. "I let it out. It's the healthy thing to do."

"But you wouldn't want to overreact to an unreturned phone call," I said, in a half-question/half-statement format. Elke resumed her task of chopping vegetables into small pieces.

"I believe that ignoring a hundred minor betrayals will hurt far more than the occasional screaming session."

From the kitchen table behind us, the sound of my phone ringing interrupted our conversation. I wiped my hands and checked the phone. The caller ID signaled it was my parents.

"Sorry Elke, I should take this. Just a sec." I walked into the living room.

"Hello?" I listened for a half minute, stunned. "Oh my God." I hung up and gathered my things from the table. "Elke, I'm sorry—I gotta go."

I wandered around my room for a few minutes, unable to

get traction on the simple task of changing my pants. Eddie called. He'd come and get me, he said. Fifteen minutes later he knocked on my front door. We headed to Mass General in sustained silence. When we got to April's room, Eddie took Melody's hand and guided her out, presumably to the cafeteria to distract her with ice cream or some other novelty. When they were gone I sat next to Liz. My cousin was sipping weak-looking tea, staring at April, who was pale and sleeping and attached by tubes and wires to the equipment around her hospital bed.

"She wants to look like Sleeping Beauty," Liz whispered. "I told her today. I told her what the doctors told me."

"Oh, Liz." My heart sank to my toes.

"She made me say it," Liz was still whispering. "She made me tell her. She wanted to know. She deserves to know." Liz's tone was almost matter-of-fact, which made me suspicious that she was in shock. I could think of nothing to say.

"Liz—"

"I'm taking her home. I want her to be home."

I nodded, unsure if that was a controversial idea, a good idea, both, or neither, but sure that I wanted Liz to feel supported. Imagining that April would be happier in her special bed than in the hospital.

"Of course."

April's experimental treatment had failed, her tumor was back and growing, and the only thing the doctors knew for sure was that she wasn't going to make it.

CHAPTER 41

When I got back to the office that night I checked my email and there was a message from Paul with the subject line *Got your message.* I clicked the email open:

Thanks for calling, Annie. I realize I've been out of touch but I've been distracted by a few big developments over here. Can I call you when I come up for air? Really hope to see you soon. Thanks and sorry.
-PJD

Honestly, it was a relief. Paul had something, probably work related, that was distracting him and I had something bigger and much more important to think about, which was how I was going to help my cousin and myself and the rest of our family get through this impossible time. And in the middle of it all, the company I worked for was having its own struggles. Yes, there was plenty to keep my mind off of Paul Dennison.

Two days later Liz brought April home, and a few days after that Eddie and I climbed into the back of Barbara and Jimmy's Maxima and drove with them, mostly in silence, to Liz's house for a visit. Heading down Route 3, Jimmy kept to the speed limit, Barb leaned her head against her passenger-side window, and next to me, Eddie tapped his knee to the Counting Crows CD playing on the stereo. It was obvious we were all thinking the same thoughts and asking ourselves the same unanswerable questions, so whatever conversation we might've had could happen without talking. Adam Duritz's voice filled the void: *And in between the moon and you, angels get a better view, of the crumbling difference between wrong and right.*

Jimmy pulled off the highway and into a 7-Eleven and he and Eddie went inside and emerged with cups of coffee and bags of Rolos and Swedish Fish and miscellaneous candy. When we arrived at Liz's, most of the lights were on and we found her sitting at the kitchen table, a cup of tea in her hand and a blank look on her face. She brightened once we were inside, knowing we would take up space and share the responsibility for keeping the girls engaged. Barbara turned on the kettle and joined Liz at the table while Eddie and Jimmy went to play cards—Go Fish, I think—with April and Melody in the living room.

Liz explained that April had been having a particularly difficult day, a delayed reaction after the shock of her prognosis sunk in. Some parents might've shielded a child from such a harsh truth, but Liz believed April needed to know she was going to die, that honesty was the only option. As I listened to my cousin, my admiration for her strength filled my heart.

"I told you, Annie, she has decided that she wants you to be engaged." Liz touched my forearm. "You have to do this." She tried to laugh as she implored, but I could sense an undercurrent of desperation, of a brokenhearted mother searching for any sliver of comfort she could provide to her child.

April had been hinting at wanting to see me have a boyfriend for months. And now, especially, since she had decided she wanted to right all the wrongs and organize all the loose ends that were even vaguely within her control, she hit upon seeing me and Eddie engaged—it was at the top of her list of things to arrange.

"Okay. But I don't know how you do it. How you can handle this so gracefully."

Liz shrugged her shoulders while glancing past me at April in the next room. "It isn't me. It's her. I'm just trying to keep it together like she is."

We moved into the living room, where April, dressed in a long-sleeved T-shirt and flannel pajama bottoms with attached feet, was carrying around a white plastic device about the size of an overstuffed #10 envelope. It was her portable pain controller, connected to her skinny body via an intravenous tube hidden by her tee that delivered doses of morphine when she pressed a red button. She seemed a little high, agitated and pacing back and forth as I appeared in the doorway.

"You have to, Annie." April spoke with pleading eyes and without hesitation. Eddie was quiet on the far end of the sofa, reshuffling Go Fish cards. April faced him next.

"Eddie, you have to."

Without looking at him—I simply couldn't—I sensed that Eddie was coming to the same realization that I was. After months of April's cajoling us to become engaged and our half-hearted compliance with the ruse, we had hit a critical juncture. April was adamant, Liz was reconciled to it, and the "groom" wasn't voicing any protest. Apparently I was the only one harboring serious doubt about the whole charade, partly because it was all so perplexing. How had April picked me as her charity case, to use one of her last wishes and limited time and energy on? If I hadn't been feeling so self-conscious I might've felt pathetic. But in the moment I was just concerned about doing it right and pleasing April.

April approached me and put her hand inside mine, pulling me fully into the room and seating me at the edge of the chenille-covered ottoman, arranging my limbs as if I were one of her Barbie dolls. In the meantime, Eddie snuck past us then returned a minute later from the kitchen. I was conflicted about lying to a child, but everyone else seemed to believe that a tiny untruth was unimportant in the scheme of things. Surely they were right.

Eddie crossed the room and stopped in front of me as I felt my face turn hot, then tugged at his right pant leg so he could get down on one knee. The whole situation was reminiscent of the wedding garter episode—maybe that's where April got her idea—and Eddie was as composed as he'd been then, while I felt similarly embarrassed. *Get it together! You're doing this for April.*

Eddie produced the light blue Tiffany box from his pocket, which made me think he really was conspiring with April, since he must've gotten it from her. He placed the box in front of me and looked in my eyes, not betraying for a moment the seriousness of the proposal.

"Annie Thompson, will you become engaged to me," he said, a bit more of a statement than a question. In a soft, confident, unembarrassed voice. Sincere. Kind. Generous.

I knew there was only one answer I could possibly give.

"Yes." A hush came over the room as Eddie opened the box. Inside was a red candy ring, in the shape of a massive diamond, wrapped in plastic. Eddie tore the plastic and then tried in vain to get the ring onto my ring finger, which proved far too big, and settled for my pinky. I was grateful that at least I'd painted my nails a lovely light pink in post-Paul anticipation and I looked at Eddie, trying to return his sincerity.

"It's lovely."

April, who'd been sitting nearby and watching intently, looked as if she was about to burst. She barged in between us, the newly engaged couple, and hugged Eddie, relief washing over her pale, ravaged features.

"Thank you. Thank you for that." With an arm still around Eddie's neck, April reached out and hugged me to them both, squeezing as tightly as her scrawny arms could. When she broke the tight embrace, she continued to hold onto us both, and turned to me.

"Don't you want to call your mother?"

"Ah, well, yes, of course, but it's late, so I'll . . . tell her tomorrow," I said. Eddie couldn't keep from smiling, scratching a non-itch so that he could cover his face without April seeing.

"When will you have the wedding?" asked April.

I eased myself out of April's arms and looked at her sweet face.

"April, honey," I said. "Since Eddie and I really just met a few months ago, do you think we could date for a little while first?" April looked deep in thought for five seconds, glancing between Eddie and me.

"Okay. I guess that would be alright." She smiled and surveyed the scene, clearly pleased with herself. She rested back on the oversized chair, legs out straight in front of her on the ottoman, nearly lying down. And though she was at first smiling and happy, her face was quickly taken over by a sheet of sadness.

"I'm never going to get married." It was almost a whisper.

Eddie and I looked in panic at Liz, who moved to sit closer.

"Oh, honey." Liz was holding her daughter's hands in her own, sharing a moment of awful truth. April wasn't going to live long enough to do many things.

"Mom, what did I do? What did I do?" April's eyes were filling with tears and confusion. Liz looked heartbroken and helpless.

"*Nothing*, honey. You didn't do *anything*."

"Well, what did *you* do?" April asked her mother.

"Nothing!" Liz said, alarmed. "Honey, I didn't. No one did

anything."

April was clearly fighting tears. "I'm never going to have a boyfriend. I'm never going to have a wedding. I'm never going to have a baby." She looked searchingly at her mother, who was doing her best to be the strong one. *"Mom, I'm never going to have a baby."* Tears spilled onto her cheeks, and Liz leaned toward April to hold her in her arms.

"I know honey. I'm so sorry. I'm so sorry . . ."

There was a long moment where Liz held April and rocked her back and forth. Barbara and Jimmy had retreated to the kitchen to keep Melody preoccupied, and Eddie and I were frozen in our places. After a few minutes April lifted her head up and looked at her mother.

"Well, if I can't have a baby, can I at least have a puppy?"

Liz laughed. Her answer was as instinctual as breathing. "Of course you can."

That night, hours after I was dropped off at my apartment, Elke and I huddled under the covers in my bed, drinking tea and looking at my engagement ring.

"This is the sweetest story I have ever heard," said Elke. "What a darling man."

"Too bad it's the wrong man." I instantly regretted saying it—there was something off and selfish about making this about me and my preferences. I was not the point of this engagement, this was about April's wish. "But it is incredibly sweet. April is so so happy about this. Liz even said she is feeling quite a bit better." I had called upon arriving home to check in, and Liz had sounded relaxed and relieved that April had calmed down and gone to bed easily.

"The spirit is a powerful part of the healing process," Elke said, placing the ring back in its plastic wrapper. "This was a very kind thing for you and Eddie to do."

"I don't deserve any credit. It was all Eddie. I felt foolish but he just took control and did it. It was quite nice, actually."

The next day, Liz called to tell me that she and April had gone to the dog pound and rescued a one-year-old flaxen-colored cocker spaniel named Frederick. April fell deeply, madly in love the moment she laid eyes on him.

"He's the one, Mom," she'd said.

Then the most amazing thing of all happened. April stabilized. In the days and weeks that followed she didn't get better, but she didn't get worse. She stayed the same, treating her pain with medication and having good days and bad days, but on balance more good, and I started to believe, deep inside myself and without knowing why and without telling anyone, that April was going to defy the odds, that she was going to make it.

CHAPTER 42

I pressed the apartment buzzer, surprised that Eddie wasn't already downstairs. It was strange to be waiting outside the place where Paul lived, since we hadn't spoken since our night together. At first I had made excuses for him, and then I was much more concerned about April, and it was easier not to notice the time that had passed since we'd spoken. My instinct was to want to lean on him in sad times like this. He'd sent his emails with apologies and references to big stuff at work and such as well as check-in emails to ask how my day was, and I wrote back in as witty a way as I could, but we hadn't had a live conversation and we certainly didn't make any references to our night together. I just thought it was better to explore that territory in person, and by his silence on the topic Paul seemed to agree. I was sure we'd eventually get together.

"Hello?" Eddie's voice was muffled through the intercom.

"Hi. I'm here," I said.

"Be right down."

I sat on the stoop, and checked my nails. An out-and-out mess! Ravaged cuticles and dull, chipped polish. A metaphor for the state of my ravaged, dull, chipped life. Absorbed in an attempt to peel and scrape off the rest of my polish, I didn't notice Paul's arrival until his shadow cut off the light for my makeshift manicure.

"Hey there."

I looked up at Paul's handsome, smiling face. What was he doing here so early in the evening? I'd left work hours before I normally would have and thought for sure my chances of seeing him were zero, or I'd have prepared.

"Hi." One tiny syllable, and it still managed to sound awkward.

"Are you waiting for me?" Paul asked.

"No!" I almost shouted and my voice was sharper than usual, though there was really no need for raised voices. "Eddie is on his way down."

Paul was smiling his best smile and tempting me with his trademark charm.

"Come here Annie, I haven't seen you in so long." He pulled me into a hug and I have to admit I melted a little. "I am so sorry about April. Eddie told me what's happening. And I'm more sorry that I've been out of touch. There is some really big stuff happening that I want to tell you about. Really big. So I've been meaning to call to see if you want to have dinner. Friday night?"

I was sure I should say I was busy. Be hard to get, all that nonsense. But I was so *very* available, feeling so easy to get, and as embarrassing as this was to admit, I was dying to spend time with Paul again and finally get to talk about us. One does not let go of her ideal man easily.

"Um, sure. That would work."

Eddie opened the door and bounded outside.

"Hey, man." Eddie slowed up upon seeing Paul, and nodded hello to me.

"Hey," Paul replied. "What are you guys up to?"

"Going to visit April," Eddie explained.

"How's she doing?" Paul asked. Eddie and I looked at each other. It was hard to say.

"She's hanging in. She keeps surprising us," I said.

"She's okay. On a lot of drugs," Eddie added. I thought he sounded pessimistic.

"But Eddie," I said, trying to suppress the defensive edge in my voice. "She's been feeling so much better. Don't you think that is a good sign?"

"Yes, but we don't know. Did you remember your engagement ring this time?"

I held up my hand in a flash to show Eddie that I was wearing the dainty sterling silver ring with the cubic zirconium stone that he'd given me after I'd eaten my first ring, in a weak sugar-craving moment after a particularly stressful night at work.

"Yes, sir." I turned to Paul. "April was very upset with me when she found out I ate my candy ring, and Eddie, being the greatest faux-fiancé ever, gave me this inedible one." I paused, remembering the night that Eddie presented me with a replacement ring that was perfectly sized to fit my fat finger, without a hint of judgment that I'd scarfed down the first one, which had been a rather yummy flavor of strawberry. "She's so smart in so many ways, but on this one she just believes what she wants to believe."

Paul smiled. I glanced over and could see that Eddie was not smiling.

"Say hi for me," Paul said. "Tell her I'm jealous she didn't find a beautiful fiancé for me."

I smiled, blushed, and stared at Paul for a second too long, as Eddie and I turned and left.

CHAPTER 43

I was getting ready for my follow-up dinner date with Paul, refusing to make the same mistake I always did. Tonight I'd be ready, dammit. I showered, shaved my legs, put makeup on carefully, took great care with my hair, strategically placed perfume, pulled off the tags and pulled on black lace panties and a sexy matching bra. As I finished dressing, Elke came home and into my bedroom.

"So, it's tonight. Your date with Paul?"

"Yes, tonight is the big night! What are you doing?" It was Friday. Elke often had plans, with one cute guy or another.

"I have a date too," Elke said.

I was distracted. "Oh, good. Anyone special?"

"Something new, sort of, we'll see. We are going to Club Passim." Elke smiled as I switched from my backpack to a small bag, trying to fit my lipstick and my cell phone and my wallet in the tight confines of the leather purse. I then checked my hair and my makeup and my watch.

"Gotta run. Have fun tonight."

"You, too."

I arrived a few minutes early at EVOO, a new restaurant at the edge of Somerville where Paul and I had agreed to meet. I stood at the bar, contemplating the wine list, considering a New Zealand pinot gris, which was made from a red grape with the skins removed, or so I'd learned at the launch party wine tasting. For a long time I had considered the details of wine too voluminous to comprehend—grapes and regions and years and vintages—so I hadn't paid any attention at all. Lately I'd changed my attitude and decided to pick up whatever I could here and there, and not beat myself up for not knowing absolutely everything. I didn't need to be a wine expert, I just needed to be able to find something I liked. I ordered a glass from the bartender/waitress, a petite twenty-something named Billie with straight dark hair that curled only at the ends, and super-short bangs. A face any less striking couldn't pull off such a look. It reminded me of the time when Melody decided to cut her bangs herself and ushered in her pixie phase.

Billie had doe eyes and perfect skin and when she stepped away to get the wine I noticed her shoes. Strappy pewter stilettos as impractical—especially for a waitress—as they were dazzling. And we were not talking just pewter colored—they looked like the actual metal. It made me want to go shopping immediately.

I felt good even though my sandals weren't nearly as fabulous as Billie's and my stomach was doing somersaults at the thought of being with Paul again. If only I'd been prepared last time with smooth legs, and if Paul had been a bit more sober, we'd have already gotten past the potentially awkward first encounter and could be venturing into the really good part of sex, when you knew what to expect from each other's bodies and fingers and lips and could count on the pleasure forthcoming. It should've shocked me how easily I forgave him for waiting so long to follow up since our last night together, no matter how busy he was.

Paul arrived almost twenty minutes late and looked sheepish, which I attributed to his principle of always being on time. I was quick with forgiveness, but the wait had been a little stressful given the circumstances and I was well into my second glass of pinot gris by the time we sat at our table. With any luck we'd be able to rush through the niceties and get on to the business of making out. I was dying to kiss him again.

I took advantage of the quiet time of menu perusal to steal a glance at my date. Hmmm. He actually needed a haircut and, objectively speaking, looked a little shaggy, especially for Paul, but that was okay—I could see past such surface matters. I who had cut my own hair for most of the past year should not be passing judgment on others. Yes, he probably did need a shave, but some stubble could be sexy, right? Although his patchy stubble tended to look unkempt rather than sexy, and I did notice he smelled a little stale when we'd hugged hello. A quick hug, I'd noticed. Nothing lingering or intimate. He was probably nervous, too.

It was stunning how quickly I could put the facts and warning signs behind me and focus on my carefully laid plan for the evening. A light, garlic-free dinner with enough wine to set the mood and then I'd invite him back to my place for "dessert." I'd bought some chocolate, Rosie's double fudge brownies, just in case, but was planning more of a naked dessert. My bathroom was clean—I could offer Paul a shower before a nightcap. Maybe I'd hop into the shower with him. At first the idea felt exciting and then my better judgment brought it to a screeching halt. No, no NO!! What was I thinking? Nothing could steal a good hair day as fast as a steaming shower. And first-time nakedness needed to be *horizontal* and with the aid of properly rigged bedroom lighting and *covers*.

Our dinner conversation consisted of small talk, which suited me because I didn't have the attention span tonight to get into anything heavy. He mentioned Eddie, who was apparently headed to Club Passim, like Elke. He inquired after April, but we didn't dwell there.

I might have expected more flirting, more accidental touching and staring through lowered eyelashes. I was distracted enough with anticipation not to notice how cool Paul was acting. An hour and a half into the meal, Billie approached our table to drop off our check and do a final refill of our wine glasses. This was my fourth. If Billie were paying attention, she might notice that I looked slightly tipsy and expectant, while Paul looked just uncomfortable. Finally—finally!—Paul brought up our last encounter. He spoke with his eyes lowered in between long drinks of pinot.

"So. Annie. I figured I at least owed you dinner so we could . . ." A brief hiatus of wine gulping left me on the edge of my seat. "So we could, um, talk about our drunken mistake."

Our drunken mistake. Talk about our drunken mistake. There was a loud buzzing sound suddenly occupying all the space in my skull. Excuse me? Did I just hear that right? Did Paul just characterize the most exciting night of the entire last year of my life as a *drunken mistake?!*

"Our drunken mistake?" I needed to check. Perhaps he was just worried that I was embarrassed by it, that I didn't want it to happen again, which couldn't be further from the truth. Instead, Paul seemed grateful that I was referring to it the same way. He let out a long gasp.

"Yeah! Exactly. That night was weird."

My hopes for the night were deflating instantaneously, hopes so big and bold and built over days and days and then so carefully wrapped in black lace fancy panties. I couldn't think of anything original to say, so I blurted out an automatic response, the kind designed to make tension go away. The kind I was so good at.

"You don't owe me anything," I said as evenly as I could, but my voice caught in my throat and the last part didn't really make it out of my mouth.

"I just, I didn't want things to be awkward between us. Obviously." Here he paused and blurted out a little awkward chuckle. "That other night was a mistake and I'm sure you couldn't believe it happened either. Or almost happened." He laughed another embarrassed laugh and I wanted to poke him with my fork. "I really value your friendship," he continued. "You've been so good to me ever since this whole thing blew up with Susie."

What I envisioned would be happening on this date and what was actually happening were so dreadfully not the same that I was speechless with disbelief. I found all I could do was stare at his mouth, a mouth that was responding to my silence by rephrasing his take on the situation. Thankfully he wasn't repeating the words "drunken mistake," or I would have had no choice but to hurl water in his face. *No, wait. That would be far too predictable and easily cleaned up.* If he said "drunken mistake" again my half-melted fallen chocolate cake with almond-tinted ice cream was heading clear across the table and into his lap. A much better idea. *Don't tempt me.*

I remembered Elke's comment that everything that was true did not have to be said, and realized that saying my truth right now might result in serious regret, a *real* drunken mistake, so I decided to take a breather and compose my thoughts.

"Paul, would you excuse me for one second?" I signaled that I was heading to the restroom.

"Of course. Sure."

I summoned my inner nonchalance to make it from the table to the bathroom without drawing any special attention to myself, especially from Paul the Bastard. Finding refuge in the empty restroom, I took a deep breath and swallowed gulps of disappointment over and over again, willing myself not to cry. I studied myself in the mirror.

"Omigod, omigod," I whispered to myself. "I can't believe this. I'm such an idiot." I checked my watch, then dug my cell phone out of my bag and dialed. Elke answered after two rings.

"Hello?"

"Elke. It's Annie." I could hear music in the background but not Elke's voice. "Can you hear me? Elke?"

"Oh, is that you Annie? All I can hear are vowels, aaa-eee-oooo."

I looked at my phone. One bar. Shit. "Okay, sorry, I'll talk to you at home. Bye."

"What? Bye? Okay, bye."

I took another deep breath, still holding back tears. I looked again in the mirror and the words came tumbling back.

and so I thought, who's the best listener I know? And I thought of you . . .

a good quality in a lover
stay, please stay
just don't piss him off
tonight's the big night
talk about our drunken mistake
you don't owe me anything.

Don't owe me anything, I repeated to myself. Don't owe me anything. Well why the hell not? Why was it so crazy to think that Paul Dennison might actually owe me, sweet doormat that I was, something beyond his fucking sob story of a life?

Something deep inside me started to come undone, and forced its way to the surface. I would probably remember that moment, that solitary moment in the surprisingly well-lit restroom of EVOO, as the moment when I officially snapped. Twenty-nine years of compromise had hit their high-water mark and were about to overflow, like a forgotten tub, or an accidental over-pouring of Diet Coke, when you misjudged how much space the fizz would take up and ended up with liquid running over the sides and onto the table. I'd simply had enough of making things easy, keeping things tension free, cleverly redirecting conversations to keep everyone and everything simpatico, going along with the flow. Not this time. I took another deep breath, fixed my hair, applied more lipstick and headed back to Paul.

I'd been gone a while. Billie the waitress was departing our table just as I claimed my place, standing in front of him and staring down at his confused expression. He surely expected me to sit, compliantly. To finish dessert and the rest of our wine. Instead I made my semi-prepared speech, rehearsed quickly into the bathroom mirror.

"I didn't think it was a drunken mistake. In fact, I pretty much came here intent on repeating it, not apologizing for it. And if you're not ready, because of Susie, well then you're a real asshole because you never should have kissed me, or touched me like that last time. You should have let me be. And if you're just not that into me, then you *really* never should have kissed me or touched me like that. We're supposed to be friends." It seemed like it was now Paul's turn to be silent. I wanted him to talk to me, to say something, but he just stared ahead. Was he thinking? Preparing a response?

"Paul. You have to have known that this would screw up our friendship. If you didn't mean it."

"I guess I thought you wanted it, too."

I did. I had. I wanted it so badly it stung behind my eyes to think about it. But now that I knew he wasn't into it, I didn't know what to think.

"Wanted what? Do you really think I would forgo my pride

and our friendship for the sake of one fuck?" *Why was I talking about my pride?* Where did that come from? And "for the sake of one fuck"? So crass! Too much pinot gris! Warning, WARNING!

"Your pride? Annie, I wasn't thinking like that. I wasn't thinking at all. And I didn't think I was risking our friendship. And . . . ," he lowered his voice again, "we didn't exactly fuck." I ignored that distinction. Didn't he understand? We *would have*, if I'd shaved my legs, if he hadn't passed out.

"I don't get it. I don't understand how you can just forget about the consequences." Uck. I was sounding like a junior high school principal. Why couldn't I say what I meant? That I couldn't believe he would do this to me, if he really cared at all about me, why he would lift me up with so much hope only to yank it away and let me land alone with a thud.

"Annie, I'm not saying I'm right here, but most people don't think all the time. Sometimes you go with how you feel. And then, yeah, I did kiss you and want you that night, even if it was selfish. I'm sorry."

"That night. Not this night." I was embarrassed and deflated. I didn't know why I gave voice to the most humiliating parts of what he'd said, so I had to live through them again.

"I don't know what to say."

I looked for signs that my dreams could be salvaged. Maybe Paul was just afraid, it was too soon after Susie. Maybe I just had to be more patient. Maybe. Maybe. Maybe *not*.

Paul's eyes dipped and I looked down. Oh jeez. To my horror, the top button of my already low-cut top had sprung open and my absurdly sexy black bra was in plain view, certainly betraying to Paul my original hopes for the night. The salt was in the wound. Enough said. *E-nough!!* I pulled the sides of my top together, turned on my heel and headed out the door. On the sidewalk, I realized I was relishing the release of actually saying what I thought. This could get addictive. Of course I was also a bit drunk. When Paul stepped up behind me, I turned to face him.

"Paul, if you want to be just friends, I can deal with that. But you have to start being my friend back. For months, it has been you talk, and talk and talktalktalk, I listen, you pay for my dinner. What am I? Some kind of amateur therapist whore? I don't want that anymore." I was literally stomping my feet. "You are not the only person with problems. You're not even the only person with major tragedy going on in their life. If we're going to be friends it has to go both ways." He nodded as if to say *Of course.* Yeah, right. Of course now that I'm yelling at you.

"Annie, I do want to be your friend. Very much."

"Now I'm leaving."

"I'll walk you."

"NO! I will take care of—I will walk myself."

"But . . ."

"Paul, I want to be alone." I really did. I really wanted to be totally alone to lick my wounds and eat my Rosie's brownies. All three of them, by myself, in a row. I took off down the street toward my apartment, hoping my ass looked okay. I wasn't expecting and hadn't planned for a long view of my behind. In retrospect I'm certain he didn't notice my ass one way or the other. I turned to see him leaning into the passenger window of a taxi.

I was still fuming, and covering ground quickly, especially considering the height of my heels and my aching feet. If I'd known my night would end like that instead of naked with Paul I'd have worn more practical shoes. I was oblivious to the late-night sounds as I limped along my street, almost home. I only realized at the last minute that Paul's taxi had been following me. This made me half-smile with relief. At least he cared enough to follow me home and make sure I was safe. That's something, right? Maybe he'd come in for tea and brownies and we could get back on track. I didn't want to hate him. I was already a little embarrassed by my outbursts.

I turned to Paul to invite him in. I looked to the back seat, a dark hollow with no person in it. Only then did it register with a jolt that there was no one in the cab except the driver, a scruffy guy wearing a plaid flannel shirt and picking his teeth with a toothpick.

"Your friend asked me to make sure you got home safe."

Of course. Of course he did. One last chance for me to get my hopes up only to have them come crashing down.

"Right. Well, I hope he tipped you well."

"Twenty bucks for a half mile. Not bad." Nope, not bad at all. At least someone got some benefit from this godforsaken evening. Well, since the cabbie was there, I thought he might as well finish the job.

"Would you mind waiting then just till I get inside?"

"Sure thing, miss."

It didn't make sense. Paul lived around the corner—why wouldn't he take the cab home, unless he really didn't want to deal with me? As much as I was the injured party here, he wasn't going to face it anymore that night.

I stormed into my apartment, kicked off my shoes, and stormed up the wide staircase. I'd never stormed before that I could recall. But tonight, I stormed. Like a three-year-old, stomping for the sake of being loud, of hearing my anger through my aching feet.

Dropping to my bed, I spotted my nemesis, the damn Relationship Box, sitting on my bedside table, mocking me. I rolled over so I could reach it. Opening the top, I took out my engagement ring from Eddie and placed it on the table, then rolled myself off of the bed and stormed some more to the far side of the apartment. I entered the kitchen and slammed down the Relationship Box on the counter. Yanking open the fridge, I pulled out a bottle of wine, left over from the roommate dinner. I cut off the casing and labored a little with the cork—where was a good screwtop when you needed it? Impatient, once it was open I drank straight from the bottle, then dove into the Rosie's brownies.

"Drunken mistake. I'll show you drunken." I drank more, in big, gasping swigs. "God, we buy cheap wine." I was seeing double. I retrieved a massive red toolbox from under the sink. Snapping it open, I pulled out a large hammer and placed the innocent Relationship Box on a nearby butcher block. I raised the hammer, and attempted to smash it. My first blow missed completely.

"Are you fucking kidding me?" I said out loud. Really loud. My next attempts to smash the sacrificial box were more successful. With a satisfying crunch, I flattened the container into a sad metal parallelogram, as stones went skidding across the countertop and onto the floor, coming to rest in the corners of the kitchen. I gave it one last hammer for good measure, drank more from the half-empty wine bottle, and popped the last of a brownie into my mouth, swallowing without tasting, or chewing for that matter, while surveying the carnage.

"My work here is done."

Retreating to my bedroom, I left on every light in the apartment and didn't care. I sprawled diagonally on my bed, and let my hair fall in a sheet over my face. I was too furious to cry, too sad to sleep, too distraught to put on pajamas. I just closed my eyes and tried to keep from playing the evening over in my mind. A few minutes later I heard the front door open; Elke was saying goodnight to someone. As she came up the stairs I feigned sleep, unable to bear repeating the humiliation of the night, especially since Elke was a witness to my careful preparation and expectations. She must have paused at my door, then crossed the room and gently placed the covers over me, smoothing my hair away from my face. I heard the familiar click as she picked up the cordless phone from its base on my nightstand, turned out the light, and left.

CHAPTER 44

The next morning, even before I opened my eyes I could tell I had a headache, blood pounding in my veins and crying out for hydration. I was in that unfortunate state of hangover insomnia where sleep was elusive despite every cell of mine pleading for silence and rest. After interminable minutes of lying face down into my pillow without falling back to sleep, I gave up and went in search of water and Alka-Seltzer. In the kitchen, over gulps of the fizzy hangover remedy, I spied the remnants of the Relationship Box and leaned over to pick up some of the stones and flattened metal.

I heard Stephen come in the front door, catching the trill of his off-key whistling as he ascended the stairs, sounding strangely awake for so early in the morning. I met him at the top of the staircase with my headache and my pieces.

"I think I got in touch with my anger last night," I said, following him into his room, showing him the stones and warped metal, explaining the cause of the sweet box's demise.

"I can't believe how well I fabricated the possibilities in my head," I said with genuine remorse.

"You're not the first person to do it," said Stephen. Perhaps he was referring to Elke. Or Blake. Or any number of the women who believed he was into them when he wasn't.

"He wasn't even a great kisser, but I was willing to let that go, you know?"

"Very generous of you."

"I bet he has a small penis."

"Whoa, Annie. That's hitting below the belt. No pun." Stephen looked at his watch. "Kiddo, I have to go. I just came home for a shower and to change. Are you coming to the office this morning?"

"Later, I need to go back to bed or I'll be useless. I think I'm still a little drunk."

After Stephen left, I was making myself another Alka-Seltzer hangover special when the telephone rang and I looked around for the cordless, which was off its base outside Elke's room, where I noticed a pair of men's shoes, fancy Italian ones, near the door.

"Hello?" I whispered, walking away from Elke's room to avoid waking her or Fancy Italian Shoe Man. I heard my mother's voice saying my name. My pulse raced; it was barely past eight a.m. and my mother would never call this early.

"Mum. What's wrong?" I could hear her doing the dishes through the phone, her silence punctuated by the occasional clang of stacking plates. Then the stacking stopped.

"Ah," she started, stammering. "Aunt Belle called us this morning. I have very sad news."

My heart stopped while my mind jumped to the worst scenario. "April?"

Then there was a ridiculous silence. A pregnant pause that said *Yes* louder than any words.

"Mum, tell me." I retreated to my bedroom and closed the door behind me.

"She—she died last night. Liz and Melody were with her. And the hospice nurse."

I dropped onto my bed. "Oh my God. I can't believe it."

"I know. It's just so sad. So sad."

"Oh my God. Poor Liz. Poor Melody. Poor April." It was impossible to process this news, especially with a hangover.

"How's Liz doing?" I asked. Sort of a dumb question, but an obvious one.

"She's with Aunt Belle and the hospice nurse. They have to make arrangements. They think the wake and the funeral will be next weekend. Are you working? Can you make it?"

"Mother, what kind of question is that? Of course I can make it."

"Well, I didn't know." I suspected this was part of my mother's coping—to focus on inane details like whether I could slip out of work for a wake and funeral of a beloved young relative.

"Mum, I'll call you later, okay?"

We said muted goodbyes and I curled up into a ball on my bed. The tears wouldn't come. Neither would sleep. I looked at my watch and wished I had someone to talk to, someone to tell. I tried Liz's house but hung up before the call connected—I just wasn't sure what would be most comforting to her. Elke always said that "pain shared is pain halved" but was that true in this case? Could anyone actually share in Liz's particular, unimaginable pain? Barbara didn't answer her phone. I couldn't reach Jodie, either. I was craving chocolate, and shuffled back down the hallway toward the kitchen, pausing outside Elke's room and noticing again the man's shoes, and after listening for signs of awakeness and hearing none, decided not to knock. In the kitchen I searched the cabinets, the fridge, the Speisekammer. There was no chocolate of any kind! I spotted Elke's box of Twinkies in the pantry and tore into one. The first bite fell in a lump to the bottom of my stomach, producing instant queasiness. I tossed the rest of it into the trash and wandered back to the far end of the apartment. I glanced into Stephen's room even though

I knew he was already gone. From the hallway, I looked out the window, through the trees.

My face felt greasy and my teeth had a fuzzy hangover film, and bits of golden sponge cake sticking to them, too. I needed a good brushing and a piece of gum. I washed my face, attended to my teeth, stared in the mirror. Willing the tears to come. Nothing.

I couldn't stand being inside the apartment a minute longer. I left, and walked and walked and walked.

CHAPTER 45

Through a teary blur, I watched my boots pass over vague stretches of brick that turned to crumbled gray asphalt as I took the corner on Broadway, moving forward but thoroughly unsure of where I was going, in search of comfort. I felt lucky that I had no experience with this kind of loss, but that left me on shaky ground for how to cope. April was barely double digits in birthdays, and even though she was what Elke called "an old soul," she was just a kid. A precious little daughter, sister, niece, cousin, granddaughter. I felt a pileup of emotions and thoughts and twitches and pangs. A tug of war played out on my insides, heaving back and forth between thankfulness for even a child-sized life, and devastation that April was actually gone. If I let myself drift to the sympathy I held for Liz, and Melody, and Aunt Belle, I would feel the tears form behind my eyes, disbelief washing over my shoulders as grief coursed through my body. After five or ten or thirty minutes of wandering—I wasn't at all sure—I was at the foot of the steps of Number 401, Eddie's apartment, Paul's temporary home. The last time I'd been inside was weeks ago, the night of Paul's so-called drunken mistake. It all seemed so unimportant now. I just needed someone to talk to, someone who would hug me. My brain was empty, a black unease pervading every part of my body and consuming my heart. I pulled out my cell and dialed the house phone, but it went immediately to voicemail. Someone was on the line.

My ability to make a decision had disappeared. At the top of the stoop, I considered the buzzer, feeling just as likely to press it as to abandon the entire idea and flee, but then a neighbor exited and politely held the door for me. It felt rude not to accept the gesture, so I mouthed a thank you and stepped into the foyer and climbed the stairs to Unit 4, knocking, hoping he was there. My watch indicated it was past nine, but he might be asleep. He was probably asleep. I knocked again anyway.

A few seconds ticked away, then not Paul but Eddie opened the door tentatively, shielding most of his body and looking puzzled, probably at the sight of my tearstained face and reddened eyes in his hallway. By that point, I surely looked like I'd been punched in the face.

"Annie?" His hair was wet. He was holding a toothbrush and wiping blue toothpaste from the corner of his mouth, and as far as I could tell, wearing only his boxers. I stared without speaking, not sure why I was surprised to see Eddie in his own apartment, wishing that Paul had answered, to finally for once be there when I needed someone. And I so legitimately needed someone.

But it was Eddie who was standing there, concern creased in his forehead, trying to make sense in those passing seconds of my unexpected appearance on his doorstep on a random Saturday morning. "What's wrong, Annie?"

I couldn't say it. It was partly that I couldn't bring myself to put words to my shock and grief. And partly because a blinding flash of the obvious came into sharp relief—Eddie would be as crushed as I was, or nearly so, and it was quite clear, from the normalcy of his teeth-brushing and by virtue of him looking perfectly composed, that he hadn't heard the news. Finally, after what felt like minutes but was probably ten seconds at most, I cleared my throat and whispered. "It's April. She's gone. Last night."

Eddie's eyes closed for a second and he seemed to take in a deep quiet breath. When he opened his eyes again he wordlessly pulled me into the apartment, placed his toothbrush on the table and wrapped his arms around me, holding me close and smoothing my hair. The gesture was so loving and generous that I could feel a fresh wave of unshed tears building in my throat, craving release.

"Oh, no," he whispered into my temple. "Oh, no."

"I tried to call. It went to voicemail." I was talking into Eddie's shoulder. His skin was cool and he smelled clean, like Ivory soap.

"Shhh. It's okay." His voice was soothing and his arms were solid around me; I wanted to lose myself in the comfort of his strength. Other than the occasional cheek-kiss hello or friendly hug goodbye, I'd never been physically this close to Eddie for more than two or three seconds. Now I felt aware of his body next to mine for the first time, his near-nakedness blending with my bone-level exhaustion. As the devastation and sense of loss seeped in, every one of my defenses was down, I was all unprotected nerves and still unshed tears, unable to pinpoint my feelings. Eddie took a breath and I could feel the rise and fall of his chest against mine, and his tender way of holding me gave way to a charge that was raw and strangely sexual. I felt traces of heat and longing escape and fill the space between us, mingling with genuine confusion. As if he came to the same realization at the same time, Eddie broke our embrace and stepped away and toward his room, apparently to pull on some clothes. I was jolted to the present moment, realizing Eddie was barely dressed and feeling embarrassed by our intimacy, but also noticing his toned and well-built body and wanting to touch it again. I wanted him to come back, to wrap his arms back around me and help me feel something other than oppressive sadness.

Eddie returned, zippering his jeans and then he looked up, but not at me. His eyes, and now mine, were taking in the pewter shoes, lying toe to toe under the coffee table like fallen angels, funky high heels that unmistakably belonged to Billie the waitress from the night before, perfectly situated in front of the sofa and beneath two empty wine glasses. I exchanged a look with Eddie.

There was muted conversation and giggling coming from behind Paul's bedroom door and it was getting louder. I turned back to Eddie.

"I have to go." The talking was louder, the giggling sickening.

Eddie said, "Let me come with you. Annie, let me come with . . ." Paul's doorknob was turning. I looked back at Eddie. I felt nauseated and desperate to be gone from there, seeing no point to adding humiliation to the layers of awfulness that were accumulating rapidly.

"No, it's okay."

Eddie reached out for me and grasped my arm.

"Annie —"

"No! Let me go. Eddie, please let me go."

I broke away and raced out of the apartment and down Broadway, oblivious to anything other than the pain. I didn't know what to make of it, but somehow I relished the scene I'd just departed, welcomed the sting of realizing Paul was with the waitress, adding insult to injury, and fueling a rage I didn't know I was capable of but that felt entirely appropriate under the circumstances. And finally, finally, I was able to really cry. I raced home and retreated to my bed, pulling the duvet around me like a cocoon, covering myself with pillows. I couldn't remember a time when I sobbed so hard, in great rhythmic bursts, until I fell asleep.

Hours later, I awoke and found Elke in the kitchen. She offered me tea and a slice of French banana bread. I had the impression that Elke simply thought I was sleeping late, so I sat down with her and shared the news about April.

"Oh, Anna, I am so very sorry to hear this."

"I can't believe it. I can't believe this sweet little girl. I can't believe she actually died." I was out of tears.

"But, you knew . . ." Elke looked at me, seeming confused, as she poured the boiling water into my mug, looking to confirm that this was expected, perhaps to make sure she remembered correctly that the doctors had told us there was no hope.

"No, I didn't. Only in my head. In my heart of hearts, I really thought she was going to make it. I think I needed to believe it could happen, that she could beat it. How stupid is that?" I looked up at Elke; it was not a rhetorical question. I really wanted to know why I'd let myself hold onto hope even when the doctors said it was hopeless. Maybe if I'd accepted it, then I would have felt more ready than I did to hear that she had actually died. I remembered a class in business school on human behavior. The big lesson was that humans will do almost anything to avoid pain. A sign of emotional health was a willingness to move *through* pain, rather than contort oneself to try to circumvent it. I was proving to be a master pain avoider.

I chose to avoid recounting to Elke any of the details of the blowup with Paul or the debacle with the pewter shoes, or of my inexplicable rebuffing of Eddie's kindness. The whole of the last twenty-four hours was one great big clusterfuck. And I still couldn't make any sense of the Eddie encounter, which was just so bizarre and the strangest feeling. He had hugged me for such a long time, and it was just so nice to be held, feeling so sad, but then it turned into this sexual thing and it went so quickly from being natural to intense to unbelievably awkward. I felt so outside of myself, like I'd lost control completely.

Elke was cutting more banana bread. I wished there were chocolate chips inside, the way my mother made it.

CHAPTER 46

I didn't need to drive by myself to the wake. I could have gone with my parents, or either of my siblings, or Barbara and Jimmy. But I wanted to be alone, to not have to talk. Shockingly, I was on time, and agreed to meet my sister and brother at their hotel before heading to the funeral home for the first set of visiting hours. I spotted my brother sitting by the window, drinking a beer. I looked at my watch; it was ten a.m.

"Andy, what are you doing?"

"Trying to deal with the death of a ten-year-old. That's what I'm doing," he replied, and took a big swig of his Coors Light. I was warming to the trend of the people in my life just saying it like it is. I went with Andy and Jodie to the funeral parlor, a majestic old Victorian home converted from a private residence a few decades before.

I looked around the generously sized rooms where the wake was being held. I was thankful that there wasn't another wake happening at the same time. The rooms across the hall were empty, the sign that would normally hold another name was blank. I glimpsed Eddie across the room. I tried to make eye contact, I wanted to talk to him, to smooth things over and apologize for abandoning him the other day. He didn't look my way and I didn't see him again that morning.

I spotted my parents across the room and closed the distance between us in a few steps. I could see that my mother brought her steely self-control. My father was teary. We exchanged heavy hugs and cheek kisses.

"How's Liz?" I asked.

"She's okay," my mother said. "They gave her a pill." We stood together for a little while without talking.

"Well, I guess I should go pay my respects." I noticed the line momentarily shrink and I could see Liz through the crowd for the first time. My father nodded his support, unable to speak. His new cell phone, which he wore attached to a holster on his belt, started to ring, so he picked it up quickly and headed outside to take the call. I felt my mother's hand grip my forearm in a tight hold. "Whatever you do, don't look at the pictures." Her lips formed a straight line, her head shook a somber, slight "no" and her eyes closed. "Too sad."

I glanced toward Liz, who was wearing a blue suit and flat shoes, clutching a tissue and Melody. Next to her, a collage of pictures, glued to a flimsy poster board, leaned in a curve against a lightweight easel. Her warning against the pictures was my mother trying to protect me, and I couldn't listen. I needed to be sad, to step into the pain, to stop avoiding. I didn't know if I could actually handle my mother being anything other than a rock, but on some level I wished she could experience the feeling that came when you let yourself really face how much you cared. How deeply and how much you could actually feel—not think, not analyze, but *feel*—about somebody.

I joined the back of the receiving line and shuffled in step with the people in front of me toward Liz. When I reached my cousin we hugged tightly and for a long time. Liz was crying again. Melody brought her a tissue, and that made her cry more.

As I was waiting to kneel in front of the diminutive casket, I couldn't bring myself to look at April. I knew she'd be there in her Sleeping Beauty dress, with daisies in her hair, surrounded by

Beanie Babies, just like she planned. Instead I focused on the collage of photographs. It included two of me and April. Near the middle was the one that Pete the Homicide Photographer had taken at Barbara's wedding. We were beaming at the camera with matching smiles. I kept my eyes fixed on the pictures until it was my turn to kneel.

When the space cleared in front of me, I concentrated on finding the kneeler, positioned right in front of the casket, inches from its shiny white exterior. Most people went in pairs. I was alone so the space next to me on the kneeler was empty. Why hadn't I waited for Jodie? I tried to remember a prayer from St. Mary's Parochial School and to think of something to do. I was my mother, staring at my own hands, unable to look up, garbling the Lord's Prayer in my head, which had little to do with what I wanted to say to God about April. Or to April about God. How long had I been kneeling there? Twenty seconds? I saw out of my peripheral vision that someone tall had knelt beside me. When I realized it was Eddie, an instantaneous wave of relief reached my throat. He didn't look at me, he just gazed at April. His presence had the interesting effect of solidifying what I wanted, which was time to focus on April, on what she had meant to me, to say goodbye. I took a deep breath and lifted my eyes. At first to the white patent-leather Mary Janes, then the silk and organza princess dress. I started to lose it when I saw Fleece, the little lamb Beanie Baby that everyone in our family seemed to have, resting near April's hands, which were clasped as if in prayer. When I spotted the daisy wreath resting on April's bald little head, I sensed the people behind me, waiting patiently for their turn. I might be taking too much time. I made a sign of the cross—possibly in reverse order, I couldn't recall moments afterward—and lifted myself and my heavy heart up and away. Eddie didn't follow me; when I turned to talk to him he had disappeared.

I suddenly, desperately, wanted to speak to him. Of all the people in this room, Eddie might understand best how I was feeling. Like me, his relationship with April had been paradoxically stronger because of her illness. He was one "outsider" who showed up consistently for April for the last six months, who played endlessly with Melody so Liz and April could have time alone. Who made April feel like she was the most precious thing in the world. Who played Pretty Pretty Princess a hundred times as if it were entirely desirable and normal for a thirty-something man to wear blue plastic earrings and covet the pink ring. Who listened to April when she asked him to marry me, and displayed the same confidence and cool that he had with the silly garter toss at Barbara's wedding when buying a strawberry-flavored candy ring and getting down on one knee and proposing. Who knew how important birthdays were. It was Eddie who gave April some of the most special gifts in her last months and weeks and days of her life. If there could be more clear evidence of decency and character I didn't know what it was and I certainly didn't know why I couldn't see this more clearly until now.

Eddie was the same guy who'd been so kind and sweet to me despite my abject disinterest. What the hell was wrong with me not to really notice him sooner? It would be easy to dismiss my behavior as longstanding blindness to what a good man looks like, or as superficial because Eddie did have a mullet, after all. And technically he was a used-car salesman, though I did finally get it that he was more of a general manager than I'd ever been, screw my advanced business degree. But that wasn't it. I was finally getting it. It wasn't the superficialities (and my own desire to upgrade my life) that were responsible for my keeping emotional distance from Eddie. It was actually the deeper parts of him that unconsciously frightened me, terrifying because he was more honest and mature and quiet and strong and *intimate* than I was capable of handling. This was striking me as ironic and sad, that I'd so far missed out on really knowing him because of my own fears and incapacity for true closeness. And I'd probably blown it—Eddie was too self-assured in his own way to tolerate my indifference forever. Interestingly, the same impulses that kept me guarded from Eddie in the months since I'd met him were waking up now that he was probably about done with me. That was messed up, and I knew it.

I spotted Eddie outside by Jimmy's black Maxima. He was wearing a dark suit and sunglasses, and the two of them were pulling bottles from a small cooler in the trunk. My siblings had joined them, and no one made any effort to hide their Sam Adams. The beer was looking tempting to me, too. I took a deep breath and prepared to approach Eddie, when Liz tapped me on the shoulder from behind.

"Annie, would you please take Melody for a walk? She's upset and she's upsetting me." I looked down at Melody, whose blonde curls were falling over her bright blue eyes, rimmed by lashes dotted with tears. Liz transferred Melody's tiny hand to mine.

"Of course I will. Come on Melody, let's go for a walk." I started toward the Maxima and Eddie, but decided against it, imagining it wouldn't be entirely appropriate to bring Melody there—there was something wrong and strange about drinking beer in the parking lot of a funeral home. Or perhaps it was because I knew I couldn't talk to Eddie for real if I was responsible for Melody. In any case, it no longer seemed the opportune time to see him. Instead I retrieved Melody's fake-fur coat, the white one with black spots that Melody called her Dalmatian Coat—and we headed for a bench at the side of the building, where I could let Melody try on my pumps, the ones that she called "the clapping shoes," and clomp around the parking lot, completely absorbed in the sound of the tapping heels.

CHAPTER 47

The funeral was a blur, but a welcome one, a quiet ritual of tribute and goodbye. I was struck by the somber feeling of the entire service, how silent everyone was, how dry-eyed. It was a collective holding it together, until the end, when Liz honored April's request to play her favorite song, the one we'd heard countless times over the months, which Liz had played twice the night her daughter died. When the familiar notes of "Angels Among Us" were heard over the church's loudspeakers, it was as if April were coaxing the tears from everyone who loved her, helping us grieve and heal from her place in heaven.

Eddie sat with Barbara and Jimmy, many pews away from me and my family, and he didn't seek me out at any point during the church service or the subdued party afterward. I started to think he was avoiding me, and if I reflected on it, I was probably avoiding him, too, since I was no longer sure he wanted anything to do with me. Could it be that I'd angered him that much by refusing to stay with him—or let him come with me—that morning we heard of April's death? There had to be more to it, and I feared that it was the cumulative effect of my indifference and disregard. I felt guilty and wrong, and I couldn't bring myself to approach him.

I had told Stephen I would be back in the office sometime the next week, Monday at the earliest, but I found it difficult to be around my family, where no one felt it appropriate to talk about anything except April's death, but they couldn't do that, so no one said anything at all. In addressing a shared need, it would seem, for some means of reestablishing order, most of my family became immediately preoccupied with other activities—clearing out the garage, making meatballs for dinner, alphabetizing a bookshelf—and I felt alone and useless. I decided to head back to Cambridge earlier than expected, and went straight to the office.

Stephen and Jeet were sitting on top of a desk in the GoodMatch.com office, clinking beer bottles. When he saw me Stephen immediately stood to hug me and whisper his condolences in my ear. Jeet mumbled, "I'm sorry." It was sweet. I wanted to change the subject.

"Tell me something that isn't sad and has nothing to do with wakes or funerals," I said.

Stephen looked more relaxed than he had in months, and announced they'd finally closed the bridge financing round, with Paul in the lead. This financing would hold us over until the bigger money came in.

"Whew, that was a close call," I said. "I'm so glad it worked out."

"Paperwork is even signed. Thanks for coming in. I wasn't expecting you," Stephen said.

"I feel better when I'm useful anyway," I replied. "It didn't make sense to sit around my parents' house and watch them practice pain avoidance. My family doesn't grieve particularly well. Everyone was back to work and their same routine the next day. And I was stressing out about getting this bridge financing done."

"I hope it didn't make things awkward with Paul," said Stephen.

"Nah. It's a non-issue. I finally got it through my head that relationship isn't going anywhere, and you know what, it's totally okay."

"Really?"

"He's not the right guy for me."

"When did you figure that out?"

"I think it was something April told me. Or showed me. Anyway, I redefined what is right for me."

I arrived home to what seemed like an empty apartment. I dumped my things at the foot of the stairs. As I moved down the hallway and approached the kitchen, I heard voices. I couldn't tell who was there exactly, but I could see Elke from behind, her long hair loose and flowing down her back, and it appeared that a guy was sitting in front of her, shirtless and with a towel around his neck, like he'd just emerged from the shower. I knew Elke wouldn't be expecting me back home until tomorrow at the earliest, so I hoped I wasn't interrupting something. It wasn't as if Elke's lovers and I hadn't had our accidental encounters in the past six months, like the time I popped into the bathroom to get my brush only to realize Elke wasn't alone in the shower, or the time when a half-asleep, possibly intoxicated overnight guest got the wrong door and attempted to climb into bed with me.

I cleared my throat to announce my presence, and Elke turned around and, in doing so, moved slightly aside, revealing the guy. It was Eddie. Well, of course it was Eddie! This was the way my life worked. Eddie sitting there with wet hair and no shirt, with Elke in exceptionally close proximity, in the middle of our kitchen. Once the scene registered fully in my brain I didn't know what to make of it.

"Oh, hey, Annie." Eddie sounded embarrassed.

"Annika, we weren't expecting you yet," Elke said. More evidence that I'd caught them.

"Yeah, I came back early. Don't let me interrupt." I felt stupid standing there and invented a purpose for being in the kitchen. I opened the refrigerator, took out a beer, then retreated quickly, back to my room.

I spilled beer on my button-down shirt, took it off and tossed it on the bed. I was wearing a white tank top underneath, and jeans. I kicked off my shoes. Eddie knocked on my door and stepped in. I was sitting on the small sofa at the foot of my bed, with my back to him. When I heard him there, I absently crossed my arms to cover up.

"Annie."

"Yes." I offered the word as if I were confirming that I was in fact Annie, not as a question inviting continued dialogue. I was mad and hadn't had time to figure out if I should show it or hide it. I gulped some more beer.

"How are you doing?" Eddie continued. "How is everyone?"

"Fine. Everyone is fine." I was caught in this confusing place of wanting to scream and cry. I allowed a long pause and I could feel Eddie standing there behind me, probably trying to figure out my chilly attitude. I was so tired of this. So tired of not getting anything that I really wanted, of having things get messed up all the time, of knowing it was probably all my fault. I turned to look at him.

"She's leaving in three weeks you know. She's going home to her boyfriend in Germany. At most she wants to fuck you. I didn't take you for that," I said.

Eddie looked taken aback. He'd never heard me talk like that. *I'd* never heard me talk like that.

"Take me for what? You don't even know what you're talking about."

I stood and turned toward Eddie, who moved into the room,

closer to me. I was still holding my beer bottle and saw again that Eddie was wearing only a pair of jeans—no shirt and no shoes. Shit, he had a hot body. How did I fail to recognize this for so long?

"Don't I? I've lived with Elke for almost half a year. I've watched the parade of men. Don't think you're the first. You probably won't be the last." Yes, that was fair. Three weeks was plenty of time for Elke to meet a new fling, or two. Bees to honey, that's just who she was, she couldn't help it. I continued to drink. I didn't really believe what I was saying. Well, yes, the facts were right, but I didn't feel the way I sounded.

"Annie, could you be more judgmental?" asked Eddie, shaking his head. "As though it's the biggest crime in the world for two people to sleep together. Why do you even care?"

I didn't care who Elke slept with, so long as it wasn't Eddie.

"I guess I shouldn't expect you to be different from every other guy I know," I said.

"I didn't know you had any expectations of me," Eddie replied.

"It just bothers me, Eddie. It bothers me how it changes things. Elke and Stephen, then she almost went after Paul. Now you? Why does she have to go after everyone in my life?"

This made Eddie angry; I could see it in his eyes.

"Am I in your life, Annie?" Eddie asked.

I didn't like anger, and tried to joke. "Well, technically you're my fiancé," I said.

Eddie looked at me with no expression, not laughing, not appreciating my joke.

"I did that for April, not you," he replied.

Ouch. This was not going well. I had never seen Eddie like this. I was intrigued.

"Elke may be a bit more free than you understand, since you

know nothing about her world, but at least she doesn't judge people the way you do. She's just enjoying herself."

I realized I was focusing on the wrong thing. It wasn't Elke's behavior that was upsetting to me. We'd actually come to an understanding over our months of living together, and I'd come to admire her confidence and appreciate her openness and carefree ways, which never hurt a soul, and Elke had been the most supportive presence in my attempts to get back out there dating.

"Eddie, Elke and I are friends. I care for her a great deal. It's not like I'm constantly judging her. But it's true, I can't relate."

"The reason you're so frustrated with Elke is because she dares to do what you can't, she actually puts her own needs first, she asks for what she needs and wants from other people, and, most egregious of all, she doesn't feel guilty when she gets it."

I looked at him funny.

"Yes, I know what egregious means." Eddie was now clearly annoyed with me. How did this all turn 180 degrees so quickly?

"Eddie, I didn't—"

"The day you start realizing that you deserve what you want is the day you'll stop being so angry at everyone who already knows that."

"What are you talking about? I'm not angry!" I shouted.

"You are so angry. You are angry and scared," Eddie said. I was completely taken aback.

"I need another beer."

As I stormed away, I stepped on a wayward, sharp-edged stone from the smashed Relationship Box, which sat repaired on a nearby shelf. I winced and limped out of the room. I walked hard to the kitchen, retrieved a beer, threw the bottle cap across the room, and slammed the refrigerator door shut. I spotted Elke's haircutting shears resting on a paper towel on the counter, wet.

Eddie had followed me, and when he spoke, I jumped.

"Annie, why are you drinking? It's four o'clock in the afternoon."

"It's called a coping mechanism, Eddie. For my anger and fear."

"And sadness," he added.

"Eddie, I've been crying for a week. I'm drained and defenseless. I don't know how to respond to what you're saying. And more to the point, I don't know why you're saying it." I looked out the window and saw Elke sitting outside.

"Annie, I've been interested in you since I met you, and you have passively rejected me at every turn. I've been patient, but there's only so much of that one person can take. And now only because you see me with Elke do you even notice . . . what is this, junior high?"

I couldn't believe what I was hearing. Eddie was right, I hadn't treated him well. I had taken him for granted, I had treated him as unimportant, and he was finally calling me on it.

"Eddie, that's not it. It's not about seeing you with Elke."

"What is it then? What?"

Eddie was really irritated with me, and I hated it. I swallowed hard. I wanted to tell him. To say something that would show my true feelings. To acknowledge that I felt amazing chemistry that morning I went to his apartment, that I'd thought about him every day since. That I was dying to be close to him again. To kiss him and to know him differently than I had before. But I was ashamed of my behavior and I couldn't do it. I couldn't risk his anger and the possibility he'd shoot me down.

"Nothing. It's nothing. You're right about the way I treated you. I'm sorry."

"Yes, it is nothing." Eddie looked at me for a long moment,

then grabbed his shirt off the back of the kitchen chair, stepped into his shoes, picked up three shopping bags that I had failed to notice before, and left. I heard the door slam behind him. I looked out the window, expecting to see him with my roommate. But he merely waved to Elke and kept going.

I rushed downstairs and crossed the short distance to join Elke. Eddie was barely visible in the distance. Elke offered a welcoming look as I approached. I didn't know where to begin.

"Anna, how are you doing? How is your family?"

"Thanks for asking, Elke. Everyone is doing okay. Not Liz, but I don't think she'll be the same for the rest of her life. But I think the funeral was good for healing, you know?"

"Yes, I do. Such markings of passing can be lovely and astonishing. I am inspired by April's strength. I cannot hardly fathom a ten-year-old with such poise and grace. What a remarkable child."

"Elke, it is so true. She's just the most amazing spirit. So much more mature than, say, me."

"Oh, Anna, don't be so hard on yourself. You've been through a lot."

We sat on the lawn, quietly, for a few minutes before I brought up Eddie.

"Elke, he looks so good. What did you do?"

"It was nothing. A little updating, that is all," Elke shrugged.

"So, you and Eddie?"

"Well, I will admit I tried for something more, but we are just friends," said Elke.

"Excuse me? But I thought . . . Elke, you don't have any male friends." I spoke with only kindness and honesty, without judgment.

"Yes, I tried it this once," Elke replied. "Was not bad. I will next try with Stephen. But what about *you* and Eddie?"

"What about?" I said in a tone that matched my depression. "There's nothing. It seems he got over me just about the time I opened my eyes to him." I paused, reflecting on the last half hour. "Why didn't I notice him before?"

"It is hard to look past a, what you call it, a mullet," Elke offered and made me laugh.

"And he wasn't putting up with any of my stupidity," I added. "That's so attractive."

"But Anna," asked Elke, "if you're interested, surely there's something to be explored?"

"I don't think so. He's so pissed off at me and he's right. I have taken him totally for granted. And I underestimated him and offended him. I don't have the right to ask anything more of him now."

Elke looked at me and sighed.

"Anna, you have this all wrong. I know for a fact that Eddie wants you to ask more of him now. We talked about it. I was helping him."

"When did you talk about it? What do you mean, helping him?"

"Anna, just because we have no secrets, I will tell you that Eddie was my date last week, when you went out with Paul and I went to Club Passim. But despite my ideas he was not tempted. He seems to subscribe to the same silly roommate rules that you do." She smiled. "You're a match. And I convinced him he needed some updating, to get you to see him a little differently. It is something I might refer to in Germany as Übereinstimmung, which in this case—Eddie's case—means roughly making his outward expression of his personality and style match his insides. I thought he needed to get your attention in a new way."

"Well, I like what you've done, but I was already thinking about him differently. Ever since the morning we found out April died."

"Anna, if you feel for him, and want him, would you please get out of your head and abandon your misplaced logic and pursue the man?"

"What do you mean? Literally follow him home?"

"Yes, I think you should move yourself over there and tell him how you feel and what you want. Now."

I moved quickly before I lost my nerve. Elke was right. I trusted her. I couldn't think my way out of pursuing something so important. If there was any chance of Eddie forgiving me and letting me into his life, I needed to try. I covered the distance between our apartments in record time. I bounded up the steps and buzzed Eddie's apartment, and heard Paul's voice over the intercom.

"Hey, Paul. It's Annie. Can I come up?"

I was perspiring and slightly out of breath, so I took the stairs more slowly than I'd been walking. Composing myself, I knocked on the door and Paul answered.

"Hey, Annie. I was just going to call you."

I was distracted, eager to see Eddie and have this sorted.

"Really," I answered, looking past him for signs of Eddie.

"Yeah, I was hoping we could talk. I know I was a jerk, but I got some news, from Susie. And now you're here."

"I'm sorry Paul, I don't have time right now. Is Eddie here?"

"Huh? Oh, no. He isn't—"

"Oh. If you see him, please tell him I came by."

"Uh, okay. Hey, what about tomorrow or next week?"

"Next week?" I was confused.

"For us, to get together."

"Paul, maybe. Call me and we'll see." I turned to leave quickly, wondering where Eddie had gone.

I heard Paul murmuring "Ah, okay . . ." as I exited. I shuffled down the stairs and exited the building just as Eddie was arriving, shopping bags in one hand and a Starbucks in the other. We nearly collided on the steps.

"Hey, what are you doing here?" Eddie asked.

"Just trying to find you," I said.

"Oh?"

"I just, I forgot to tell you something, at my house. I wanted to tell you . . ."

"Yes?" Eddie put his bags down and sipped his coffee, watching me squirm.

"I realize that you're right about some things and I'm sorry. But you're not right about Elke. It wasn't Elke that made me snap."

Eddie leaned against the stoop railing, settling in, it would seem, then tossed his coffee cup into a trash can a few feet away.

"Remember the day April died, when I came over?"

"Of course," Eddie said.

I tried to figure out how to explain this. Did I go chronologically? Hit on just the highlights? Or jump to the punch line, that I'm all of a sudden hot for him? This lack of preparation and rehearsal was unsettling. "I was surprised by how that made me feel, seeing you that day," I stammered.

"It was a terrible day. I also remember you ran away pretty quickly," Eddie said.

"I know, but it wasn't about running away from you. It was Paul, and the waitress. I'm so sorry about that. You were being so kind and I was a . . . freak."

"Sounds about right."

I implored with my eyes for him to be nice to me, like he'd always—*always*—been. I so wanted to regain his kindness, his warm regard, his quiet presence in my life.

"I knew you were upset, Annie, but so was I. And it's those kinds of situations that tell you how someone really feels, and all I know is you were running away."

"I was confused. About a few things."

"Excuse me?" Eddie seemed curious. My eyes were averted. This sucked. I didn't have the words.

"I don't know what it was. Something felt different. And it caught me by surprise. But it was such a sad time, then the shoes, and the laughing, oh God, I had to go. But I looked for you! Later at the wake, and the funeral. I did want to see you."

"Why?" He sounded irritated.

I looked at him, unable to express how I was feeling. Better put, I knew words wouldn't cut it. I took a deep breath.

"Why, Annie? Why did you want to see me?" Eddie asked again.

"What is with the questions?" I asked. "Why. You want to know why. I think you know why. I think, but of course, I'm not totally sure anymore."

Eddie looked completely confused. "Annie, has anyone ever told you that you talk too much? Sometimes you talk a lot without saying anything." He smirked, which looked a bit like a smile, and with his smirk-smile it seemed to me like he'd moved from annoyance to amusement at my fumbling inability to express myself. I sensed this was my chance. I needed to act. If there was a chance of recapturing Eddie's interest, the time was now. I looked again at him, taking in his face, realizing he had one of those faces that became more and more attractive especially once you could see the depth and beauty coming through from the inside, too. He was standing above me; I was on the second step to his third.

"What I'm trying to say . . ." I began. I bit my lip and Eddie tilted his head to the other side, this time not interrupting or responding to me, but looking incredibly attractive, thoughtful, patient.

"... is maybe I should stop talking ..." Eddie grinned. It was time to silence my inner critic, the one telling me I was undeserving of Eddie because I had dismissed him for so long. The truth was, before then I couldn't see past my own misguided priorities and preoccupation with Paul to really *see* Eddie, who had been nothing but wonderful and loyal and kind in the entire time I'd known him. Now that I knew I felt chemistry with him, well, all bets were off. I just hoped I wasn't too late, hadn't blown it completely. And with that thought I lifted my eyes and took in his, and it hit me. I needed to kiss him. Okay, wanted to kiss him. Needs, wants, whatever. It was all good and pointing in the same direction. Without giving myself time to analyze whether he would kiss me back, I touched his arm and pulled myself onto his step and moved forward, closing the gap on platonic, and with our height difference, I could no longer see his eyes, just his lovely mouth. Omigod, how could I have not realized before what a great mouth he had! With my hand still resting on his arm, I leaned forward and kissed him, at first slightly hesitant, then when I could feel him responding, sexy and full. I could feel his lips smiling between kisses.

"That's better than talking," Eddie whispered to me and kissed me again, this time pulling me into him so I could feel the firmness of his chest and his lean arms wrapped around me. "So, I guess it wasn't just the haircut?" Eddie asked between kisses.

"Don't even think about growing it back."

CHAPTER 48

I was using the whiteboard on the wall adjacent to my desk to brainstorm a new marketing idea, trying to keep from being distracted by thoughts of Eddie, when Stephen walked into the office, grinning.

"Anyone have a bottle of champagne?" he asked in my direction.

"What's up?" I asked, wondering what the good news was, always eager to hear it.

"Just finished meeting with DNGI. They're in. Probably for fifteen. We have to work out the details."

"Fifteen? Million?!" I was astonished. In a good way.

Stephen couldn't stop smiling.

"No champagne, but I have a couple of Diet Cokes," I offered.

"Good enough."

I retrieved the beverages and took a seat atop my desk while Stephen flopped onto the nearby futon.

"Cheers to financing," I offered.

"Cheers to you and the team for keeping things going while I've been so preoccupied," Stephen replied.

"You know, the magic ingredient here is Jeet. He's the one you have to thank," I said. "And keep. Make sure you don't let that guy go anywhere." It was true. The kid was a prodigy, and without him we'd never have been able to launch the site, develop innovative marketing partnerships, or keep the development team on track and engaged.

I hopped off the desk and walked around so I could access the file cabinet underneath, and retrieved a document from the bottom drawer.

"Stephen, there's something I want to tell you."

"Yeah?" Stephen had no idea what I was giving him.

"I don't think I want to go on the VC ride with GoodMatch.com. I know it's the right next step for the company, but I've worked too hard to become assistant vice president of promotional emails or whatever will happen when the new VP of Marketing gets hired."

"Annie, it wouldn't be like that," Stephen said.

"Hear me out. I'm just saying that the stuff about a start-up that I love—the creativity, the responsibility—changes when you grow as fast as the venture guys will require."

"Well, I can't argue with that," said Stephen.

"I may not be General Manager of the Universe," I said. "But I'd like to be general manager of something. So I have a proposal for you."

I handed him the document, with "GoodMatch.com Events" typed on the title page. "I want to start my own company. I will handle the live events part of the business and you'll give me an exclusive contract and a marketing agreement." I watched to see Stephen's reaction.

"Interesting."

"And you'll sign these agreements before you sign the DNGI deal, so the venture guys can't squash it," I said. "I'll make it work for both of us. I won't siphon GoodMatch resources. I put it all in this plan. Take a look."

"Okay, Anna-belle. I will do that today."

CHAPTER 49

I moved quickly through the apartment, readying it for the swarm of guests that would soon be arriving for the bittersweet occasion of Elke's goodbye party. I passed the bathroom mirror and paused to note the depressing predictability of my all-black party outfit, and frowned.

"What is wrong?" Elke asked as she appeared behind me in the mirror. She was smashing in silver-gray silk pants and satin bustier and a magnificent necklace she'd found in a vintage shop in Porter Square.

"Oh, nothing. I wish I had something other than this to wear," I sighed.

"Aha! But you do!" Elke disappeared and returned a moment later with a dry cleaning bag draped over her arm. "I forgot to pack this, and I have decided to bequeath it to you, Anna." She held up the sock dress and handed it to me. "This is perfect for tonight."

"Elke, I couldn't possibly!" Seriously, a sock dress? On me?

"Yes, you can possibly, and you must."

After a few minutes of cajoling I'd relented and tried on the magic sock dress. And it *was* magic—the cut, color and fabric were a stunning combination and even though it looked entirely different on me than on Elke—for one thing, longer, given our height difference—it was undeniably spectacular.

Elke was heading back to Germany the next morning, and we'd packed and shipped her things earlier in the day and turned her bedroom into a dance floor by hanging flashing white Christmas lights at eye level around the perimeter of the room. We invited everyone we knew to the party, and pored over Elke's GoodMatch.com listing, selected the best of the best of her many suitors and invited them all to come. Then we filled our guest list with equal amounts of fabulous women so that the balance would be right, because to my delight, the party was doubling as market research for my business, which would be launching in three short months with a series of launch-party style events in Boston, New York and San Francisco.

As our guests started to arrive, I made a final appraisal of myself and the sock dress in my bedroom mirror and decided to tie a silky cardigan around my waist, which dressed it down just a little but happily achieved the effect I was going for.

Jodie and Christopher were among the first to arrive.

"Annie, I love the dress," said Jodie, while Christopher stashed their coats. "But nothing screams *I'm trying to hide my ass* like a sweater tied around it."

"I'm not hiding my ass!" I said, as Elke joined us and made a face at my attempt at accessorizing.

"Good. Then this has to go." Jodie untied the sweater and tossed it above my head to Elke before I could object, and pulled me toward the bar.

Soon our apartment was swelling with the good mood of dozens of friends and acquaintances. All of my special guests from the GoodMatch launch party would be making a reappearance tonight, and I was amused to see Milly Knight, the wine proprietress, hitting it off with Stephen in the corner. Jeet was flirting. Jodie and Christopher were tasting Milly's wine and talking into each other's ears over the music, my brother Andy was chatting about politics with Chris Macadamia, and Barbara and Jimmy were just arriving. As I watched my family mixing with my friends and colleagues, I felt happy.

I found Elke in the kitchen and pulled her aside.

"Elke, I really cannot believe you are leaving. I don't want you to go," I said, and meant it.

"Oh, Anna, I feel the same. I wish I could stay. For you, and also for *this!*" She indicated the throngs of men eager to make her acquaintance. "I am eating this up, as you say, all this attention!"

"But Elke, you *always* get this much attention!"

"It is not true! Once I am back in Germany, my looks, they are a dozen for a dime."

"What did you say?"

"Ah, yes, this is the last I will expect of ceaseless attention from the men."

It had never occurred to me that Elke's daily life would be that different in Germany than here, and in an instant the past several months snapped into focus.

Elke continued, "This is my last night of this outrageous situation, and I think I should take full advantage, don't you?"

"Of course I do!"

Stephen came by with a tray full of Jaegermeister shots and handed one to Elke. They had managed to forge a warm friendship and found it easy to laugh with each other now. I slipped past them and headed back into the living room. Then I saw him. Coming down the hallway, looking handsome as ever, was Paul Dennison. And that could mean only one thing. Yes, as Paul stepped into the party, there was Eddie, carrying a gorgeous bouquet of peonies, which he placed in the center of the buffet table. In an instant I was beside him, smoothing my dress over my hips.

"Hi, you," I smiled and he did a double-take at my magic

sock dress.

"Look at you," he breathed into my hair and hugged me tightly. He was handsome in a casual sport jacket and jeans. "And look what I found." Eddie reached into his jacket pocket and held up a blue beaded bracelet that I recognized from April's Pretty Pretty Princess game. I smiled at the memory of the three of us and our frequent competitive bouts, late into the night. "Here," he said, as he reached for my hand and slid the bracelet on.

"But it doesn't go with my sock dress!" I smiled, not really caring if I made another accessorizing error.

"Yes, it does." Eddie held my wrist, and gently pushed the bracelet under the sleeve of the dress. "Just tuck it inside," he said, smoothing the fabric, kissing me softly, holding my hand.

ACKNOWLEDGMENTS

My greatest expression of gratitude goes to my angel muse, Kaitlin Zavalcofsky, who inspired me to write and showed me the heart of this story with her enormous spirit. I am forever grateful to Mary, Crystal, Joey, Amanda and Eric for letting me share so many special moments with your family. My love and sincerest appreciation go to Mary Zavalcofsky, Frances Richard, Beverly and Joe Carrieri, Ralph Carrieri, Susan Kiernan, and to my entire extended family for demonstrating the kind of unconditional love that Nana taught us and that I've tried to honor with the message of this book.

My earliest and most influential reader, the incomparable Eve Bridburg, one of the smartest, loveliest people on earth, provided advice and support that sustained me throughout. Heb Ryan, your early encouragement and thoughtful feedback were instrumental in motivating me to continue; thank you! I'm forever indebted to Steve Almond for his personal example, for advising me to %&^# *style, tell the truth,* and for his friendship. Mike Connell, thank you for your insightful edits, writerly camaraderie, general brilliance and good humor. I'm grateful to Belinda Borelli, Milissa Day, Shandor Garrison, Marie Claire Guglielmo, Courtney Welsh and Janet Wu for their contributions and thoughtful critiques of early chapters.

Alethea Black, you are truly a kindred soul and being on this writer's journey with you has been a gift. Thank you for your support and feedback and friendship. Jeannine DeLoche, your friendship has sustained me through so much in life. Thank you for being part of this, too. Your insights and wise counsel have made everything better, and more joyful.

My heartfelt thanks to Grub Street, the most important community and resource for a writer in New England and most definitely for me. First, to the amazing staff—especially Eve, Chris Castellani, Sonya Larson and Whitney Scharer. I cannot possibly express how much your help and encouragement at every step has meant and how much you are appreciated. And without Grub, I would not have the following list of incredible people to thank, for various forms of support and inspiration: Alison Adair, Lisa Borders, Linda Button, Lynne Griffin, Marc Foster, Amy MacKinnon, Hank Phillippi Ryan, and Lara JK Wilson. A special thanks to Sophie Powell for her editing expertise, support and enthusiasm for this project. And to Jocelyn Kelley of Kelley & Hall Book Publicity for her expert guidance and optimism.

Thank you to my early readers, especially Salima Remtulla, and also Maria Aliferis, Amanda Curtin, Diane DeLoche, Christine Manning, Erica Milligan and Tobi Rifkind.

Thanks also to the original Boston/HBS/Tuesday Night Club crew, memories of which helped provide the dot-com context for this book, particularly Warren Adams, Scott Friend, Dominic Ianno, Frank Levy, Julie Schramm, Megan Weeks Adams, and especially, our Schmetterling, Katja Reinhold.

For the special forms of encouragement (sometimes words, sometimes wine) of beloved friends, my deepest thanks to Ondine Brendt, Laura Gould, Laura Johansen, Samia Kirmani, Catherine Lee, Marthe Stanek, Karin Stawarky, and Pauline Tsirgotis. Love always to the Posse and the Six Pack. And JJP.

To Hillary and Jeffrey Rayport, I'm beyond grateful for your friendship, your generosity, and your insights. Jeffrey, special thanks for teaching me so much of what I know about technology and its capacity to change the way we live.

To Irene Cross—you've taught me more than any other person in my entire life, but it is your friendship that I treasure most. Thank you for helping me to imbue my characters with some of your wisdom. To my fellow dreamer Michael Noel, thank you for being an inspiration with every hilarious insight and vote of confidence. To Beth Whittaker, your immense talent, creativity and artistic determination have always inspired me, and your friendship is a blessing.

For cutting across every category of support and for being the best sisters I could hope for, love and appreciation to Joanna Christensen and Laura Phillips. I thank my wonderfully supportive parents, William and Mary Toth, and my brothers, Bill and Michael, for being unwavering sources of love, confidence and stability. To all of you and to Kim, Kelly, Brian, Craig, Madison, Connor, Isabelle, Marinna, Ryan, Preston, and Audrey, I'd like to paraphrase Dad: family is everything, and you are mine.

ABOUT THE AUTHOR

Michelle Toth divides her time between New York City and Boston, where she serves on the board of directors of the non-profit Grub Street Writers. *Annie Begins* is her first novel. Visit Michelle on the Web at www.anniebegins.com.

Block Photography

Made in the USA
Charleston, SC
09 April 2011